Echo

Katie Frankey

Saved by Grace Publishing—Fairfield Township, OH
ISBN: 978-0-578-53872-3
Library of Congress Control Number: 2019910811
Echo | Katie Frankey
Available Formats: eBook | Paperback distribution

Dedication

I would like to dedicate this book to the loves of my life, my extraordinary husband and our beautiful, tenderhearted daughters. It is my hope that you each follow your dreams and don't lose sight of your passion. Trust in God to guide you. When you aren't sure what to do, turn to Him. He will guide you to whatever is right. Keep Philippians 4:8 close to your heart. I love you all so very much. Thank you for all your love and support.

CHAPTER 1
Just Trying to Help

"Tamara Michelle, if you don't get your butt down here within the next six seconds, you can bet you will be walking yourself to school for the next month!"

"Mama! Chill out, I'm coming! Dang!" Tamara yelled back at her mother from the top of the stairs.

"First of all, watch your tone, little girl," her mother waved her finger and stared at her as Tamara grabbed her backpack by the front door. "We have zero time to play. You wasted twenty minutes straightening your hair, and now you're about to be late to school and so help me God, if I'm late to work again this week you better know you goin' be in a world of hurt!"

"Yes, ma'am," she nodded as the two of them climbed into the Cadillac Escalade parked in the garage.

As they pulled out of the garage, Tamara realized she left her English homework on her desk in her bedroom. Knowing better than to ask her mom to let her run in and get it, she decided it would be better to just redo it once she got to school.

Her mom's phone began to ring into the car on the Bluetooth connection. "It's the office. Jerry is going to kill me if I'm late," she said as she gave Tamara a sideways glance. "Hello?"

"Sharon?"

"Good morning, Jerry."

"Hey there. So, I'd like to run through some numbers this morning before we go into our meeting with our new potential client. Are you almost to work?"

"Actually, I'll be there by eight but not a second before. I am about to drop Tamara off at school. I will call you back after I do so and we can discuss those numbers along with a few new hires we made earlier this week while you were out."

"Excellent. I'll grab the coffee."

"Sounds great. Talk to you in a few," she said as she pressed the red end button on the dashboard. "Tamara, now this is a really big week for us at the office. We have a huge client we are looking to land and I'm going to need to stay late tonight."

"Ugh," Tamara sighed. "Please don't tell me I have to deal with Eric and the boys by myself tonight?"

"You can call him Uncle Eric, and yes you do. What's the problem?"

"Mama, he is clearly not my uncle. He is white."

"Tamara Michelle, I'm warning you!" she looked at her daughter. "I have told you several times that he was my foster brother growing up. He is in a rough patch in his life and ever since your father," she paused and took a deep breath. "Ever since your father died last year I have been trying to keep it together and Eric has been incredibly helpful to me in providing the necessary daycare I need for your little brothers. We are helping him get on his feet and he is helping me by providing child care."

"I know," Tamara sighed, feeling guilty because her father had died in a car accident about a year and a half ago on his way to pick her up from her first and only afterschool detention. "He's just so creepy. He is so sketchy, I honestly think he is bipolar, Mama. That or he is high all the time."

"He better not be high. The second I catch him doing drugs again, he is out of my house. He knows that too," she said as she pulled the car into the school parking lot. "Listen, baby. Uncle Eric is working through some stuff right now. I agree that he is a little off at times. I don't think he is sketchy though. He just wants to help out. He had a really tough childhood. Cut him some slack. He has come a long way since he got out of rehab a year ago.

Right now he needs us as much as we need him. We need to love him, not push him away," she said as she looked at her tall daughter and stroked her hair.

"Fine. But he is still creepy. I'll just ride the bus to get home," Tamara agreed.

"Thank you. I should be home by nine or ten. Eric is going into his job around nine, I think, so you won't have to deal with him for too long. There is leftover food in the fridge," she said as she leaned in to let her daughter kiss her on the cheek.

"A'ight. Love you," she smiled at her mother as she got out of the car.

"It's alright. Not a'ight. I raised you better than that!" her mom scolded as Tamara shut the car door. She rolled down the window to yell out, "Love you too, baby."

She rolled her eyes and walked into the school building.

"Hey, girl! Where you been? We was suppose' to meet twenty minutes ago. How we gonna practice for the talent show if you keep punkin' us? Or were you hangin' with your new man?" Maysha teased as Tamara approached her group of friends.

"What?" Tamara responded with her large brown eyes opened widely, raising her eyebrow slightly to show Maysha she knew she was trying to sneak dis.

"What are you talkin' bout? I just got here. I already heard it from my mom so I don't need to hear it from you too." Tamara stood next to her group of friends in the school hallway which also happened to be across from her first bell class. "The best part about being late though is I don't have to sit next to your loud self for too long," Tamara snorted back and then looked at the rest of their friends to let them know she was playing.

Tamara had Ms. Panacinni first bell for Advanced Calculus. Ms. P. had been teaching for about fifteen years at Vector High School. Tamara admired her on so many levels. She sometimes found it fun to imagine Ms. P. with a life outside of teaching high school;

perhaps bartending late nights.

Typically Ms. P. was kind to Tamara. She seemed to recognize something special in her. Ms. P. knew Tamara was incredibly intelligent and thoughtful. She always seemed to be in tune to Tamara's compassion for other people. Ms. P. had told Tamara one time when the class was being rowdy that Tamara was her calm in the storm.

Recently, she had started trying to convince Tamara to take College Credit Plus math courses. Tamara was a math wizard. She loved it. The one thing keeping her from taking college level math courses, as Ms. P. suggested, was how nervous she was to fail it.

The rule was if she failed the course then she would have to pay for the course, but the F would stay on her college transcript forever. She lacked confidence in herself and was so afraid that if she failed she would let her mom down and not get into the school of her dreams.

Her dream was to go to Howard University to study medicine. Both her mom and dad went there, so it was expected that she would go there too. But, ever since her dad died Tamara started to feel afraid to fail. She wanted to make her dad proud and follow in his footsteps. He received a full ride to Howard and had straight A's all through high school and college so she wanted to do the exact same thing.

Ms. P. knew Tamara's situation and promised to help her get in if she stayed focused on her grades and made the right choices.

Ms. P. was standing outside of her classroom door talking to another teacher.

There wasn't really room anywhere in the building to practice for the talent show so the group of girls decided to set up their practice spot in front of Ms. P.'s room because she was cool enough not to care about the music and the hallway was a little wider here since the bathroom was right across.

"So, we have the first part down, right? Should we run through it so we can start the middle solos?" Maysha asked as she looked at the clock realizing the first period bell was going to ring and they only had about fifteen minutes left to practice for the talent show.

The school's talent show was coming up, and the entire community around the city showed up for the Vector High School Event. Even parents called off work, including Tamara's mom, to come watch their babies be the star for the night. The school's Multicultural Student Union, a group of students who all wanted to bring equality to the school, put it on.

Not that equality didn't exist at Vector, but there was a lot of racial tension in the school, mostly stemming back from the racial profiling that happened in Cincinnati many years ago. Most people had long forgotten about it, but the racial tensions remained present throughout the city, hidden or not. The administrators and teachers all supported the idea of the talent show, hoping to bring a sense of community to the school's atmosphere.

Just as she and her friends began to take their places to start rehearsing, a loud commotion started coming from the boys' bathroom.

Tamara looked toward the bathroom and realized that a fight had broken out in there, and within seconds, the hallway flooded with onlookers.

As she tried to figure out what was happening and who was involved, swarms of students started to bump into her. Trying to hold her own to get a look, she saw two boys, both white, swinging and landing punches on each other. Blood covered both boys faces and it was obvious neither one was going to go out easily.

The thick crowd of students started to hoot and holler only to escalate the fight.

Tamara glanced over her shoulder and saw the school security officer running down the hall toward the fight. She knew the fight had to be stopped so she tried to help clear the hallway and the group of kids around her. She started shoving anyone around her to get them out of the way so that security could come and stop the fight.

She wasn't alone in the clearing. Several of her friends and other students realized that the fight and crowd were getting dangerous quickly.

"Move it!" she exclaimed. "Get out of the way!" She shoved a white girl out of the way so hard that the girl went flying into Ms. P., knocking them both to the ground.

`The kindness on Ms. P.'s face quickly transitioned to shock and frustration. Hurriedly, the teacher grabbed herself and the white girl off the floor and gave Tamara the *"I'm disappointed in you"* look, taking the girl into her classroom.

Tamara's heart sank. She knew in that moment that she was going to be in big trouble with her favorite teacher. She hadn't meant to hurt her or the girl she flung. She was just trying to clear the way to help out.

As the officer got the boys into order and into handcuffs, the crowd started to back away from the scene.

Officer Bolvain, the school's main security officer, was good at getting extremely ugly and potentially dangerous situations under control quickly. No one wanted to rumble with him. Rumor had it that he used to be an Ultimate Fighter. His six foot, five inch, two-hundred and fifty pound frame made the rumor even more believable. Even the gravity in his voice implied the magnitude of the trouble you would be in if you didn't comply with his request.

"A'ight! I'm goin'. I ain't do nothin'. He started it," one of the boys in cuffs started yelling at him.

"You just actin' crazy and need to chill out. We goin' down to the office so you can cool off for a minute, then you goin' downtown," Officer Bolvain sneered at the boy and tugged him harder as he escorted him down to the office.

The other boy was much more agreeable and walked obediently on the other side of him.

Maysha, who also had a quick temper but an even sassier demeanor, started to disperse the crowd of students by saying, "Ain't nothing here to see. Keep it movin', no one else gonna get beat up today."

The kids in the crowd didn't give her much attention and all started comparing their phones and video footage they got of the fight and began to disband.

Tamara rolled her eyes as she turned away to walk toward Ms. P.'s classroom. She looked at her best friend, Porsha, who was standing next to her in the hall.

She and Porsha had been best friends since they were in sixth grade. Porsha was Tamara's confidant.

She looked at Porsha and slumped her shoulders, "How am I going to get into Howard if Ms. P. thinks I'm a part of nonsense like that, Porsha? I can't have her thinkin' that I'm a fighter too. I'm gonna be in so much trouble. I can't believe I just threw that girl into her. I was only trying to help. You know she gonna write me a letter of recommendation once I'm a senior to help me get accepted. I need that, you know?" Tamara stewed, almost in tears thinking about the look that Ms. P. just gave her. "I have to get into Howard, girl. I have to."

"I know, girl. You will. Ms. P. jus' mad, she'll get over it. She likes you. Don't worry. Besides, you only a sophomore. You know you gonna have plenty of time to make it up to her. Plus, you ain't do nothing wrong. She knows that. You stressin' too much, girl," Porsha consoled her friend and smiled at her. Gently, she pushed her, "Girl, lighten up. You good."

"Ugh. I know. It's just annoying. I hate when people act like they hard and they be fighting and then it makes all the other people around 'em look bad too. An of course Maysha's loud mouth over there ain't helpin' nothing."

"You don't got nothin' to prove to me. I hear you. I got to go though, for real. I'll catch you at lunch. You good?"

"Yeah, thanks, Porsha. I'm good. I'll holla atcha," Tamara nodded at her friend and headed into her classroom with Ms. P., who was standing with the white girl.

Tamara noticed a quiet exchange of words between the two of them and then the girl walked out of the class.

Ms. P. was sometimes hard to read but Tamara could tell immediately that she was in a no-nonsense mood. She looked directly at Tamara and asked if she did her homework.

"Of course I did," Tamara quietly replied thankful she hadn't left that on her desk at home too.

"Good, because you are going to demonstrate how to use derivatives to find areas under curves today," she took a step closer and continued, "and don't think for a second that your mother won't be getting a phone call about what just happened."

"Yes, ma'am," Tamara murmured. *I swear, what did that girl just say to Ms. P.? She probably made me look like a bully when I didn't even do nothin'. She don't even know me. Who does she think she is trying to make me look like the bad guy? I ain't do nothin'. Ugh. I can't wait to get out of here, out of Cincinnati.* Tamara thought to herself reflecting on the commotion. She opened up her Calculus homework to double check it since she was going to need to make amends with Ms. P. and get back into her good graces.

CHAPTER 2
In the Way

Honk, honk!

"Sarah Nicole! There is no need for you to blare the horn like that. It is too early to be waking up Zoe's neighbors," Mrs. Benson, Sarah's mom, scolded from the passenger seat.

"Uh! Mom, seriously. I really don't need to be yelled at, thanks," Sarah, who was just about to turn sixteen uttered from the driver seat of the family's new Expedition. "Besides, Zoe's parents are cool, they actually let her have boys over in her room and she doesn't have to keep the door open. They're not going to care about a horn."

Mrs. Benson gave her daughter the wide-eyed look letting Sarah know she was walking a fine line.

Sarah flicked her brown layered hair over her shoulder and stared out the window toward her best friend Zoe's house.

Zoe came prancing out of her house in a short pencil skirt and high heels. "Yay! There she is. She's gonna be so excited that I'm driving!" Sarah exclaimed as she rolled down the window.

"Shut up! What is this? You actually get to drive the Expedition to school today? Mrs. Benson, are you crazy? This car is amazing. It's so awesome," Zoe excitedly called out from her front porch as she pulled the door behind her. Just before she headed toward the car she made sure the glass storm door was shut and doubled checked her outfit in her reflection.

"Well, Sarah's father said she needed the experience in driving a bigger vehicle since she is getting her license in a couple months. Aw, my baby girl is going to be sixteen," Mrs. Benson lightly teased as Zoe got into the back seat.

Sarah gave her mom a secretive grin, but then quickly said, "Whatever, Mom." Sarah and her mom had just recently begun growing apart. Sarah was growing into her teenage self and becoming more popular at school, and because her mom had started becoming distracted on her new phone within the past few months. Sarah wasn't quite sure how to react to this change in her mom, but there was definitely something going on. "Okay girl, you buckled up?" She looked in the rearview mirror at Zoe.

"Yep."

"Check your mirrors and your blind spot before you pull out, honey."

"I know, Mom."

"Oh my goodness, Sarah did you hear about Toby?" Zoe exclaimed from the backseat.

"What? No, what happened?"

"Sarah, you need to pay attention to the road, dear," her mother chimed in.

"Mom, I am, she is just telling me a story, there's no crime in that!" Sarah rolled her eyes as she argued. "Okay, so what happened? I knew Abbie was mad at him, did they break up?"

"Yeah, like in front of the whole school. So last night right, they were at the mall and you know that smoothie stand outside of Gap?"

"Yeah."

"Well, I guess Toby was waiting for Abbie outside there and these two girls from Saint Mary's High School came up and he started to check them out."

"No he didn't?"

"I know, right! So anyway, I guess Abbie saw this so she walked right up to him from the store and pushed him out of his chair."

"Shut up!"

"Sarah Nicole, use your turn signal."

"Mom, I am. Anyway, what did he do?"

"What could he do? She made him look so stupid and everyone was there watching and laughing. I feel so sorry for him. She was so controlling. I think he is so cute, she didn't deserve him anyway," Zoe exhaled and grinned toward her friend in the driver's seat.

"You would." Sarah turned into Vector High School's parking lot. "Alright girl, we're here."

"Turn your blinkers on and park over there," Mrs. Benson gestured to an open spot in front of a school bus.

"Mom, I know!" She pulled into the parking spot her mom indicated and looked back at her friend. "So, am I the best driver you have ever seen?" she grinned as the two girls opened their doors to get out of the SUV.

"Bye, honey, have a good day. I love you. I'll pick you up at three."

"Okay. Bye," Sarah quickly said as she and Zoe hurried from the car into the building.

"Well, you did okay. I mean, you don't have on heels like me so I'll let you know when I see you drive in a pair of these."

"Ha. Right. I don't think I can. I think I'd get the heel stuck under the gas pedal and plow right into the building."

They giggled as they entered the school building. Their usual band of friends, Brody, Toby, Jesse, and Caitlin all greeted them as they walked up.

Sarah and Jesse had been friends since they were little. They grew up together in the same neighborhood and went to the same babysitter. They knew each other better than anyone. People used to tease them and say they would end up marrying each other but the thought of it always made both Sarah and Jesse laugh at the absurdity.

Jesse had a girlfriend anyway. He and Caitlin were the couple in the group, but Brody and Sarah were quickly becoming an item. Brody was far more experienced in the girlfriend department than Sarah was but there was no question that she was the girl he was currently pursuing.

Sarah felt the same way for him, but only being a sophomore and young in the dating world she didn't know how to make it official and be his actual girlfriend, the girl every girl wanted to be: Brody Paulson's girlfriend. She tried to play it as cool as she could and not do or say anything stupid as she walked up to them.

"Hey, guys," she practically shouted as she approached the group.

"Hey, girl. What's up?" Brody responded with a smile trying to help her not feel silly for being way too loud. "How'd you sleep last night?" he continued with his hair sweeping across his face and tilting his head. He coolly put his arm around her neck to embrace her. His chin fell right on top of her forehead and he placed his lips at her hairline, to enfold her neck and upper body into his.

Sarah gave Zoe a shy smile and hugged Brody around his waist. "Hi. I slept fine, but someone kept me up texting until three o'clock in the morning. Uah-hm," she teased. "I'm gonna have to start turning my phone on silent when I go to sleep so I can actually survive this relationship!"

"Ah, don't look at me, I didn't force you to do nothing you didn't wanna do," Brody contended. He leaned over and whispered in Sarah's ear, "Talking to you is worth losing a little sleep over anyway," he gave her a quiet smile and a wink causing her to grin bashfully and wrinkle her nose.

"Oh my God, you two are so stupid cute," Zoe added her opinion. "You guys just need to start going out and make it official already!" She put her hand on her hip and stared down Brody.

"Um, so I'm gonna run to the bathroom real quick, I'll meet up with you guys in the cafeteria," Sarah awkwardly broadcasted.

They all giggled for a brief moment and Sarah headed toward the bathroom across from Ms. Panacinni's classroom.

Caught up in her own thoughts she hardly noticed the large crowd of students forming outside of the bathroom. *Oh, he is so cute. I can't believe he hugged me in front of everyone. His hair looks so good today…I can't believe Zoe just said that! Ugh. What is going on here?*

As Sarah approached the hallway near the bathroom she slowly snapped out of her love trance and realized that there was a huge fight taking place. She couldn't see who was fighting but she knew it was bad.

The students in the hallway were screaming and shouting at the commotion egging it on even more.

Sarah was trying to avoid it all realizing that the situation clearly wasn't safe. Within seconds of being there she started getting bumped and knocked around by people trying to get a look at the fight. Everyone had their cell phones out recording it all go down.

The screaming of the crowd started getting louder. Some people were trying to clear the way for security to get by.

Sarah was trying to get out of the way when all of a sudden someone hurled her across the hall. She was heaved into Ms. P. and they both collided and fell to the ground.

Quickly, Ms. P. scooped her up and took her into her classroom to get her into safety.

As she picked her up from the floor Sarah turned around to see who had shoved her and saw a tall, light-skinned black girl staring at her. She couldn't tell if the girl was giving her a mean look or an I'm sorry look, but Sarah reciprocated it with a look of disgust.

"Oh, my dear, are you okay?" Ms. P. asked as she closed the door behind them.

"Yes, ma'am. It was my fault, I shouldn't have cut through

there. I just really had to pee," Sarah groaned and put her hand on her face, knowing that she really was thinking about Brody but didn't want to tell on herself.

Ms. Panacinni slightly smiled, "I don't know what has gotten into those kids out there but you need to stay in here until it's safe."

"Yes, ma'am. I'm sorry," Sarah said as she straighten out her clothes. "Are you okay, Ms. P.? Did I hurt you?"

"Heaven's no. I am fine. I've seen plenty of fights here and this isn't the first time I've been knocked around," she smiled. "Perhaps next time you need to pay a bit more attention before you go walking straight through a fight like that."

Just then the same girl who had stared at her, the one she thought shoved her, walked into the room and put her backpack down on the floor next to a desk in the classroom.

Realizing that the crowd in the hallway was dispersing and the noise had died down Sarah looked to make her exit, "I'm going to go to the bathroom now, Ms. P. Thanks for your help. And sorry," Sarah whispered to her teacher.

"Okay. See you in class this afternoon."

Sarah scurried out of the room and darted to the bathroom. Once she finally made it back to the cafeteria, she told her friends all about her fiasco. "Zoe, you will never believe what just happened!" Sarah proceeded to tell her story, leaving no detail uncovered.

"Are you kidding me?" Zoe said with her hand on her hip and her opposite leg twisted to the side. Her long legs seemed longer when she stood like that, especially in the tight skirt she was wearing.

Brody and Toby only partially paying attention to the story in between swapping headphones and talking about the upcoming drinking opportunities both looked at Sarah and in unison said, "Screw it!" they looked at each other and laughed as if it was the most genius thing either one had ever said.

"I can't believe she did that to you, Sarah. Who does that girl think she is? Some people are so mean and act like they run this school. It's so annoying," Zoe's ranting was beginning to fade into the background as Sarah's mind was replaying the incident in her head.

What was I thinking? I should have just used the other bathroom. I'm still shaking. I'm an idiot. Arrh. I am so mad! Just then, the bell rang and the entire cafeteria cleared out and the students filed into their classes.

Brody pulled Sarah nearer to him and kissed her gently on her cheek. "It'll be alright, babe. I'll protect you," he sounded so manly and so confident in this moment that Sarah felt comforted and kissed him back.

They exchanged smiles and she hurried off to her first bell class, Biology.

CHAPTER 3
I hate homework

"Did those boys from the fight this morning get suspended?" Porsha asked Maysha as they strolled into their Social Studies class behind Tamara.

"Yeah. Of course they did. They going up for expulsion. They were still cleaning up the blood on the floor at lunchtime. My mama called me and said she saw it on Snapchat and wanted to make sure I was okay," Maysha said with a smile as she took her seat.

"Tamara," Porsha said as she nudged her, "You get to talk to Ms. P.? You guys cool now?"

"Ms. P. was for real upset. She made me prove all my work on the board, and gave the class all the odd and even numbers for homework tonight because of what I did," Tamara whimpered. "She normally only assigns the odd numbers."

The girls rolled their eyes at her.

"For real, I think she even called mine and that white girl's house cause she was so mad."

"Ah, that's skept, she just being a hater. White teacher had to go save the white girl," a girl named Kenna laughed as she chimed in.

Tamara couldn't stand Kenna. She was loud and obnoxious and she always had something nasty to say about anyone.

"No, it wasn't like that, Kenna," Tamara said as she gave her a glare and cocked her head at her.

"Yeah. Okay," Kenna retorted as she gave Tamara an equally tough glare and looked the other way.

With her left eyebrow raised, Maysha nodded her head toward the classroom door as the white girl Tamara had shoved walked in.

Porsha and Maysha looked at each other and giggled and then they looked over at Tamara who rolled her eyes at their immaturity.

Students began to file into their last class of the day, Mr. Zohng's Social Studies. Tamara glanced at the white girl giggling with one of her friends, and couldn't help but roll her eyes as she took her seat.

"Okay, class, take your seats," Mr. Zohng announced to the rambunctious group of sophomores that had just piled into the room. "How is everyone today?"

A faint, "Fine," responded from the teens.

"Hey. Tamara. Tamara!" Maysha whispered while Mr. Zohng continued on about the new unit they were about to start today.

Tamara often found herself annoyed by her seat next to Maysha, who was always talking too much trying to distract her from her work, "What?"

"You think he's actually married?" Nodding toward the disheveled Social Studies teacher with his shirt half way soaked through with sweat.

"Girl, bye," Tamara smiled trying to politely ignore her and listen to Mr. Zohng go on about President Nixon and the Watergate Scandal.

Since Tamara wasn't going to give Maysha the attention she wanted she turned to her other side and started giggling with Kenna.

Tamara shot them a look that demanded silence, but the girls just continued to giggle and talk.

Porsha and Tamara exchanged annoyed glances and Tamara then looked at the white girl across the room who was busy taking notes.

"Ladies, could you please pay attention. You are going to need to know this for your homework tonight," Mr. Zohng nervously said toward the now noisy chatter that was coming from Maysha and Kenna.

"What? What I need to know about some stupid dead white guy for? The way I see it I don't need to know crap about 'em," Kenna snorted to the teacher trying to provoke him. Her body language was begging for an argument; her eyes pierced through his forehead, daring him to call her out on her combativeness. She sat there with a smug snarl lighting up her face and waited.

The whole class waited.

"Uh… Kkkenna."

"Whatsa matter? Can't talk? You zoning me out! You for real a crazy ass Asian. How you gonna teach us about American History if you ain't even American?" Kenna tried to act innocent as she stared down the teacher waiting for his response knowing that she was fueling a fire.

"Girl, shut up," Maysha whispered to Kenna, realizing her friend had taken it too far.

"Uh. No. No. Not okay. You don't get to talk to me like that, or anyone for that matter," Mr. Zohng implored anxiously as he scampered across the room near the doorway and pressed the security button.

Tamara could do nothing but just stare at Kenna in wonderment.

Within seconds Officer Bolvain pounced into the classroom.

"Get Kenna out of this room. She is being extremely disrespectful," Mr. Zohng was almost in tears.

Officer Bolvain gave Kenna a very disenchanted look then walked toward her and with a deep intonation said, "Get up, get your books, let's go."

Kenna didn't even attempt to argue. She simply gathered her belongings and with the continued brash look plastered across her face, she sauntered out of the room with Officer Bolvain behind her.

In sync, the entire class put their eyes on their desks. They were hesitant to even look at Mr. Zohng.

After about a minute, he excused himself from the room. Still no one said a word. No one even looked at each other. Everyone busied themselves with their notes.

When Mr. Zohng reentered the class Tamara noticed how his attitude had changed. His demeanor seemed more confident than it did only minutes prior. Tamara thought perhaps he had gone to the bathroom to give himself a pep talk in the mirror.

"Okay. There has been a change of plans," Mr. Zohng began.

The students all started to look around at one another to see if anyone had a guess about what he intended to do.

Porsha gave Tamara an inquisitive look as Tamara shrugged her shoulders.

"Apparently," Mr. Zohng continued, "there are some students in this school who don't understand culture. As a Korean-American, I find it disturbing that in a country as great as this one, kids don't have a basic respect for others. So that is why there is a change in plans. Each one of you will be given a partner of a different ethnicity and the two of you will explore each other's lives. You will go to each other's houses, you will meet families, and you will find things you have in common. You will learn to understand each other, respect each other."

As he was saying this, the class began to groan and sigh.

"I don't want to hear it," he said. "I know I want to be respected as should the rest of you. And the best way to respect someone is to learn about them. This project needs to be done together and not over the phone. You must go to each other's houses. You will each turn in a summary of events and a two-page reflection over how this experience made you feel. In this reflection, you should include any pre-notions or judgments you had before your meeting."

"You can't be serious?" Sean, the kid to the right of Tamara argued.

"I am entirely serious, Sean."

"Can we pick our partners?" Pam, a straight A student, asked.

"No, I will assign them right now," Mr. Zohng responded.

Sighs and groans continued from the group, some louder than others.

"Let's see," he began to look over his class roster, and glanced up at each kids face. "Seth Cringle, you are going to be paired up with Derrick Moser."

The two looked at each other and grinned. They played football together so they spent time together already.

"Zoe Drisdale, you are going to be with Pamela Chin."

Tamara noticed the two of them glance at one and another and nod as if in agreement that the pairing would be suitable.

Mr. Zohng continued down the roster and quickly approached the H's. Tamara Hudgenson, you are going to be with,"

Not the white girl, not the white girl, not the white girl.

"Sarah Benson," he continued.

Tamara looked up and saw the white girl looking right at her. She rolled her eyes in Sarah's direction and it was returned with a deep sigh and a head tilted rolling of the eyes as well.

Are you serious? He can't be serious. He has to be crazy. I'm not working with her. I'm not doing this. Ugh. She better be smart and not slack off. I'm not going to do her work for her. This is so stupid. I hate homework. Especially homework that involves other people. I hope she's smart. She looks like she might be smart. At least she doesn't look as ridiculous as her friend behind her. Ugh. We can just meet and get it over with, as long as I get an A, I don't care. This is so stupid. Kenna needs to learn to keep her mouth shut.

Tamara was being tapped on the shoulder by Maysha, which pulled her out of her thoughts. "Don't even say it. Shut up."

"Ha. Looks like it's your lucky day, girl," Maysha teased.

Mr. Zohng continued to pair up students in the room and once he finished, less than five minutes remained in the class. "Now, everyone go sit by your partner and make arrangements for how and when you are going to meet. This is going to be due on Monday."

"Dude, it's Thursday," Seth argued. "We have a game tomorrow night, and J.V. has an away game Saturday."

"Yeah, and I got church on Sunday," Derrick assisted Seth in his argument.

"Plus, I got a big party to attend Saturday night," a voice announced from the back of the room.

"Well you will just have to find a way. You can do it on the sidelines if you have to, but this is due Monday. And I'd be more than happy to email Coach Daniels to let him know you have this assignment due Monday and are afraid you won't have time with the game and all?"

The boys snorted and shut their mouths quickly so they didn't stir him up any more.

Tamara looked at Sarah, her new partner, and flared her nostrils. Tamara noticed the other kids all moving toward their partners so she too got up and headed in Sarah's direction. She plopped down in the seat next to Sarah and just stared at her.

"I don't want to do this anymore than you do so don't give me that look," Sarah said as she turned her neck to face Tamara.

"Whatever," Tamara inhaled. "Look, I didn't shove you on purpose. I was just trying to clear the area. I'm sorry it happened like that," she glanced at Sarah who seemed to be studying her. "When you wanna meet?"

Sarah let out a sigh. "Well, thanks. I don't care when we meet. Saturday morning? Here?"

"Fine."

"Fine. What time do you want to meet?" Sarah asked without

making eye contact.

Tamara took a deep breath and almost as if exhaling her disdain she responded, "Nine o'clock, by the flagpole."

"Fine," Sarah agreed, and the bell rang to dismiss the students.

Both girls exchanged glances and Tamara turned to Porsha and together they walked out of the room.

"Kenna's gonna get it, girl," Porsha whispered as they headed toward their lockers.

"You have no idea," Tamara quietly mumbled and gathered her books to head toward the bus stop.

CHAPTER 4
This is Stupid

"Toby totally grabbed my butt today. Well, not really, but kinda. We were in gym class and I was taking a shot with the basketball and he was behind me and I felt him touch it. Aw, I am so in love. He is so cute!" Zoe rambled on to Sarah who was daydreaming about the intimate kiss she and Brody shared just after lunch. "Are you listening to me? Sarah?"

"Oh, yeah, I'm listening. You said Toby grabbed your butt."

"I know, right! Can you believe it? I mean we are totally gonna hook up. Are you okay? Where are you?"

"Oh, I'm here, I'm glad for you two. You guys would be cute together."

"Maybe we could like go on a double date. You know, me and Toby and you and Brody."

As Zoe said this, Sarah's face started to blush and a smile grew across her cheeks revealing her dimple on the left side.

"Oh, I get it. You are still thinking about that kiss. Oh, you are so totally going to hook up with him."

"No I'm not. What does that even mean? I'm not going to have sex with him."

"Yeah right! Do you see your face? You are totally going to. You are in love. Besides, it's fun!"

"Shut up!" Sarah was turning scarlet with embarrassment. "I could never do that. Besides, I wouldn't even know what to do. What do you mean fun? Sex is fun?"

"Uh, duh. Get with it girl. You are like the only virgin in the tenth grade. You totally need to hook up."

"This conversation is so totally over. I can't believe we are even friends. I mean are you serious? We are so opposite."

"Yeah, but that's why you love me so much," Zoe winked at her friend and the two girls strolled into their Social Studies class with Mr. Zohng. "I'm so glad school is almost over. Are you riding home with Jesse? I think Brody is. Text your mom and tell her you have a ride."

"Do you think Jesse would take me? Caitlin has him so wrapped around her little finger now."

"Shut up. He's like your best friend, besides me, of course. You guys have been friends since you were in diapers. If he doesn't take you home then he has some serious priority issues. He lives almost right behind you. Plus, he'd be stupid to say no. Brody would like kick his butt if he didn't take you."

"Ha, true. I'll text him just to make sure." As Sarah sat down in her seat she got out her phone to text Jesse.

Zoe, who was sitting right behind her, nudged her to look across the room at the black girls staring at her.

Sarah realized it was the girl from the morning fiasco that came into Ms. Panacinni's room. Sarah just looked away as if she didn't even notice they were staring at her. "Seriously, are they really going to try to stare me down now? I mean really. Get a life," the two girls laughed and Sarah's phone vibrated in her purse.

She opened her purse and looked at her phone.

"YOU ARE DUMB! Why do u even think u have 2 ask? Of course I'll take u home. IDK why I don't everyday anyway."

Sarah smiled at Jesse's message.

"Jesse said he'd take me home," she whispered to Zoe.

"See I told you. Now you can cuddle up next to your man," Zoe teased.

Sarah rolled her eyes and turned forward to face the teacher. Sarah sent a text to her mom to tell her she was going to ride home with Jesse. She then pulled out a pencil and began writing down information about the Watergate Scandal.

Sarah really didn't like Social Studies, but it was better than Science. Her favorite class was English, but her English teacher was out on maternity leave currently so they were doing some pretty generic learning. She loved to write. Writing was a fun place to escape to whenever she needed a break.

Mr. Zohng, however, was discussing President Nixon. Sarah's dad would sometimes talk about his childhood years and he would refer to Nixon being the president at the time. Her dad was a Lawyer for Broker and Donaldson, one of the biggest Law firms in the city, but he had a deep appreciation for history and literature.

As Sarah was taking her notes, the girls across the room were getting noisy. She looked their direction and noticed they were laughing and looking at her. She tried to block them out by going about her note taking, but the chatter annoyed even the teacher.

"Ladies, please pay attention. You are going to need to know this for your homework tonight."

Sarah noticed how nervous Mr. Zohng was when he said this to the girls across the room.

Much to Sarah's surprise, one of the girls responded with, "What? What I need to know about some stupid dead white guy for? The way I see it I don't need to know crap about 'em," the girl snorted and just sat there with a self-satisfied expression.

Sarah wasn't sure what was going to happen next. All she could do was watch the event unfold in front of her. So she just waited with the whole class and watched.

"Uh… Kkkenna," Mr. Zohng stuttered.

"Whatsa matter? Can't talk? You zoning me out! You for real a crazy ass Asian. How you gonna teach us about American History if you ain't even American?" The girl's tone was hateful. Hurtful.

Oh my goodness. What is she thinking? She is going to be in so much trouble. What is wrong with him? Why isn't he saying anything? Aw. It looks like he is about to cry.

"Uh. No. No. Not okay. You don't get to talk to me like that, or anyone for that matter."

Good for him. Sarah thought to herself as she watched him call for security.

Officer Bolvain was in the room almost immediately and Mr. Zohng instructed him to take the girl out of the room. Officer Bolvain walked right over to the girl and towered over her. "Get up, get your books, let's go."

She didn't even argue. Like a mouse she gathered her things and stood up. As she walked out of the room she stared down Mr. Zohng with a menacing look.

Sarah immediately put her eyes on her paper. She knew she didn't want to make eye contact with Mr. Zohng. She really didn't want to see if he was crying or not. He excused himself from the room.

While he was gone no one said a word. Normally in a moment like this, Zoe would be tapping on her shoulder and start up a conversation about her boyfriend or something that lacked depth, but not this time. No one said a word. No one even looked at each other. Everyone seemed to make themselves busy in their textbooks and notes.

Mr. Zohng came back into the class with a new attitude. Sarah thought maybe he had gone to the bathroom and given himself a pep talk in the mirror. "Okay. There has been a change of plans," Mr. Zohng began.

Sarah turned around to look at Zoe who just shrugged her shoulders.

"Apparently there are some students in this school who don't understand culture. As a Korean-American, I find it disturbing that in a country as great as this one, kids don't have a basic respect for others. So that is why there is a change in plans. Each one of you are going to be given a partner of a different ethnicity, and the two of you will explore each other's lives. You will go to each other's houses, you will meet families, and you will find things you have in common. You will learn to understand each other."

As he was saying this, Sarah, along with the rest of the class began to groan and sigh.

"I don't want to hear it," he said. "I know I want to be respected as should the rest of you. And the best way to respect someone is to learn about them."

Several students questioned him and complained, "Can we pick our partners?"

"No, I will assign them right now. Let's see," he began to look over his class roster, and briefly glanced up at each kid's face. "Seth Cringle, you are going to be paired up with Derrick Moser. Zoe Drisdale, you are going to be with Pamela Chin."

Sarah turned around to look at Zoe who nodded at Pam and gave Sarah a look that said it was okay.

Mr. Zohng continued down roster, "Tamara Hudgenson, you are going to be with,"

Please no, please no, please no.

"Sarah Benson," he continued.

Dang it! Sarah looked up at the black girl, Tamara, who returned eye contact. Sarah sighed and tried not to roll her eyes but she just couldn't help it. *Are you serious? He can't be serious. He has to be crazy. I'm not working with her. I'm not doing this. She better be smart and not slack off. I'm not going to do her work for her. This is so stupid. I hate homework. Especially homework that involves other people. Hopefully she is smarter than her dumb friend that got us into this mess. At least she's not as loud as her friends. We can just meet and get it over with, as long as I get an A, I don't care. This is so stupid.* As Sarah reflected to herself Mr. Zohng continued to pair up students in the room.

After all the students finished their grumbling and Mr. Zohng put a few whining football players in their place, the class started to move around toward their newly assigned partners.

Sarah looked at Tamara, her new partner, and noticed her nostrils flare.

Tamara got up and headed in Sarah's direction. With all the body language that expressed hatred for the partner assignment, she threw her body into the seat next to Sarah and just stared at her.

"I don't want to do this anymore than you do, so don't give me that look," Sarah said as she intentionally just turned her neck to face Tamara.

"Whatever," Tamara sighed. "Look, I didn't shove you on purpose. I was just trying to clear the area. I'm sorry it happened like that," she glanced up at Sarah.

That was out of the blue. I didn't expect that. I kinda thought she was the one that pushed me but that was big of her to even admit it and apologize.

Tamara continued, "When you wanna meet?"

Sarah let out a sigh, "Well, thanks. I don't care when we meet. Saturday morning? Here?"

"Fine."

"Fine. What time do you want to meet?"

"9:00, by the flagpole?"

"Fine," Sarah agreed, and the bell rang to dismiss the students.

Before either one got up to leave the room, they added the dates into their phone calendars so they wouldn't forget. Both girls exchanged glances and Sarah turned to Zoe and walked out of the classroom to head for their lockers.

"This is so stupid," Zoe complained.

"I know right!" Sarah rolled her eyes again and then felt her phone vibrating in her purse. She got out her phone and saw she had two text messages. The first one from her mom approving of her ride home but reminded her to get home quickly because they needed to pick Ben, her little brother, up from practice. The second text was from Brody.

Sarah read it aloud to Zoe, "Meet me by gym locker rooms b4 we walk out I got something for u."

"Ohhhhhh. Girl, okay. You better not miss out on him," Zoe teased.

"Hmm. I wonder what he wants? Okay. Well, I'll meet you at Jesse's car. See you in a minute."

"See ya!" Zoe winked at her friend who was briskly walking toward the gym locker rooms.

CHAPTER 5
The Bus Ride Home

"Yo, T, you got a dollar I can get for the bus?"

"Chance Armstead, are you for real? You ain't paid me back from last week when you bummed money from me for the bus then," Tamara pretended to be annoyed with Chance, one of her close friends, who also happened to be best friends with Brandon, the guy she had a major crush on.

Despite her slight agitation toward his constant borrowing money she knew he was good for it and it gave her an excuse to bug him about Brandon. She searched through her purse and scrounged up three quarters, two dimes and a nickel. "Here. That's all I have. You need to stop forgetting your bus card. You better pay me back too."

"Aw, you the best girl. I know Brandon done made a good choice when he tol' me 'bout you." Chance gave a silly smile at Tamara and strutted ahead of their group of friends all walking to the bus stop to catch the 3:15 Metro.

"Hey, what time is it?" Porsha asked the group.

"It's 3:05. We got time," Tamara responded looking down at her phone. The bus stop was down on Atkins Blvd., the main road about a quarter mile from the school in front of the gas station.

As they approached the road to cross over to the bus stop she glanced at her phone to make sure they still had plenty of time because she wanted to get home to her little brothers.

She saw a text from Brandon on her phone. "Hey, lady. Headed to practice. Coach got us runnin all the lineups and film stuff for the big game tomorrow night. I'll try to text u later but it might be late. Just thinkin bout u and that perfect smile."

Her heart swooned. *Could he be any sweeter?* She tried not to show her joy but it definitely added a little spring in her step. As she approached to cross the street she looked down at the row of black teenagers all hugging the curb waiting for the walk signal.

Almost simultaneously, a silver four door Chevy Cavalier blared it's rock music as it approached the right turn lane beside them.

It all happened so fast as if time stood still for Tamara for a brief moment and she was in trance watching it all unfold.

She glanced in the car and noticed it was a group of white kids from school all gawking at them on the curb. If tension could be cut with a knife, Tamara thought to herself this would be the moment that it would sever.

It was almost like an old western movie, where the cowboy stares down the bank robber on a desolate town road and they both challenge one another with the look that echoes this town ain't big enough for the two of us.

Piercing through the window were white kids in the car and the black kids on the curb. If looks could have killed every last one of the students, both white and black, would've fallen dead on the spot.

As the car was turning, the white boy in the driver seat decided to hug the curb so tightly his tires squeaked against the concrete barrier forcing two of the black kids standing on the curb to backup or be whipped by the side view mirror.

Tamara looked down at the boys that were pushed back and one of them held up his hand in the air like a gun being held sideways and pointed it at the front passenger and gestured his hand forward as if it were popping bullets.

"Dang!" He put his hand down. "I'm not even playin', y'all, white boy gonna get popped if they keep playin' like they do," Troy, a basketball player who towered above the group continued,

"Dang."

"Na, Forget that. They ain't got no right rollin' up on us like that. Who was that, for real?" Chance shouted as the car disappeared down the road.

"Shut up, y'all. You don't need to be talking like you hard. You ain't gonna do nothin' anyway so don't even play," Porsha argued with the boys.

"Yo, I think that dude is in my English class. He's dumb," Troy started to make light of it with Porsha. "He'll get his."

"Hey, y'all, there's the bus," Porsha pointed to the Metro headed in their direction.

The walk signal appeared and they sprinted across the street to get on the bus.

Tamara looked up and saw the bus, which shook her out of her trance. She shook her head disappointedly and sighed.

As Tamara got on the bus, she swiped her bus card and the driver verified its approval and nodded for her to go find an open seat.

The group slowly filed onto the bus one by one, some used their bus cards, while the others clinked their money into the coin machine.

She headed for the usual spot near the middle of the bus. While the rest of her friends piled into the seats behind her taking up the back half of the cabin.

"Girl, you okay? You awful quiet. What's up?" Porsha asked Tamara once the bus started down the road.

"Yeah, I'm fine. I'm just sick of these fools. They act hard, and the white kids be sellouts, but ain't nobody never do nothing. How's things ever supposed to change if ain't nobody never do nothing to make it change?"

"I hear ya, girl, but you can't let it get to you."

"I know, but it's like that garbage in Social Studies with Kenna. You know? Why did she have to get all hard like that? I mean for real, Porsha. When is it going to get better? When are we all just gonna be cool with each other and stop all the charades?"

"You going deep with this one T. You can't change anything about people. You just gotta deal with it. You just gotta let it ride," she gave Tamara a small smile and tapped her leg. "So, did you and that white girl decide when to meet?"

Tamara rolled her eyes, slightly thankful for the change in conversation. Tamara relaxed her shoulders and replied, "Yeah, we gonna meet on Saturday up at school. Hopefully it won't last too long cause I have a date with Brandon that night," she strummed her words to a beat as she spoke and shrugged her shoulders back and forth.

"Haa---what? Hey! You ain't tell me that. When did that happen?"

"He asked me at lunch today. He is so fine. So sweet too."

"Don't he have a football game Saturday?"

"Na, he plays varsity. So he just has films in the morning but he'll be done by the time Sarah and I are."

"Sarah?"

"The white girl."

"Oh, yeah. So where y'all gonna go?"

"Who, me and Sarah?"

"No, you and Brandon, dummy. I don't care about you and Sa-RAH."

They both giggled at the emphasis Porsha had placed on her name.

Smiling, Tamara responded, "Well, I think he wants to go to dinner or something. He didn't really say, but he was so sweet when he asked me. He seemed so nervous. He was like, 'Um Tamara, you uh, wanna, uh like, maybe, uh go to dinner with me Saturday night?' He wasn't even breathing when he said it. He seemed so shy."

"Brandon? Nervous? He must really like you? I didn't think

varsity running-backs got nervous."

"Na," she said as she smiled into her shoulder.

"So, what'd you say?"

"Girl, what you think I said? I was like sure."

The two girls smiled at each other as the bus bounced over the train tracks heading to Porsha's stop.

"A'ight, girl, I'll catch you later. Gots to get Moms up for dinner. I'm hungry, those hot fries ain't do it for me today at lunch."

The bus pulled up on the outside of the Weldon's Apartment Community. Several little girls were playing double-dutch in the parking lot outside of a three story, six-unit building.

An older black woman walked out of the building when the bus pulled up and just waited there for her child to get off.

"Hey, Chance, get your booty up, boy. Your aunty is waitin'. She don't look like she playin' no games today neither," Porsha teased as she got off the bus.

"Oh, dang, she musta got my cell phone bill. You know how I roll!" Chance tried to act as if he was a big baller and gave Troy a slap and hand shake. "A'ight."

"Bye," Tamara waved as the door closed behind him.

I don't want to deal with Eric. I hope he is asleep. I wonder what time Brandon will call? I have so much homework. Ms. Panacinni's gonna stroke me if I don't do her work. I'll make sure Dom and Wes are good, and I'll get my homework done. I have Science homework too. Dang, I gotta write that English paper too. I got a lot to do.

She pulled out her assignment tracker and continued to think to herself as the bus pulled up to her stop. She waved to Troy and her other friends sitting near her and began her stroll down the road toward her house.

CHAPTER 6
The Car Ride Home

Where is he? He did say meet him outside the locker rooms right? Maybe he's in the gym. Sarah thought to herself as she walked toward the gymnasium door and opened it.

The volleyball team was setting up the net getting ready for practice but Brody was nowhere in sight.

I guess I'll text him. Sarah shut the gym door and began to fumble through her purse to find her cell phone.

Just beside the gymnasium entrance was a janitor's closet. Sarah was so busy looking in her purse that she didn't see Brody sneak out of the closet behind her.

He grabbed her by the arm and pulled her body into his.

Startled, Sarah yelped and jumped around to see Brody laughing.

"What are you doing?" she yelled at him.

He didn't say a word, but just smiled and grabbed Sarah's hand. Looking around to make sure the coast was clear, he escorted Sarah into the janitor's closet.

"What are we doing in here? Didn't you say you have something for me?"

"I do, come here." Brody held onto Sarah with one hand and shut the door behind them with his other. He placed his hands on the back of her head and tilted his head for their lips to embrace. It started with small gentle kisses and quickly escalated to heavy breathing in between tongue exchanges.

Brody started to pull Sarah in closer by grabbing the waist line of her skirt near her bellybutton.

Sarah, feeling uncomfortable, squirmed a bit to shake off his hands, but instead he dropped his hand and put it on her skirt.

Oh my God. What is going on? What is happening? He doesn't want to do this here. We can't. I can't. How do I get him to stop? I don't want him to be mad at me. I really like him. Oh, he kisses so good. No, I can't. What do I do?

Sarah tried to move away but at the same moment Brody grabbed her by the back of her thighs and hoisted her into the air to sit on top of a wooden box in the room.

As he did this Sarah tried to catch her balance and accidentally brushed her hand against the front of his jeans.

Taking this as a sign he started unbuckling his jeans. While he was fuming with his belt buckle, he kissed her even more passionately.

Sarah heard the zipper unzip and she knew she was in over her head.

Oh my goodness. We can't do this. She thought to herself.

"Wait," she whispered.

Unwilling to listen he continued to kiss her.

Sarah stopped his wandering hands on her thigh and pulled her body backward saying more loudly this time, "Wait. We can't do this."

"What? What are you talking about? Sure we can. No one will see us." Brody pulled Sarah's waist closer to his.

"No, Brody, not like this. Jesse, and Zoe, and everyone, they're waiting on us."

"Let 'em wait." He continued to kiss Sarah's neck.

"I'm, I'm… I'm just not ready yet. Not like this. You know? In a closet? I, uh. I want it to be special. You know?"

Letting out a deep sigh and running his hands through his straightened, messy, yet perfect hair he said, "Are you for real Sarah? Really? You're gonna let me get this far with you and just cut me off. When we gonna actually do something more than just kiss? We been kissin' for like two weeks now. I think it's time we embrace what's been given to us." He put his hands on her waist and tugged slightly. Seeing that Sarah's body language wasn't exactly saying no, he gently placed his hands on her legs and leaned his body into her ear and whispered, "Besides, you're my girl. I think I'm falling in love with you. I just can't help myself. You're just so damn sexy," he said as he softly kissed her ear and neck.

It was true that they had been sneaking little kisses for a few weeks, but definitely nothing this extreme. She didn't even know if they were officially an item yet. *Is this his way of asking me out? Are we official now?* Sarah's mind was racing.

"Aw, Brody, I really like you too. And I totally want to. I think. Just not like this. Not yet. Let me think about it. This is all so quick. My mom needs me to get home too. Let's just save it for another time."

Realizing that he wasn't going to win, Brody sighed a deep breath and leaned over to pull up his jeans now lying on the floor atop his flip-flops. "Whatever, Sarah. I just poured my heart out to you, and you don't even want it."

"No, I do, I mean, I think I feel the same way too. But, I don't know. Just let me think about it. K?"

"Alright. Fine," sounding annoyed he continued. "So, you going to Connor's party this weekend?" He tucked his boxers into his jeans and adjusted himself to walk out.

"Oh, yeah, I think so. As long as my mom lets me," Sarah responded as Brody hoisted her off the box and onto the floor. Sensing frustration she asked, "Are you mad at me?"

"No," his tone softened. "I understand. I just really like you, and I want to show you how much I like you. I can wait as long as you want. Well, as long as you don't want to wait too long. You're so hot and I don't know how long I'll be able to stop myself," he sighed, then winked in her direction. Realizing her discomfort, he pulled her into his arms once again, and kissed her on her forehead. "You ready, beautiful?"

"Yeah." Sarah knew he wasn't satisfied, but she was too confused about what she was feeling to know what was right. On one hand, he was hot. He was the guy every girl in the school dreamed of being with and he did make her feel sexy, almost too sexy. But, on the other hand, she had never had sex before. She kept hearing her dad's voice in her head telling her that if she ever got pregnant he would be so disappointed in her. Not to mention how she felt about God. She knew she was supposed to wait until marriage, and up to this point in her life she figured she would. Now, all of a sudden, she wasn't sure if she wanted to wait that long. Nevertheless, she thought she would probably just wait until she knew what was right, and in the janitor's closet, it just didn't feel right.

Quietly opening the door, Brody grabbed Sarah's hand and led her out of the room. He held her hand all the way to Jesse's car but neither one said a word.

As they approached the car his demeanor went back to being the fun loving, too cool guy and Toby began giving him a high five as if it were an unspoken message that he had just taken care of business and he was to be admired.

"Girl, where were you? You guys took forever," Zoe impatiently squawked to Sarah.

"I know, sorry. Are we ready? What time is it?"

"It's like 3:05, let's go," Jesse announced to the group.

Everyone began to pile into his four door, silver Chevy Cavalier.

"Jesse, man, let me drive this beast!" Toby shouted as they all climbed in.

"I wouldn't constitute this ride as a beast, but, ever since I installed those new performance cylinder heads, she is faster than ever," he smiled as he nodded in appreciation of the affirmation. "But, if you wanna drive, then it's all yours," he said as he tossed Toby the keys.

Jesse then took the front passenger seat and Brody sat immediately behind him, squeezing Sarah right next to him with Zoe and Caitlin to her left.

"Sorry, babe, If Toby's gonna drive my car, I need to be up front. I'll make it up to you though," Jesse apologetically said to his girlfriend, Caitlin, who was giving him an annoyed look because she had to be squeezed into the back seat.

Brody took up almost half of the back seat because he couldn't sit with his legs together. He looked like he was trying to be stylish by putting his arm around the ladies to his side, as if he was posing for a designer ad.

"Brody, where is your truck?" Caitlin asked, obviously still unhappy at not getting to sit up front.

"Oh, I had to take it to the shop to get some work done on it. I should have it back today or tomorrow though."

Once everyone was piled in, Toby chauffeured everyone out of the school parking lot toward the main road and turned the music on to some old school rock.

"I can't believe you still listen to this crap," Sarah teased him from the back seat.

"What? Sarah, we can't be friends if you're gonna hate on some Metallica."

"I would much rather be listening to something better," she looked at the other girls and smiled.

Just then Brody started to whisper into Sarah's ear, "Did my heart love till now? Forswear it, sight! For I never saw true beauty till this night," he kissed her shoulder after quoting Shakespeare sending shivers down her spine. "Is that a better tune for you?"

"Oh, okay then, Romeo!" she giggled to Brody, and they smiled at each other, reassuring her that he wasn't mad at her about earlier.

Toby took a side street and headed up to Atkins Boulevard. As he approached the corner to turn right a large group of black kids were standing on the curb waiting to cross.

"Ah man, look at them. Dude, give me five bucks if I run them over with your car," Toby said to Jesse as he turned down the music slightly and began to stare down the group of kids on the corner.

"Ha, heck no, dude, don't wreck my car."

"Dude, watch this," just as Toby spoke he rolled around the turn slowly inching as close as he could to the curb where the kids were standing.

Sarah noticed the stillness in the car as he approached. It was like you could cut the tension with a knife. Brody and Toby stared down the black kids with hatred. They looked at the kids on the curb loathingly, as if it came so naturally, like they were born to hate each other.

The kids on the curb stared back, but Toby got the car so close that one of them was almost knocked over by the passenger side mirror.

An uncomfortable feeling came over Sarah.

"Jesse!" Sarah shouted from the back seat.

"What?" he turned and looked at her

"That is so mean. You know better. You need to be nice. I know you were raised better than that!" she scolded him without realizing Brody was raising his eyebrows out of concern until she looked at him.

"Why you yelling at me? I didn't do it. Toby is the one driving."

"I don't care. This is your car and if you can't control the people in it then you shouldn't be allowed to have it," she said as she realized everyone in the car was staring at her as if she had three eyeballs.

"What?" she said to Brody.

"Uh. Nothing. I just didn't realize you were his mom. Pretty sure Jesse has a mom and Caitlin can handle putting him in his place. Not your job," Brody was being playful, but his tone was mildly harsh.

"Oh." She looked at Jesse. "Sorry, Jess." Then she turned to Caitlin, "Sorry. I didn't mean it any type of way, I just, you know."

"Whatever, you guys," Zoe interrupted the tension. "If we didn't have Mama Sarah in the car then you know we would all be living recklessly. No big thing."

Jesse turned and winked at Sarah just as Zoe nudged her on the shoulder.

As Toby continued down the road the car was mostly silent, except for the music on a low volume.

Sarah felt her phone vibrate as she got a text from Zoe who was sitting right next to her. "U ok? Did something happen w u and Brody?"

Sarah typed her response, "Yeah, I'm good. I'll call u later. I think it's fine." She glanced over at Zoe reading her text and the two girls just nodded and smiled.

Jesse had turned the music back up and the three boys in the car were bobbing their heads to the beat of the drums.

Brody took his right hand that he was leaning on and brushed Sarah's leg with it.

Sarah looked up at him, doe like, as he winked at her. Reassured by this, she wiggled her right shoulder into his chest as if nestling in, feeling comforted by his warm demeanor. There was something about him that intrigued her.

Maybe he's not mad at me. I wonder if he really does love me? I think I love him. He makes me feel something I've never felt before. Is it love? If I am in love, I should just go ahead and have sex with him. Right? Ugh. I don't know.

Toby pulled up to his own house, and he hopped out. Punching fists with Jesse as he got into the driver's seat, he gave a quick glance back at Zoe and smiled.

She reciprocated it with eye batting.

He winked back and said, "See ya'll tomorrow."

"Bye."

"Later, dude."

"See, ya," Caitlin said as she climbed into the front seat, which gave more room to the three of them in the back seat.

Zoe lived right around the corner from Toby so she was the next to go.

Brody lived out even further. He lived in a small house on a busy road outside of the city limits. His house was a dirty grey on the outside with several older cars and trucks in the driveway waiting to be fixed.

As he started to get out of the car Brody kissed Sarah on the lips but pulled away quickly as though he was trying to tease her.

"Later, I'll text you later," he winked at her and effortlessly stepped out of the car before Sarah could respond.

Jesse drove over to their neighborhood about ten minutes down the road into a bigger subdivision.

Sarah's large house had five bedrooms, four bathrooms, a finished basement, and a chandelier hanging from the cathedral ceiling in the foyer.

Jesse pulled into her driveway and Caitlin immediately noticed the golden retriever waiting at the glass door wagging its tail furiously, "Aw, Sarah, is that your dog?"

"Yeah, that's Miss Emma. She's my baby. She's so sweet."

"Aw, I want her. She is so cute."

"I know, right. Okay, Jesse, thanks for the ride. I'll see you guys tomorrow. Bye, Caitlin."

"Bye."

Sarah walked up her driveway alongside the Expedition and up the brick walk to her front door to be greeted by her loving pup. "Hi, Emma!" she said as she pet her dog on the head. "How are you today?"

"Sarah Nicole, is that you?" her mother's voice echoed from the upstairs.

CHAPTER 7
Whatcha Wanna Eat?

As Tamara approached her house she began to smile to herself thinking about how sweet Brandon was at lunch today. *I can't believe he likes me. I mean, I know I'm pretty but he is a varsity football player. He is a junior and already getting offers to go to Notre Dame, Duke, Michigan, Ohio State. He is so sweet. He was so shy today. Aw, I can't wait to talk to him tonight, I really like him.*

As Tamara approached her house, she saw Ms. Grangle, her next door neighbor sitting outside on the lawn in her rocking chair. Ms. Grangle was the Mother Goose of the neighborhood. No one gave her trouble because she never seemed to be in her right mind and she was just too sweet. She would talk to anyone who'd listen.

"Hi there, Ms. Grangle. How are you feeling today?"

"Ohhhhhhhhooooooo. You are such a gem. Look atcha! What a precious blouse you have on there. Come 'ere, darlin'. Let me get a closer look atcha."

"I have to go in and check on my little brothers today, Ms. Grangle. I'll come see you later this week though okay?"

"Oooweee. I remember when I was a looker like you. Boys just loved me. Have you seen my kitty cat, Sniffles?"

Smiling Tamara responded, "No, Ms. Grangle, I haven't."

She had once told Tamara that she named her cat Sniffles because she would always get a stuffy nose when the cat sat on her lap. That's why she sits outside, because the cat doesn't give her the sniffles if she is breathing the fresh air.

"Okay, sugar, I'll be seeing ya. You go wash up for dinner

now."

"Yes, ma'am," as Tamara smiled toward Ms. Grangle she put the code into the garage door keypad to open it. As she opened the door she was greeted with a cloud of cigar smoke and Tom and Jerry cartoons blaring from the television set.

"Tamara!" Dominick, Tamara's three year old brother, came sprinting to her from the floor in front of the TV.

"Sissy!" Followed by Dominick was her youngest brother, Wesley, who was two years old.

"Hi, guys! How are you? I missed you today." Tamara knelt down on the floor and grabbed the running boys with both her arms and hugged them tightly.

The hug was reciprocated with jovial laughter and a wet peanut butter breath kiss on both cheeks, followed by a G.I. Joe climbing up her leg to attack her nose with his machine gun.

"Bang, bang, bang, bang. Look, Mara, he's gettin' your nose," giggled Dominick.

"Uh, oh. He better not get my nose," Tamara raised her body to a standing position with Wesley clinging to her back. "You know what happens when he gets my nose don't ya?"

The boys couldn't stop giggling. Dominick ran toward the couch and belly flopped on it.

Pounding her feet to the couch with Wesley gripping her neck and giggling uncontrollably she said, "The cave monster will get you! Arghhh!" as she said this she flipped Wes over her back and gently tossed him to the couch, and in the same motion she pinned both her giggling brothers against the couch and started to tickle them and make monster noises.

"Hey! What the hell is going on out here?" Eric, her uncle, came around the corner. "Oh. Dang. Tamara. I ain't know it was you. What you doin' home so early?"

"Eric, what is going on? Why are these boys still in their pajamas and why does this entire house smell like cigar smoke?

Mama is gonna kill you if she finds out you smokin' in here," she cocked her head and looked at the tattooed white man standing across from her.

"Whatever. It's cool. I already talked to her. She knows. I tol' her I was gonna have some friends over to play some cards. Ain't no big thing," he said, trying to sound hard.

This man was certainly not Tamara's favorite person. There was something about him that she just didn't trust, his eyes perhaps. She couldn't figure it out. But she knew the longer he stayed in this house, the more she didn't like him.

Tamara didn't say a word to him, she just looked at him and rolled her eyes as he turned away back to the dining room to continue his card game with two of his friends encircled by a cloud of cigar smoke.

As soon as he yelled at them in the living room, the boys' laughter silenced and their bodies went limp on the couch.

Tamara noticed how scared they looked so she hid her anger toward Eric and asked the boys, "What are you silly monster fighters still doing in your PJ's?"

"Jus' watchin' cartoons."

"Carsoons," Wes echoed his older brother.

"Oh, yeah?" glancing at the cat on the television screen with a bandage on his head and a mouse smiling and shaking a bulldog's hand. "Well, I know two boys that need to get into some big boy clothes so we can eat. I'll race you to your room…Ready…Set," she paused and acted as if she was about to get a head start but the brothers leaped over the couch and started screaming. "Go!" she shouted as she allowed them to dash ahead of her to the room they shared next to hers.

The boys were practically twins anyway, being so close in age, so it just made sense that they would end up sharing a room at some point. Tamara's dad was in the process of having the basement finished when he died. However, since it wasn't finished, Eric had to stay upstairs. They turned Wesley's nursery into Eric's room and Wesley moved into Dominick's room sooner than expected.

"Okay, let's see, Wes, where is your turtle shirt?" Tamara said as she sat down in the rocking chair in their room. "Dom, where are your jeans Mama bought you last month?"

The boys had already stripped down to their underwear, which had obviously not been changed since Tamara put them in their pj's the night before.

"Here is," Wes exclaimed from the dresser the two boys shared. He also pulled out a green shirt for Dom to wear. "He' go Dommy." He handed his brother the shirt and the two of them giggled at their naked belly buttons.

Dom hurried over to the bunk beds and pulled the laundry basket out from underneath. "Are deese mine or his?" he asked as he held up a pair of jeans he retrieved from the basket.

"Look at the size, Dom," Tamara patiently said to him. "What is the number?" She had taught Dominick to count to ten and he was about halfway through his ABC's. Wes was still learning one, two, and three.

"Uh. I dunno."

"Yes you do, here, look." Tamara took the jeans from his hands and showed him the tag. "What does this say? What number is that?"

"Tree!"

"Good. So who in this room is three?"

"Me!" Dom triumphantly shouted.

"Good, so those jeans must belong to you, right?"

"Yep. Let's find Wesie's." Dominick rummaged through the basket and looked at the tags of the other clothes saying aloud each number. "Here go. Deese says two. Here you go Wesie," he smiled as he handed the pair of blue jeans to his little brother standing there in his Spiderman undies and Teenage Mutant

Ninja Turtles t-shirt.

After she got the boys dressed and put on their socks, Tamara asked, "So, what did you guys really do all day?"

"I already tol' you, we jus' watched cartoons."

"Yeah? Did Eric watch some with you?"

"No, he was sleepin'."

"Yeah? Did he get up and feed you guys today?"

"No. A lady came o'er and she got the cereal for us."

"Lady? What lady?"

"I don't know, the one with the yellow hair."

Tamara knew exactly who Dominick was referring to. Candice. She had been Eric's girlfriend before he went to jail several years ago. The two of them were toxic together and part of the deal he made with Tamara's mom upon moving in was that he wasn't going to see Candice again.

Eric had spent the majority of his childhood and adult life in and out of jail for petty crimes and drug dealing. He and Candice were high school sweethearts but neither one of them ended up graduating. Their relationship was always one of two temperatures, scalding hot, or ice cold. They only knew how to fight and it was only a matter of time before he ended up back on drugs if she was hanging around. Which is why Tamara's mom made him promise to stay away from her this time.

He had been doing a fairly good job for the past year or so, but lately the boys had mentioned Candice on more than one occasion so Tamara knew things were going to get ugly soon.

Eric had promised his sister when he first moved in that he would never let anything happen to her kids. He said that he loved her that much and since her husband died, it was his job to step up and take care of things.

Obviously, wanting to believe the best in him, she allowed him to move in with the understanding that if her kids got involved in anything scandalous it would be his last day in her home.

Often times when Tamara heard her little brothers talk about some of the ignorant things Eric would do during the day while they were alone with him, she would feel extremely guilty. She often tried to fill the role of their mother for the boys so they could feel the love that Tamara had felt for so long when her dad was alive and everything was perfect.

"So you had cereal? Well that's not enough. How about we go find some food for those bellies of yours and then go outside and play for a bit?" Tamara tried to sound excited, but her guilt was taking over and her voice cracked a little. "Whatcha wanna eat?" she asked the boys as they hurried out of their room down to the kitchen.

"Cookies!"

"Cuukie!" Wes copied his brother.

"No sillies, no cookies. How about spinach?" Tamara teased.

"Ewhh. Yuck."

Tamara browsed through the cupboards and fridge to try and find something easy to fix before heading outside.

"Hey, T, bring me three beers since you in there," Eric's voice made Tamara's spine shiver.

Eric had an explosive personality. Little things would set him off and make him lose his mind for no reason. About a month ago, Tamara had borrowed his cell phone charger and instead of asking her for it back, he raided her entire room screaming at the top of his lungs that he wouldn't be stolen from.

Not wanting to start another fight with him or aggravate him since the boys were right there, she quietly grabbed three beers from the refrigerator and took them to the adjacent dining room. Without saying a word she set them on the edge of the table for Eric and his two buddies. She didn't make eye contact with him because she knew she would go off on him if she did.

Not to her surprise, he didn't even say thank you as she walked away.

"How about some mac-n-cheese?" Tamara asked the boys who were sitting on the kitchen floor anxiously waiting her return from the dining room.

"Yeah, yeah, yeah," the boys agreed.

This was one of Tamara's favorite things to eat. Macaroni and cheese with hot sauce mixed in it. As she prepared the food, she engaged the boys in a conversation about letters.

Mostly, Dominick answered, but Wes was always mimicking his words.

Once the food was ready Tamara glanced into the dining room where the cigar smoke was looming overhead and realized they didn't have a place to sit at the table. Instead of starting a fight with Eric, she got three bowls down and filled them each with macaroni and cheese and the three of them sat at the island in the kitchen where she usually did her homework when her mom was cooking dinner.

Tamara put the bottle of hot sauce in between them. Wesley tried to pick up the bottle to put into his bowl and dropped it on the floor. Luckily, it didn't spill, but the trio giggled at his failed attempt.

"I don't think you are quite ready for hot sauce yet, buddy."

"Yeah, Wesie, you not big enough like me. I'm a big boy, you still a baby."

"Hey," Tamara frowned at Dominick. "Wes, is a big boy too. Wesley is your best friend, Dominick, and you need to be nice to him. He is your brother and you need to look after him and help him. Don't say mean things to him."

Dom tilted his head and looked at his little brother. "I sorry Wesie. You so big!" Simultaneously, both boys put their arms above their heads in a "so big" motion.

"Did you get enough to eat?" Tamara asked them as she scooped up their bowls off the counter and put them in the sink.

"Yeah. Can we go outside now?" Dom asked.

"Sure. Run to your room and get your shoes on and we'll go out."

"Yay!" they both scampered up off the floor and back up to their room.

While they were getting their shoes on, Tamara washed out their bowls and the pot. She put the leftovers in an extra bowl and covered it with tinfoil then placed it in the fridge to save for later.

"You guys ready?" she hollered from the living room.

"Where y'all goin'?" Eric yelled, trying to sound like the man of the house.

Pretending not to hear him, she stood by the door and waited for her brothers to come down from their room.

"I asked you a question." He was standing in the walkway between the dining room and the living room now.

Still not saying a word, she raised her eyebrow and glared over in his direction.

"Where you think you goin'?" he spoke a bit louder to try to prove his authority.

"We are goin' outside. They need to go play cause they been sitting in front of the TV all day while you playin' your little childish games with someone you know Mama tol' you not to see."

"Childish games? What you mean someone I ain't supposed to see?" He put his cigar up to his mouth and let it sit in between his puckered lips.

"You know as well as I do that Candice isn't supposed to be anywhere around here, Eric," she tilted her head.

"What? Dang, T. How you know about that?" he started to back pedal.

"Uh, do I look like I have stupid written across my forehead?" she mimicked her mother.

"It ain't nothing. She just came over here once. I told her to leave. It ain't no big deal. She knows I gotta be the man in this house now since your daddy died. She knows I gotta take care of y'all. She ain't coming back," he shook his head in hopes of convincing Tamara as much as himself. "I promise. Please don't tell your mom. She will kick me out. We got a good thing going here. Please don't tell her."

"Fine. Just get your little friends and the smoke out of the house," she rolled her eyes as she walked toward the back door. She knew it was only a matter of time before her mom found out just how bad it was getting with him around.

The boys came out from their room and the three of them walked outside to the swing set in the back yard.

The boys hurried over to play while Tamara walked over and sat on a lawn chair beside them.

She got out her phone and texted her mom, "Boys just ate a snack. We are outside playn' now. I got a lot of HW. What time you comin home?"

A few minutes later, she got a text back from her mom saying she would be home a little after ten and to get the boys bathed and in bed.

Tamara remembered her mom saying that Eric had to be to work at nine so she knew if she got the boys to bed by eight she would have plenty of time to get her work done. She looked at her phone and realized it was almost 5:30. It was a beautiful October evening so she decided she would let the boys play until 6:30 if they wanted.

She walked over to the swing and began to sway a little bit while keeping a close eye on the two crazy dragon slayers under the monkey bars.

Looking down at her phone again after some time had passed, she realized it was twenty after six. "Hey guys. It's getting late. Think we should head in?"

"Nooooo," they both whined.

"That crybaby stuff might work with Mama but you know it

don't work with me," she teased with a smile in her voice. "Let's head in and get a bath, then I'll let you guys have some cookies before you go to bed. Sound good?"

"Cuukie!" Wes shouted as he jumped down from the slide. He ran over to Tamara and hugged her leg.

She picked him up and hugged him.

"I wan' cuukie."

"Yeah, well let's get you cleaned up and eat some dinner, then we can get one. Okay?"

"O-tay." He jerked his body out of her arms and ran over to his brother who was still pretending to be a dragon trapped in a dungeon. "Dommie, les' go!"

Dominick crawled out from under the playset and wiggled the grass off his jeans.

The three headed back toward the house and raced over the patio to the sliding back door.

"Take your shoes off at the door guys," Tamara shouted. She walked the rest of the way into the house, exhausted from her long day. When she walked in, Eric's friends weren't there any longer and he was upstairs in the spare bathroom shower.

The shower made a loud noise all throughout the house so Tamara took the boys to their room and let them get out their toys until the bathroom was open for use.

She heard the water stop and a few moments later the door opened. She heard him rustling around then he closed the door to his bedroom.

She left the boys in their room for a few minutes while she went down to the kitchen to open the window to help some of the lingering smoke clear out. She glanced down at the microwave and noticed the clock said 7:03.

She walked back upstairs toward Eric's bedroom and tapped on the door. "Eric?"

No answer.

She knocked again a little louder this time. "Eric?"

The door flew open and he was standing there with a green towel wrapped around his hips and his chest showcasing tattoos of dice and cards on one pectoral muscle, and an old woman's face on the other, who he claimed to be his deceased grandma. "What?" he blankly stared as he stood there still dripping from the shower.

I swear, I honest to God think he is high. One second he's cool, then next second he's a jerk. I don't get it. He is bipolar. He is off. There is something so off about him. She thought to herself.

"The boys need to get a bath. I wanted to make sure you were done in there so I can get them in the tub."

"Yeah, I'm done," he said as if he was annoyed. He stood there staring at her like he was waiting for her to say something else. "What else you need?" his voice getting louder and rude this time.

"Nothing. I was just checkin'," she snorted as she walked away and into her brothers' room.

She got her brothers into the tub and washed up.

Dominick was only a year older than Wesley but if you asked him, he was Wesley's father. He liked to show Wesley how to do everything, and Wes just hung onto every word he was told by his older brother. Dom showed him how to wash under his arms, but every time Wes put his arm in the air to wash it, Dom would tickle it and the two would just giggle and squirm around in the tub.

Tamara sat on the floor against the bathroom door just watching the two boys be silly and making sure they were being productive. When they needed help, she would help, but she mostly allowed them to do it on their own.

After the bath she heated up some leftover meatloaf, mashed potatoes, and peas and the three of them ate together. She gave them each a cookie once they finished their dinner. She brushed their teeth and got them both into their bedroom.

Dom loved to sleep on the top bunk because according to him, he is bigger and stronger.

Tamara sat down in the rocking chair in their room next to the bunk bed and read them a Dr. Seuss book.

The boys both fell asleep rather quickly so she kissed them on their foreheads, flipped on their night-light, and went downstairs to start working on her homework.

She plopped down on the couch with her ear buds in and her schoolbooks to begin working. *I don't understand this problem. Am I supposed to factor here? Oh. I see. I get it. I hope Ms. P. don't make me demonstrate again, this stuff is hard.*

Interrupting her thoughts, Eric stood right in front of her.

She just looked at him and took her ear buds out.

"Hey, so thanks for getting the boys to bed. I know you mad about Candice coming over but for real, ain't no big deal. No need to go tell your mama." He stepped closer to her. "Your mama is helping me out right now while I save up for my own place, and I'm taking care of those boys upstairs while she is working hard all the time." He leaned in closer to her. "You know she wouldn't have to work all the time like she does if her husband was still alive instead of dying in a car crash coming to pick you up. Maybe you should think about that before you go and tell her anything crazy about me."

Tamara felt partially threatened by his demeanor so she nodded her head.

"That's a good girl, Tamara." He put his hand on her upper thigh. "I think you and I will get along yet," winking at her, he stood up straight and poked her nose with his finger then turned and walked out the door.

Ugh. I can't stand him. He makes my stomach hurt. Her body quivered. It wasn't the first time he had touched her leg like that. He didn't seem to think there was anything wrong with it and had done it several times in the past year. It never made her comfortable though. Every single time he came anywhere near her like that she shivered at the thought of his inappropriateness. *Ugh. He is so awful. I hope he moves out soon. I know Mama wants to help him but she is just being naïve. He is no good.*

She put her earbuds back in and tried to focus herself back into her Calculus book.

About a half hour into her homework, she got a text from Brandon, "Hey lady. How r u? I've been thinkn bout u."

"Hi. Yeah? What about?" she responded.

"Our convo at lunch earlier. How beautiful u r. How much I like you."

Tamara didn't know how to respond to this so she sent a blushing face emoji.

"See ya tomorrow," he responded followed by a winking emoji.

"See ya." She smiled and took a deep breath in and exhaling for a long time. *He literally just made my whole evening so much better. He is so sweet. I hope he's for real.* She put her phone down beside her and put her nose back into her homework.

CHAPTER 8
Was That Mom?

"Sarah Nicole, is that you?" Sarah's mom shouted again from upstairs.

"Yeah, Mom. It's me. Did you take Emma out yet?"

"Yes I did. She was outside playing with Ben and Ethan in the backyard most the afternoon before they went to soccer practice."

"Aw, her's a good girl aren't ya?" she whispered to her dog as she leaned over to pet her excited companion. "What's for dinner?" Sarah shouted up the stairwell in her mom's direction.

"Huh?"

Rolling her eyes Sarah shouted, clearly articulating her words, "I said, what's for dinner?"

"Oh," her mom responded walking out of the bathroom at the top of the stairs to stand against the railing that overlooked the foyer and hanging chandelier. "Well, I have to go pick up Ben from soccer and Daddy's gonna be home late so I was thinking we might just have leftovers from last night."

"Ehw, I don't want beef stroganoff again," taking a deep sigh, Sarah continued, "Can I drive to pick Ben up?"

"Don't you have homework? You should just stay here and work on that."

"Yeah, but I really wanna drive, Mom. You never let me drive unless Daddy tells you to. Please?"

"Well," Mrs. Benson looked at her watch and stared out the adjacent window for a moment, then looked down at her anxious teenage daughter. "Okay."

"Yes! Thanks, Mom." Sarah skipped into the kitchen and took a juice box out of the refrigerator. They always had juice boxes and snacks around because Ben, Sarah's six year old brother, got home at 1:30 from school every day.

Within a second of her opening her juice box, her mom came down from the upstairs holding a laundry basket.

"Wow. Look at you. You look nice. What's the occasion Miss Sandy?" Sarah noticed her mom was wearing a pink skirt and sparkly sandals with a white button down blouse. Her mom usually dressed to impress but she typically only wore skirts if it was really hot outside or if she had an important meeting of some sort.

"Oh, this old thing? I was just cleaning out the closet the other day and found it. It's just so nice outside and I don't want to miss out on any good weather before the snow hits," her mom dismissed the question. "So, honey, how was school today?"

"Fine." Sipping on the juice, Sarah grabbed the magazine that was resting on the island in the kitchen.

"Just fine? Nothing major happened?"

Forgetting all about the incident from the encounter with the girl and Ms. P., Sarah shook her head as she peeled back a banana.

"Hm. Okay, well, how's that Bobby you're dating?"

"Mom, it's Brody, and we're not dating. We're talkin'. You know. Like hangin' out."

"Well, Bobby, Brody, or Bimby, I'm sure he's great."

Sarah noticed her mom seemed a bit distracted, "What's wrong with you?"

"Oh, nothing, I'm just worried about getting to Ben's practice. We should probably head on over there. I don't want you to speed."

Flipping through the pages of the magazine, Sarah tossed it aside and walked to the front door.

"Sarah Nicole, are you finished with this juice and banana?" her mom sternly pointed to the juice box and banana peel she left lying on the counter top.

"Oh, yeah, I'm done." Sarah knew what was coming next, *then get in here and throw it away. We aren't raising wolves around here.*

"Then get in here and throw it away. We aren't raising wolves in this house."

Sarah did exactly as she was told because she knew her mom meant business when it came to keeping things clean and tidy.

"Thank you, sweetheart. You are such a good daughter. I'm so lucky to have such great kids."

"C'mon. Let's go," Sarah excitedly pleaded with her mom so that she could practice driving some more.

The two of them grabbed their purses off the hutch next to the door and headed out the garage entry.

"Bye, Emma. Luvs you!" Sarah patted her dog on the head as she headed out the door.

Sarah skipped ahead of her mom and climbed into the driver's seat of the Expedition in the driveway. Once they were both in she pressed the automatic garage door button and buckled her seatbelt.

"Check your mirrors, honey."

Sarah lightly rolled her eyes at her mother's annoying words but she knew if she was going to drive she had to deal with it. She checked her mirrors, then adjusted the rear view mirror slightly.

"So," her mother began to small talk, "tell me more about this Brody guy. What grade is he in? Have you two kissed? Should we be worried? Should we meet him? Has Jesse met him? What does Jesse think about him?"

"Geeze, Mom," Sarah rolled her eyes. "What is this, twenty-one questions?"

"No, I just think it's important to know what is going on in your life."

"Okay, well, he is a senior, and no, you shouldn't be worried. He is super sweet. And yes, Jesse knows him and they are friends, so it's cool."

"Oh, okay, does he go to church?"

"I don't know."

"Well you said he was friends with Jesse, so I figured maybe you guys all met at youth group or something?"

"Well, I mean he's not like best friends with Jesse. He hangs out with me so he has to be friends with Jesse."

"Oh, I see," her mother smiled.

"What?"

"Oh, nothing. You and Jesse are a package deal I guess."

"Oh my God, whatever, Mom. You totally don't get it."

"I get it alright. You will too someday, my dear. You'll see. You and Jesse are going to end up walking down the aisle together. Mark my words."

"Ugh. Whatever, Mom. I like Brody. He likes me. Besides Jesse has a girlfriend. Jesse is my best friend, not my boyfriend," she snipped back. "Can we please stop talking about this?"

The rest of the car ride was mostly silent except for an occasional, "Turn right at the light," or "There's a red light," from the passenger seat.

Sarah obeyed the orders, relaxing a bit when her mom pointed out what a great driver she's becoming. Sarah pulled the vehicle into Saint Luisa Catholic Church and pulled around behind the school building. There were soccer fields filled with teams of kids, all with their parents surrounding the fields in their lawn chairs.

"Just park here, dear," her mom pointed to a spot away from the rest of the cars.

As they approached Ben's field they saw him dribbling the ball all the way down the field to kick a goal. Missing, the goalie jumped on top of the ball, and looking like fun, four more kids piled onto the goalie.

"Aw, aren't they so cute? Sarah bear, will you stay here and wait for Ben? I'm gonna run to the bathroom real quick."

"Sure." Sarah watched her brother high five his friends as her mom walked to the bathroom across the parking lot. To Sarah it seemed like an odd bathroom to use when there was an outhouse right next to the field, but she quickly dismissed this thought reminding herself that her mother is just a clean freak and an outhouse isn't suitable for her.

After a few more tackles, high fives, and tumbles, the practice came to a close. One of the boy's parents was the coach. Mr. Kosta. He was young and good looking with his trim dark hair. Secretly, the mothers loved him, but all being married, pretended not to notice his good looks, charming personality, and the blatantly obvious lack of a wedding ring on his left hand. They would just drool from the sidelines behind their sunglasses as their husbands paid no attention to their sudden interest in the game.

Once, it was rumored that his wife had died during childbirth, but it was mostly just speculation.

"Alright, boys, you did great today. I think we have a real chance against the Ducks this weekend. Don't forget, be to the fields by eight to warm up. Game time is at nine," his voice was deep but playful, which matched his athletic appearance.

The boys all pushed each other as they rushed over to their moms and dads waiting for them.

"Hey, Turd," Sarah enjoyed taunting her little brother.

"Hey, Sarah bear," Ben didn't even notice the name calling.

"How was practice? I saw you almost score a goal."

"Did you see it? It was so great. I almost scored. I'm gettin' so good."

"Yeah, before you know it you'll be playing on the professional team."

Ben smiled because he loved watching the Cincinnati soccer team and would beg to go to as many games as possible. "Where's Mommy?" he questioned as he followed his sister toward the car.

"She just ran to the bathroom real quick. Let's get in the car. You can watch your cartoons in the back on your tablet." She looked up to see if her mom was coming from the bathroom and noticed Coach Kosta headed to the same bathroom. *That's so weird. What is wrong with the outhouse? Ehw! It probably overflowed or something.*

Ben climbed into the backseat and Sarah pulled out the tablet from the center console and connected it to her phone's hotspot so he could watch his shows.

"Hey, are you good? I'm gonna go check on Mom. I'll be right back, k?"

He was clearly more into his show than the outside world, offering no response.

Sarah walked into the bathroom her mom had entered but didn't hear or see anything. She looked under the stalls but she only saw a pair of sneakers and legs, which didn't belong to her mother. *Hmm. I wonder where she went. Maybe she went out the other door when I came in. Oh well. I guess I'll pee real quick since I'm in here.*

Sarah quietly walked into an empty stall and began to hear whispers and what sounded to be heavy kissing in another stall. *Uh. Are you serious? What is that?*

The whispers were followed by a man's voice murmuring. Then a woman's voice followed, "Shhh."

Oh my God. Tell me this isn't happening. Are there two people in that stall? Didn't they hear me come in? Oh my God. Thank God Mom's not in here to hear this. She would be mortified. No way. This can't be for real?

At the same time, she heard the woman's voice quietly giggle, and that's when it hit Sarah. Like a tidal wave against an edged cliff, *No, it can't be.*

She knelt down to look under the stall and simultaneously a sparkly flip-flop touched the floor with a leg pressed against the owner of the sneakers. She realized it wasn't just any woman's sparkly flip-flop, it was her mother's. *Oh my God. I uh. Uh. What? Uh. Why? Mom?*

"Mom?" she accidentally voiced her thoughts out loud and a loud gasp escaped from the woman's mouth and Sarah's in chorus.

Sarah frantically fumbled the lock on the bathroom stall and after what seemed like a thousand attempts, she burst through the stall and bolted straight for the exit. Behind her she heard rustling but she didn't turn around to see if they saw her. She just made a dash for the car and threw herself into the backseat with her little brother.

"Hey. Watch it. I'mma tell Mom."

"Shut up, Ben. Go sit in the front."

"But I'm watchin' my show."

"I don't care, Ben! Go sit in the front seat before Mom gets in." Sarah looked toward the bathroom and saw her mother walking in the direction of their car. Sarah hoisted Ben off the seat and shoved him toward the front. "Seriously, Ben, I'm not playing. Get in the front."

"Hey. I'm telling you been mean to me."

"Shut up, Ben."

Just then her mother got into the driver's seat and looked back at Sarah who refused to make eye contact with her.

"Ben, buckle up," she said still looking back at her daughter.

If body language was a weapon that killed, Sarah's body would have killed her mother in that moment. Her arms folded across her chest, and nostrils flared. Her breathing was so heavy she could have easily been mistaken for a dragon.

"Sarah, buckle up. We will talk about this later."

Shooting her mother a look of hatred, she thought to herself, *Are you serious? You are such a horrible person. Ahh. I can't believe this. I hate you. How could you? What about Dad? I can't believe you would do this to him.*

Tears started to well up in her eyes. Trying not to let the floodgates release but it was like fighting against a hurricane.

There was no stopping the tears. She was so full of confusion, and questions, and grief, she could do nothing but cry.

"Mommy? What's wrong with sissy?" Ben quietly asked from the passenger seat.

Glancing in her rear view mirror at her heartbroken daughter in the back, she reached her arm to place it on Sarah's knee. "She'll be alright, honey. She's just upset right now," she said as she patted Sarah on the leg.

Quickly flinging her legs away from her mother's reach, Sarah could say nothing. She was choking on her tears as snot smothered her face and make up for the rest of the car ride home.

As soon as the car pulled into the garage of their home, Sarah threw her body out of the car and stomped into the house and ran up to her bedroom slamming the door behind her. *I hate her. I hate her. I hate her.*

"Sarah, I will come talk to you in a little while."

She heard her mother call from the stairwell in a calm, controlled tone.

How can she be so calm? Reckless? I can't even. I can't even. Her thoughts drifted into a land of nothingness as she was flooded with grief and pain. She just put her head on the floor of her bedroom and stared up at the ceiling in a puddle of tears. There were no words or thoughts going through her mind. She was motionless, almost ripped apart in despair over her discovery.

"Sarah?" her mom said as she tapped on her bedroom door.

Sarah refused to answer.

"Sarah. I'm coming in. We need to talk."

"I don't wanna see you! I hate you!" She rolled over onto her stomach and the tears came flooding back.

Her mother opened up the door and gently walked in closing the door behind her and sat down next to her crying daughter. "Sarah? Honey, I know you're confused right now. I know you must hate me for what you think you heard."

Sarah interrupted, "What I think I heard? Mom! You were with Ben's coach in the bathroom. It's not like you were just accidentally in the same stall! God!"

"Sarah, quiet down. It's not like that."

"It's not like what, Mom? You cheating on Dad?"

"Now listen, Sarah, I love your father very much, and I never wanted to hurt him. Sometimes adults do things that we can't explain."

"Well try explaining this one to Dad! Or are you even going to tell him?" Sarah was still yelling.

"Sarah, I don't want you telling your father. I will tell him when I am ready. I love your father very much and it isn't that serious."

At the same time the garage door opened, and her mother's demeanor stiffened.

"Sarah. He is home. I'm asking you to please not tell him. I will tell him. I will end things with Ben's coach, then your father and I will have a heart to heart about it. I know what I did is wrong. I know that. I will fix this with your father. Please allow me to do on my own terms. Okay?"

Refusing to answer, Sarah turned her back to her mother and sniffed in the snot that had accumulated under her nose.

Uneasily, her mother stroked the back of Sarah's hair with her hand, stood up, and quietly walked out of her room to leave Sarah with her thoughts.

I can't believe she would do this. What? I'm not allowed to tell Dad because she wants to keep doing it. I don't understand. Doesn't she love us anymore? Daddy loves her, he is going to be so sad. I can't tell him. I don't wanna make him mad at me. Oh, I don't know what to do. Sarah just lay there crying until she began to fall asleep.

"Sarah bear, dinner's ready." Ben was standing right next to her with his face almost touching hers.

Startled, Sarah jumped back. "Ben, what do you want?"

"Dinner's ready."

"Okay. I'll be down in a minute," she was almost whispering as she rubbed her eyes to adjust and look at the alarm clock next to her bed. *7:34. I slept for almost an hour. I have so much homework.* All her thoughts came abruptly back to her about her mother and her sadness crushed her. *Oh my God. I can't believe she would do this. I wonder if she told Dad yet.*

She followed her brother downstairs and as she did she heard her dad in the kitchen laughing with her mother. When she turned the corner around into the dining room she saw the two of them laughing over the sink.

Her mother saw Sarah from the corner of her eye and tensed up. "Sarah, did you wash your hands? Ben?"

"I did," Ben shouted.

"Yeah," Sarah whispered, knowing full well she didn't wash her hands but she really didn't want to right now. She didn't want to do anything other than go back to her room and cry.

"Hey, baby girl! How's my princess today?" her dad asked as he came in for a hug.

"Hi, Daddy."

"Oh no, What's wrong with my Sarah bear?" He could sense her uneasiness.

"Oh nothing," her mother interrupted, "she had a run in with a girl at school today so she's just feeling down." Her mother shot Sarah a look that told her she knew about the incident she was in this morning.

How could she know about that? I didn't tell her. Did Ms. Panacinni call?

"Ha. Did you give her a sharp left hook?" her dad teased as he motioned his left hand in an upward direction and smiled.

"No, it wasn't like that," she whispered, still hesitant to smile.

The four of them sat down to the table.

"Okay. Who's gonna say the prayer tonight? Ben? You want to?" Mrs. Benson's voice sounded extremely cheerful.

"Yeah, Yeah."

The four took each other's hands and closed their eyes.

"Dear, God," he began, "thank you for this food today. You are awesome. Thank you for my mommy and Daddy and Sissy. Please let hungry kids like me have food too. Amen."

Everyone followed with an amen and looked at Ben and smiled.

"That was real good, Benny," her mom encouraged.

"Yeah, kiddo. That was great," her dad winked across the table at his wife and grabbed the peas and passed them to her. "So, what was this incident about, honey?"

Sarah could tell that her dad really wanted an answer this time. Sighing, she looked at her mother as if betrayed. "It was nothing. There was a big fight at school this morning and a black girl pushed me out of the way and I fell into Ms. Panacinni and knocked her down. It really wasn't a big deal. No one got in trouble. No biggie really."

"No biggie, Sarah?" her dad protested. "What do you mean no biggie? Someone pushed you and it's not a big deal? What kind of school am I sending you to anyway? Don't they teach those kids any respect? Don't parents these days try to teach their kids how to handle things using their smarts instead of their fists? "

"It's really no big deal," Sarah contended.

"Well, Sarah," her mother interrupted, "your teacher made it sound like you perhaps need to learn a little self-awareness and not walk right through a chaotic situation. Perhaps you were daydreaming about your new boyfriend?" she tilted her head at her daughter and raised her eyebrows.

Feeling betrayed, Sarah shot back, "Yeah, you would know a lot about self-awareness wouldn't you, Mom?" Sarah gave her mother a look of animosity.

Quickly interrupting, Sarah's dad raised his voice, "Hey. Sarah, don't speak to your mother like that. What's gotten into you, kid?"

"Why don't you ask Mom what's gotten into her? Or better yet, why she was alone in a bathroom stall with another man!" Sarah knew the second those words spilled from her mouth that she had betrayed her mother. In that moment though, she didn't care, she didn't care about anything other than making her mom feel the impact of her betrayal.

Her mother's eyes opened wide and stared right into Sarah's. For a brief second, the two locked eyes and the only sound to be heard was the ticking of the grandfather clock in adjacent living room.

Her dad's voice interrupted their trance, "Sarah? Sandy, what's she talking about?" He looked back and forth from his daughter to his wife, both beginning to well up with tears, then across the table to his son who was just staring in confusion at the commotion.

Sarah couldn't hold back her tears any longer. "I...I…I," choking on her words, "I…God!" The tears were now a waterfall, not knowing what to do with all this emotion, "I… I hate you!" staring through her mother's eyes, she pushed herself away from the table and her chair went flying backward as she rushed for her bedroom.

She flung herself onto her bed and buried her tears and snot into her teddy bear that had shouldered many soakings throughout the years.

About a minute later there was a tiny scratch at her door and then a timid, quiet Ben, peeked in and just stood there waiting for a look from his big sister.

She turned and motioned him to come in and he quickly scampered with Emma tailing behind him as he closed the door and ran to Sarah's open arms. Without saying a word, Sarah just hugged her little brother and cried into his hair like he was her teddy bear.

Ben, being too frightened to say anything, was just grateful for the consoling hug from his big sister.

Sarah heard dishes being slammed around in the kitchen, and the two of her parents yelling, mostly her father's voice asking, "Why," and, "How could you?"

A loud crash of dishes shattering came from the kitchen followed by her mother's apologies, and stomping across the floor.

Sarah and Ben both jumped at the crashing of each dish, and for a moment they paused in silence waiting for what was next.

The garage door opened and she heard a car start.

She stood up and walked to the window only to watch her dad's car squeal out of the driveway and into the dusk of the fading day.

"Sarah?" Ben quietly asked.

Looking back at him on the bed she noticed how little he seemed.

"What's going on?"

Wiping the tears from her face, she walked back over to her brother and sat next to him on the bed. "Mommy and Daddy are having a lot of problems right now. But I need you to be strong for me, okay? I'll be strong for you if you can be strong for me. I know you are confused, but I am always here for you no matter what. Okay, Ben?" She placed her hand on the back of his head and sadly looked at his bewildered appearance.

"Is Daddy coming back?"

"I don't know. But I'm here, I'm not leaving you."

Hearing a loud thud downstairs, she realized that her mom was probably beside herself in this moment. "Ben, how about you go get in the bath and I'll be in to check on you in a bit?"

"But, I wanna go see Mommy," he whined.

"Mommy is probably cleaning up right now, I'm going to go down and help her and then she will be up to see you in a bit."

Not satisfied at all with this answer, Ben stuck out his bottom lip about to cry.

"I know. I promise, it's gonna be okay. Just go take a bath, take your toys in there and I'll be in shortly. I promise."

"Alright," he whispered and sulked out of Sarah's room and into the bathroom.

Sarah quietly tiptoed down the staircase toward the kitchen. When she walked in, she didn't see her mother at first, but when she walked closer to the island, she heard a sniffle come from the floor behind it. She saw her mother on her knees with her face in her hands crying above a shattered plate.

"Mom?" Sarah whispered. "Mom?" She walked over to her crying mother who peered up at her with a look of desolation and despair.

"Oh, Sarah. I'm so sorry." Tears drenched the porcelain pieces below her as she coughed and choked. She was miserable and weeping. "I never meant to hurt you. Or Ben. Or your dad. Sarah, I am so sorry."

Sarah, put her hand on her mother's back and knelt down to hug her. "I'm sorry I told."

"Oh, Sarah. You didn't do this. Don't you be sorry. You hear me? This isn't your fault. This is all my doing. I did this. And I know you don't understand and I know you," blubbering over her agony, "I know you hate me." More tears and choking.

"I don't hate you," Sarah interrupted.

Continuing over Sarah's rebuttal her mother said, "I promise, I will make this up to you and your brother." She collapsed into Sarah's hug, and the two of them just sat there on the floor amidst the shards of glass sobbing and choking.

"How long has your affair been going on, Mom?"

"Honey, it really isn't yours to worry about. Please don't," her mom sniffed.

"Was it just this once? Maybe Dad can forgive you if it was only once?"

"Sarah," her mother leaned back and looked at her daughter to continue, "it's more complicated than that. The bottom line is that I made a mistake. I need to fix what I broke, but I have to want to fix it first. Your father and I will get through this, but I just don't know if I want to anymore."

"What do you mean, Mom? You are the one who has always said that marriage is sacred and forever. That once you get married you are stuck with that person forever. Why wouldn't you want it?"

"Oh, Sarah," her mother's crying continued, "you're right. I know," she sighed.

Sarah didn't know what else to say because she didn't have any words for the disarray of feelings she was experiencing. On one hand, she was so angry at her mom for cheating on her dad, but on the other hand, she had never seen her mom cry like this, and she felt sorry for her and the disaster that had been created. So instead of saying anything else, Sarah just picked up the dustpan and broom and began to sweep up the dishware surrounding her heartbroken mother.

Her mother stayed on the floor weeping, so Sarah left her to her thoughts and went upstairs to check on her brother in the bath.

"Hey, you. You wrinkly yet?"

Splashing around, he smiled and looked at his fingers, "Yep."

"Alright then. Let's get you outta here and into bed." She put a towel on the toilet and left the bathroom.

He was getting old enough that he didn't need or want anyone helping him dry off.

As she shut the door she reminded him to brush his teeth. She then headed into his room and turned down his sheets and turned on his soccer ball lamp next to his bed.

When he came into the room she pointed to his bed and he dutifully climbed in. She pulled the covers over him and sat next to him on the edge of the bed. "Mommy isn't feeling well so I'm tucking you in tonight. But don't you worry about her, okay? I'll be right next door if you need anything."

"K," he responded with a bit of wonder in his voice. "Sarah, is everything okay? You can tell me you know. I'm not a little kid anymore. I'm a big boy."

Very matter of fact she replied, "Ben, everything is fine. Mom is just sad that she and Dad got in a fight. Dad is just mad so he left for a little while. If you want you can say a prayer for them. But then you need to get some sleep," she said as she lightly tickled his chest.

Giggling he responded, "What about you? Are you okay?"

"Yeah, I'm good," She was surprised by his maturity. She kissed him on his forehead and as she got up she pinched him on his arm. "And that's for being a dorkus!" she teased and winked.

"Hey!"

"Hey yourself. G'nite."

"Night-nite."

Sarah went to the bathroom and washed her face, then to her room and started on her homework. Realizing that she hadn't talked to Brody all evening, she scrambled for her phone.

Four missed FaceTime calls. Eight new messages. Six from Brody. Two from Zoe. Geesh. I'd better text these people back. Don't want them to send out a search party for me. She reflected on the messages she received and responded to everyone telling them it was a crazy night with family and that she would catch up with everyone tomorrow.

Brody responded within thirty seconds, "Is everything ok?"

Smiling she responded, "Thanks for caring. I love that. Its fine. Or it will be. Just crazy parents."

"Did you just tell me you love me?" he texted back immediately with a winking and kissing emoji.

"Good Night, Brody!" she smiled as she messaged him back.

"Can I see you tonight? We can FaceTime?"

"No way. I look like crap. My makeup is all washed off. No way! I'll just see u tomorrow."

"You don't need makeup. Ur perfect just the way u are. Ur sunlight to me. You are so beautiful. Ok, I will just dream 'bout u instead. G'night."

She sent him back a kissy face emoji and smiled and began to feel somewhat lighter.

Shortly into her homework Zoe texted her back, "Girl? What's up? U ok?"

"Yeah, jus' been a long night. Still doin' hw. mom n dad in big fight. It's been crazy."

"Aw. girl u need 2 talk?"

"No. I gotta get this hw done. I'll tell u 'bout it tomorrow. Thanks."

"K. Ttyt."

Sarah heard her mother coming up the stairs and she thought for sure she was going to be yelled at for not being in bed yet. Much to her surprise, however, her mother didn't say a word. She just walked right by her room and went into her own room, shutting the door behind her.

She didn't even look my direction. I wonder if she's mad at me? I wonder if Dad is okay?

She refocused herself as best as she could to get her homework done, but as she stared at the literature book she was reading her eyes grew heavy and she fell asleep.

Startled out of her slumber her phone started to buzz next to her. She looked at the clock and realized it was two o'clock in the morning.

"U up?" It was a text from Brody. She didn't feel like talking to anyone, so she just ignored it. She sat up on her bed, put her school books into her back pack and stood up to walk across the room and close the blinds on the window.

She changed into her pajama shorts and tank top, crawled into bed, and turned her light off. After she pulled the covers over her body her phone buzzed again.

"Good night my lady. Sweet dreams. Love u," Brody texted her again. She looked at the phone and smiled feeling like somehow he must have known she was going to bed and had just turned out her light. *Love you? Love you? Did he mean to say that?* She thought about those words over and over until her thoughts faded away and she drifted into sleep.

CHAPTER 9
Friday Night Football

"Okay, girl. I'll be over in a little bit and we'll head up to school for the game tonight," Porsha hollered back at Tamara as she was getting off the bus.

"Text me when you get close to my house so you don't have to deal with Eric," Tamara reminded. When the bus finally stopped in front of Tamara's street, she pulled herself out of her seat, exhausted from her week.

"Sissy!" Dominick greeted his sister from the couch cushion.

"Hey, big guy! How are you? How was your day?"

"Good."

"Where's Wesie?"

"He's in the bedroom. He in trouble."

"In trouble?" Tamara asked. "Why? What happened?"

"He peed in his pants."

"Yeah. And? He's two."

"Eric's mad."

"So he told him to go to his room?" Tamara interrogated the three year old.

"No. He throwed him."

"Are you serious? He threw him?" Tamara went rushing upstairs toward the boys' bedroom.

"When did that happen, Dom?"

Like a puppy, Dominick followed her. "Um. I don't know. 'Bout long time ago, I think."

"Before lunch?" Tamara asked as she opened their door. "Oh my God! Wesie. Baby. Come here. Are you okay?"

The two year old was huddled into the corner of the room sucking his thumb and shivering. Tears were dried up against his face, which lit up as soon as he saw his big sister.

She knelt down next to him as he crawled over to her knees. She picked him up and wrapped her arms around him. Tamara noticed his clothes were soaking wet and when she grabbed him he winced as she touched his back. "Aw. Baby. You're okay. It's okay. Sissy is here," she whispered into his ear.

With those words, Wesley's body went limp in her arms as if it were the first time all day he felt safe.

I'm gonna kill him. I'm literally going to kill him. What in the world happened? How dare him hurt my brother like this. Who the hell does he think he is? He is only two years old. Oh, I'm gonna kill him. I have to tell Mama about this. She won't get home till after eleven tonight. I can't go to the football game and leave these kids with him. Oh, I'm gonna kill him. Tamara held onto her baby brother while she thought about what to do.

"What'd you say we get you out of these clothes and get ready for a football game? You two wanna go to the football game with me tonight?" Tamara had no clue how she was going to pull this off but she knew her brothers couldn't stay alone with Eric all night. "Where is Eric?"

"I don't know. He left after he throwed Wesie in here. He was mad so he left. That lady came an got him. He hasn't come back yet," Dominick answered trying to sound grown up. "Mara, can I go to the game too?"

Smiling at him, she scooped Dominick up with her arm and squeezed both of her brothers together. "Of course you can silly. Let's get the two of you ready."

Once she got the boys cleaned up and dressed, she texted her mom, "Mom.... I swear, I'm gonna.... I'm taking Dom and Wes to the football game with me. Eric isn't home...Mom, I.. I.. never mind. We can talk when you get home. I need to find the right words because I am so angry. Love you."

As she put her phone on the counter a knock came at the door. Tamara opened it to see Chance, Troy, Porsha, and Maysha standing there all ready to go to the game.

"Girl! You ain't ready yet?" Maysha asked.

Chance and Troy saw the little boys eagerly waiting for their entrance and swooped under Tamara to greet them.

"You guys! Eric's gonna be here soon. You can't stay. We gotta go."

"We can't go nowhere till you get dressed. What you need us to do for you?" Porsha asked recognizing that her friend was slightly discombobulated.

"Uh, can you just watch them for a minute?" pointing to her brothers. "I'll just be a minute. Lemme change right quick."

"Yeah, girl. Go on. I got you."

Tamara gave her friend a thankful look and headed to her bedroom. She went into her room and picked out a fresh pair of boots and jeans, accenting them with a tightly fitted long sleeve tee and a cropped vest.

"Ooooo woman! Look at you gettin' that swag on," Chance announced as he let himself into Tamara's room.

"Boy! What you doin' in here? Get out! There ain't nothin' about my room that is any of your business!" Tamara scolded him as she pushed him out of the doorway and into the hall. She pulled her door behind her and shut her brothers' door as well following Chance down to the living room.

"Ah. You know, I'm just lookin' out for my boy, is all. I hadda make sure you ain't got no other dudes up in here hidin' out. I know how you women be skept," he teased as she rolled her eyes and pushed him down the hall once more.

"Hey, so, Dom an Wes are coming with us. Eric is gone and for real, I really don't want them here with him anyway. Is that cool?"

Without hesitation everyone agreed and the group rolled out of the door with Dom on Troy's back and Wesley on Chance's back.

"Hey, Tamara," Maysha paused before they closed her house door. "You got anything to eat?" smiling at the absurd timing.

"Yeah, girl, there's some leftover mac-and-cheese in the fridge," Tamara smiled at her. "Go ahead and get yourself some. Just shut the door behind you."

"Thanks. I ain't eat nothing today, for real. I'll meet ya'll at the bus stop."

As Maysha trotted down to the bus stop she had the entire large leftover mac-and-cheese container in one hand and a large serving spoon in the other.

"What?" Chance, still carrying Wes started laughing hysterically at the sight of her. "Girl," he shouted. "You so fat! Haaa!" he bent over and started slapping his knees in laughter.

"Boy, I ain't fat, I'm thick!" she protested. "I'm gonna punch you in the face if you don't stop laughing," she playfully snarled back at him and whacked him on the top of his head with her oversized spoon.

"Ah, watcha doin'? I got a baby in my hands," he held Wes up in front of him. "That's child abuse. You can't hit me cause I got a baby." As he held Wes up he took off running and Maysha went chasing after him.

Wesley found the entire scene amusing and kept giggling as Chance dodged around avoiding Maysha.

"Hey! The bus here," Chance shouted to his friends as they approached the bus stop.

"You lucky you got a baby in your hands. Don't you put him down or bet!" Maysha teased with her fierce attitude.

While they were all climbing onto the bus Porsha asked Tamara what was up.

"Girl, Eric is ridiculous. I'm gonna kill him. He ain't been home all day. Wes peed his pants and he threw, no joke, picked him up and threw him into his bedroom. Porsha! He's two years old. He's gonna have accidents. I'm so mad. I'm gonna kill him." The two girls followed their friends toward the back. "I mean for real, I know he is a hot mess, but he is so dang temperamental. The boys aren't safe with him. Mama is going to lose it on him when she finds out what he did," she sighed and looked out the window. "He must be back on drugs. I think for real."

Once everyone settled down into their seats, Porsha looked directly at Tamara and said, "Girl, it ain't your job to raise them kids. Your mama needs to know what's going on with Eric. She workin' so much it's a wonder she even know her own name. She doesn't need to work all the time like she does. You guys have money. She is just burying herself in work so she doesn't have to feel the pain of not having your dad around. She needs to take a break from all the pressure she puttin' on herself."

"I know. You're right. I just don't know how to tell her. I just don't want to stress her out you know. Eric is super special to her. She always talks about helping people out, especially people who need the help the most. She told me once that she remembers when CPS brought Eric to her house when they were kids. She said he was so scrawny and was covered from head to toe with bruises. She said had he stayed in his biological home for another day he would have probably been killed. It's like from that day on she made it her mission to keep him alive and protect him," Tamara paused and looked over at her little brothers. "I know she misses my dad. I can't help but always feel like its my fault. Like I need to just deal with it since I'm the one who killed my dad."

"Girl, you didn't kill your dad," Porsha put her hand on Tamara's shoulder. "He died in a car crash. It was on I-75, the same route he would have taken to get home. Nothing about the accident was your fault. You need to stop blaming yourself. No one else blames you, especially your mama. You need to talk to her about Eric, she's a good mom and she would die if she knew half of what you had to deal with as far as Eric is concerned," she said as she turned her body in the bus seat to look directly at Tamara. "You think she'd be happy if she knew her foster brother was beatin' her kids and harassin' you? That kinda game ain't right, girl. You know it as well as I do."

"No. I know. I'll tell her. I have to tell her. I guess I will tell her tonight. I jus' don't know how."

"You'll figure it out." Softly, Porsha smiled at her.

Tamara knew she had to find a way to tell her mom about Eric. She knew he was constantly crossing the line with her, and especially with her little brothers. *What if she doesn't believe me? What if he finds out I told her? Will he hurt me?* She looked over at her little brother Wesley who was listening to one of Chance's earbuds. *What if he hurts them? Wes is so sweet, he is gonna grow up and be such a good man. If Eric keeps hangin' around they are gonna turn out just like him. I can't let that happen. I gotta tell Mama.* Tamara looked out the window. *I gotta tell her. I just wish he'd mess up in front of her so I didn't have to tell her. She really is workin' herself too hard. Okay, I'll tell her. I will. I'll tell her next time I see her.*

Tamara's thoughts were interrupted by a pothole in the road and everyone shouting from the painful thud.

Tamara looked back at Dom also sitting with Chance and she started to feel a little more at ease knowing that her friends were there to help her when she needed them. She looked out the window to relax for a minute, and allowed herself to think about Brandon. *He is so sweet. I can't believe he kissed me after lunch today. He's so cute. Oh. Those. Lips. I just. Mmm. He makes me feel so safe. He is so dang sweet. And I have a date tomorrow night with him. I can't wait. Just to be with him and none of our friends. I can't wait.*

Oh dang. I forgot, I got that stupid project with that Sarah girl tomorrow morning. Argh. I really don't want her coming over to my place. She probably has a perfect mom and dad who kiss all the time and are both alive. They will probably have country music blaring from the living room and NASCAR on the TV. Then she'll come to our house and not see my dad and just think that I don't have one. Oh God, I hope Eric ain't there when she comes over. Maybe we should meet at the library. Dang. I hate Eric.

Lost in thought, Tamara didn't even realize when the bus pulled up to their stop.

"Sissy? Sissy?" her brother Dominick was pushing her shoulder when she snapped back to reality. "You comin'? We here."

They exchanged smiles and the crew of friends got off the bus.

When they approached the gates Kenna came running up to them. "Hey, ya'll," she flicked her hair and popped her hip out.

"Girl, didn't you get suspended for how you talked to Mr. Zohng?" Porsha asked, shocked to see her at the game.

"Yeah, but I just got three days out so it ain't no thing," she smirked.

"You gonna get caught and get kicked out," Maysha interrupted and cocked her head.

"Okay, oh, well," she snorted back. She bought a ticket just like the rest of them. Her plan was to act like it was no big deal and not make a big scene. Nothing about Kenna, however, goes unnoticed. It would only be a matter of time before she found a way to let her presence be known and stand out in the crowd.

Tamara looked at her phone to check the time and realized she had a missed text from her mom.

"Sounds like you want to talk about something, baby. What's up? You wanna talk when I get home? Is this about the message your math teacher left me the other day about an altercation in the hallway? If you are up when I get home we will chat then. Thanks for taking the boys with you. I can't get ahold of Eric."

Tamara took a deep breath and sighed and sent her mom another message, "Its cool. All good in math. Ms. P., just be stressin' over nothin'. We can talk tonight. Boys are good w me." She put her phone away in her jacket pocket and looked up at the field to try and find Brandon.

Much to her surprise, he was turned around on the sideline looking directly at her. Through his helmet he smiled at her and nodded.

She smiled back and gave a secretive wave in return.

Around half time of the game, Tamara and her friends were standing on the ground on the far side of the bleachers when a large group of students began making a loud commotion behind the stands. Tamara turned to see what the ruckus was about and she saw about thirty of her classmates, mostly African-American classmates, bouncing around to a beat and waving their hands in the air, shouting oh's and ooo's, ah's.

Tamara quickly looked for her little brothers and saw them on the hill behind the end zone playing tag with some other kids their age so she hustled over to the group to see what all the fuss was about.

Kenna was in the middle. There was dancing involved. That is one thing about Kenna that Tamara loved, she was always dancing. She couldn't get enough of it. Porsha and Tamara squeezed in behind Chance and saw Kenna dancing with another girl named Ahnistee in a battle of sorts. It was clear the girls were having fun. The girls really knew how to dance which made the crowd hype it that much more.

Ahnistee was a straight A student and president of the sophomore class government. Her caramel complexion and light brown eyes made it hard for anyone not to vote for her. She and Kenna were good friends so the battle of dancing was all in good fun. Ahnistee twisted and jerked her body all over to the beats and Kenna synchronized herself to her friend.

Everyone around was smiling and having a good time. They were shouting and dancing in a big circle, egging the girls on.

Amidst the excitement Tamara didn't notice the ten police officers sprinting their direction until one of them shouted and slammed into her in effort to break up the assumed chaos.

That's when the chaos truly began. The officers busted into the middle of the circle and two of them slammed Kenna and Ahnistee on the ground telling them to calm down. The remaining officers pushed the other kids out of the way and shouted at them.

"Get! Go on. Get out of here!" a white officer yelled at the surrounding students.

"Boy, if you don't move on you're gonna be in a world of hurt," another officer said looking directly at Troy.

"Who you callin' boy? I ain't your boy."

"Troy, shut up, com'on." Porsha pulled at Troy's hood.

A voice from the crowd of students shouted at the officers, "They ain't done nothin' wrong. They was just dancing."

"Lemme go." Kenna squirmed from under the officer's grip. "I ain't done nothing. Let me go."

"Miss, you're gonna need to calm down or you will be tased," the officer holding her down threatened.

Tamara felt a tugging at the back of her. She turned around to see her brothers staring at the pinned Kenna.

"Kenna Jackson? What on earth are you doin' here?" Officer Bolvain exploded as he approached the scene with Principal Whitley and Vice Principal Harris. "Girl, you suspended from school, and you know you ain't supposed to be here, and fightin' at that." He grabbed her off the ground and the tackling officer stepped back.

Ahnistee was being completely compliant so the other officer stood her up and looked at the principal.

"Ahnistee Grant. Figures. Figures it would be you. You've managed to stay out of trouble this whole year so I figured your time would come," Vice Principal Harris scolded.

She didn't respond. She just looked at the ground. *What does he mean he figures?* Tamara thought as she continued to look at the spectacle unfolding and picking Wesley up into her arms. *She is such a good student. She got one detention her sixth grade year for not doing her homework but she's never been a problem. What just happened for real? They really was just dancing. Talk about racial profiling. See a group of black kids dancing automatically they assume we up to no good. That ain't even fair.*

Both Kenna and Ahnistee were paraded out of the stadium and into the school building by six of the police officers, Officer Bolvain, Principal Whitley, and Vice Principal Harris. The other officers remained near the area to make sure the dispersed kids didn't try to come back and cause more commotion.

"Dang. I can't stand that crap!"

"That ain't even cool, for real," Chance and Troy jawed back and forth.

"How they just gonna assume that we is up to no good when they weren't even here?"

"That's discrimination! Tamara, you smart. Why don't you become a lawyer and put those crooked cops in jail. Ha!"

Tamara, surprised by the whole incident, remained silent, unsure how to react to the situation and just watched as the friends blasted their feelings about it.

Once the commotion settled down they had made their way back toward the stands to watch the second half. A loud uproar from the crowd in the bleachers started up as the game continued.

"Ladies and gentlemen, he has done it!" the game announcer came over the loudspeaker above the deafening cheers from the stands. "Junior, Brandon Harris has broken the school record for most tackles ever. Wow! Look out division one college coaches, you have a real player heading to you in a couple years."

"Did he just say Brandon?" Tamara shouted as she ran to the fence to see the game.

"Heck, yeah, he did. Thats my boy! Woooooo! Yeah!" shouted Chance along with the crowd as he climbed on the fence.

Distracted by the shouting and cheering for Brandon's big tackle Tamara didn't notice Brandon run up to the fence to slap Chance's hand.

Right as she turned to look, Brandon was standing on the other side of the fence from her taking off his helmet. Surprising her he leaned over the fence and kissed Tamara right on the cheek then slapped Chance's hand again and ran back to the field to continue his game.

Aw. Did that really just happen? Did he really come over here and kiss me. Oh my God. How sweet. Did anyone see that? Tamara wondered, as she felt as red as his jersey and like the entire stadium was staring at her.

When the game came to an end, the group of friends all waited outside the stadium for Brandon to come out of the locker room. As Tamara was standing there waiting for him, she heard loud, girly yammering coming her direction. She looked up and saw her Social Studies project partner, Sarah, being thrown over the shoulder of her boyfriend who was also slapping her butt and acting macho. The two of them were being followed by their friends who were also being just as loud and obnoxious.

"Now, how come white boy can throw a girl over his shoulder and slap her around, and ain't nobody pay no attention? But bet, if I picked you up right now, T, and put you over my shoulder and started slapping your ass, every member of the doughnut squad in a four block radius be right here in a quick minute," Chance playfully argued.

"Chance, you know the answer to that. It's cause you scream louder, so since you scream louder, you get more attention. I'd look at it from the bright side of things, if you ever do got a problem, all you gotta do is start shouting, and you gonna be surrounded by crime stoppers real quick," Tamara sassed him back and cocked her head to prove her point.

Tamara looked over her shoulder at the group of white kids

and noticed Sarah, now on her own two feet, look up at her. She noticed a subtle, gentle smile from her. Tamara pretended not to notice and turned around to see Brandon as he came out of the locker room. He was quickly surrounded by his friends and family congratulating him for his record breaking game.

He hugged his grandma and his sisters who were just beaming with joy. His dad had his arm around his mom right behind them.

Tamara and her friends all waited patiently while he talked to his family, but out of nowhere a little girl came running up to Tamara and grabbed her by the hand and started pulling her toward his family.

Brandon noticed that his little sister was pulling Tamara and quickly ran over to her, "Kia, what you doing, silly girl?" he asked as he put his arm around her. At the same time, with his other hand, he grabbed Tamara's fingers and gently continued to lead her toward his family.

"I saw you go kiss her Brandon. I think it's only right if we get to meet her," his ten year old sister pointed out.

Blushing, Brandon said, "Aw, you saw that. You was supposed to be playing with your dolls, not watching me."

"I wasn't playing with no dolls! I was watching you! And I saw you, so ha!" She clearly had a knack for making him smile.

He looked at Tamara and winked, "Grams, this is Tamara. Tamara, this is Grams, Kia, Mom and Dad, or Carla and Daniel Harris."

"Hi. Nice to meet all of you," Tamara very politely responded as she shook each one's hand.

"Aw, honey, the pleasure's all ours," His grandma said in a southern sweet voice and grabbed Tamara's hand with both of her hands.

Tamara noticed the warm hazelnut smell coming from his grandma.

Brandon's mom and dad both shook Tamara's hand very

politely as well and then Kia gave Tamara a smile and said, "I don't play with dolls."

Tamara leaned over and shook Kia's hand and whispered in her ear, "That's okay. But if you ever want to, just give me a call, cause I love to play with dolls." she leaned up and smiled down at the little girl who was trying to contain her coolness toward her new found friend.

"Tamara, who are these little guys? They yours?" Carla, Brandon's mom gave her a serious look as she questioned her.

"Oh, my goodness! No, ma'am. They are my little brothers," Tamara stammered nervously. "Mom had to work late tonight so I brought them with me."

She nodded an approval in response to Tamara's answer, then gave her son a big hug and kiss on the cheek.

"Yo, dude, you comin' or not bra?" Chance shouted from behind them.

"Ah," he looked at Tamara and then at his family. His dad gave him a nodding smile and Brandon turned toward her, "I think I'm just gonna hang with the fam tonight if that's cool with you. I ain't seen Grams in a minute, and she's goin' back to Atlanta on Sunday."

"Oh my gosh, yeah, that's cool," Tamara responded earnestly.

"We still on for tomorrow night though, right?"

She smiled, "Of course we are. I wouldn't miss it for the world."

"Well, I be hearing the Patterson brothers throwin' a big party tomorrow night. You sure you ain't wanna go to that instead?" He looked at her with his head twisted to the side.

"Ha. You got jokes huh! No way. You stuck with me tomorrow."

"Good, that's what I like to hear. I can't think of a better place to be stuck."

"A'ight then," she leaned around him, "it was really nice to meet all of you!" She looked back at Brandon, "I'll see you tomorrow."

He put his arms around her waist and hugged her.

"I'll text you later," he said, then kissed her sweetly on the corner of her mouth and then again on her lips. "Bye, beautiful."

"See ya." She waved at his family again as she turned toward her patiently waiting friends who were playing tag with her little brothers.

Tamara checked her phone to see what time it was. "Oh, snap. It's 10:15. I gotta get these boys home. I told Mama I'd be home by eleven. I'm gonna have to skip out on the pizza place tonight."

"Girl, it's cool. It ain't like it's going anywhere. Troy, you still down for some pizza? Chance?" Porsha looked at the two of them as they began breaking out in a sweat from chasing Dom and Wes around.

"Man, I'm always down. Everyone's meetin' up down there, so I'm game," Troy answered.

Chance looked at Tamara and then back at his friend Brandon getting into the car with his family. "Na, I gotta get home too. Besides, someone's gotta look after my girl T. Since B-Dog gotta go home, Tamara I got you," trying to sound masculine he put his arm around Tamara's neck.

Chance knew the bus route wasn't always the safest thing to ride this time of night, and since Tamara's mom wasn't able to pick them up they were going to have to take the bus again, so no one argued with his decision.

"Plus, if Maysha goes then there won't be no pizza left," he smiled and winked as he spoke.

Maysha gave him a playful glare and rolled her eyes.

"A'ight, ya'll, I'll catch you tomorrow. I got that thing at nine with Sarah, but I'll call you tomorrow afternoon," she said to Porsha.

"Sarah? Who is Sarah?" Porsha asked confusedly.

"The white girl I gotta do that project with."

"Oh, yeah. That's right. Have fun with that."

"See ya."

The bus ride home was pretty quiet. Wesley was asleep in Tamara's lap and Dom was falling asleep on Chance's side.

"Thank you, Chance for getting us home. I really appreciate it."

"Well, I know how you women is, and I don't need my boy being cheated on, so you know, I'm just doing my brotherly duty."

She knew he was just teasing her, but nonetheless, she was glad for his company. When the bus came to her stop, both the boys were asleep; so Chance got off with Tamara and carried Dom, while she carried Wes.

Once they got inside he laid Dom on the couch in the living room and gave her a fist bump as he started to head out the door.

"Thanks again, Chance. You're the best!"

"Hey, don't go spreadin' no rumors now. I don't want the ladies thinkin' I'm a pushover," he smiled at her, and she smiled back as she closed the door.

She heard Eric in the shower as she carried Wes to his bedroom, so she quickly and quietly got Dom upstairs too and the boys put into their pajamas and into bed.

Once she closed the door to their room she went to her bedroom and started changing out of her clothes when she heard a voice at her bedroom door. She looked up and saw Eric staring at her half naked body.

"Damn girl. You look good," he said as he reached his hand down toward his towel wrapped around his waist.

Embarrassed, but more so disgusted, Tamara stood up quickly and grabbed a towel off her desk stool to cover herself up. Inhaling slowly then exhaling, she walked over to where he was standing in the cracked doorway. "There ain't nothing 'bout you that I would ever want anything to do with. You are sick. You disgust me." She went to slam the door in his face but then realized he was closer than she thought and the door bounced off of his foot.

He gave a sneery smile and licked his teeth with a popping sound effect, "Mmm." he puckered his lips at her.

She sensed that he was definitely high on something because he had no depth in his blue eyes. It was like she was staring into an empty abyss which made her extremely uneasy. She tucked the towel she was holding around her and said, "Eric, what did you do to Wesley today? Where did you go? What happened?"

"What? What you talkin' 'bout?" he asked as if he truly had zero recollection of what went down earlier on in the day.

"What are you on, Eric?"

"Settle down, I ain't on nothin'," he said as he leaned back onto his heels. "But, I could be on you if you want me to?"

"Are you kidding me right now? God, you are so disgusting. When Mama get's home I am going to make sure she never allows you to step foot in here again." Realizing she wasn't getting anywhere with him, she rolled her eyes and went to close her door again.

He got closer this time and she could smell alcohol on his breath. "Feisty. I like my women that way. One day, you wait, I'mma show you what kind of man I am," he winked at her appalled facial expression, gave her entire body one last look as if he was undressing her with his eyes and turned away back toward his bedroom.

Tamara shut her door and shivered all the way down her spine with repulsion. Quickly, she scrambled for her pajama shorts and tank top so she didn't feel so naked. Her stomach was turning at the thought of him being anywhere near her. Trying to distract herself she laid down in her bed and pulled the covers over her.

He has got to be high out of his mind. He has never been this aggressive. I don't know what he is on but Mama is going to kill him.

She started scrolling through her phone to see what her friends had been posting over the last few hours. As she started to doze off her phone buzzed.

It was her mom. "Hey baby. I'm running behind tonight. I won't be home probably until after midnight. We had to fire several people today and we landed that new client. I'm so sorry baby. I'm off all weekend though, so I will make it up to you. I just texted with Eric and he said everyone was good and tucked in for the night. He said he has to be to work by 12 so you may have to be there on your own for a little while. You good with that? Love you."

She looked at the time on her phone. 11:12. *Ugh. I am so tired. I can't wait until tomorrow though. I have to tell her tonight. She will be home soon.*

"Yeah. We for real need to talk as soon as you get home. Eric is not okay. He is high on," she paused her message to try and think about what drug he could possibly be on. As she tried to figure out what it could be she fell asleep before pressing send, allowing her phone to fall on her chest.

As Tamara was asleep, she thought she had heard her mom open her door to check on her. She was in a daze and didn't think much about it until her nose alerted her that it wasn't her mom at all. The smell of marijuana wafted into her nostrils as she rolled over to see Eric standing above her. She froze. *Oh my God. What is he doing in here? Oh God. What does he want? He is clearly high out of his mind.* Her thoughts raced.

He stood in silence towering over her stiff body lying on the bed. All she could see though, was his silhouette. Just standing. Silence. Staring at her. More silence.

Her stomach fell to the floor. She knew exactly what he intended to do next and she was frozen in fear. Horrified. She knew her mom wasn't home yet, but she thought maybe if she yelled for help her mom would miraculously appear. As she tried to call for her mom her voice was nowhere to be found. She was out of her mind afraid that she couldn't even articulate a single word to call for help. Silence filled the room.

He took a wobbling step toward her, then another.

Her heart raced. She went to scream again, but still nothing came out.

His arm began to move as he slowly pulled the covers off her and she heard her phone thud to the floor.

Still frozen in fear she didn't know what to do. She wanted to kick him. Fight. Stop him in his tracks, but her body wouldn't do what her mind wanted it to do.

He slowly reached down to her. Her heart began to pound so fast she could hear it in her ears. She realized that tears were streaming down her face now.

He got on top of Tamara pinning her body down with the weight of his. Tamara wriggled herself to try and escape, but still paralyzed, her effort was in vain. She stopped breathing. She started shaking uncontrollably. Fear. Panic. Dread. Horror. She knew in moments he was going to take her innocence from her and she would never get it back. Tears soaked her ears and the sheet under her head as they surged down her face.

"Tamara?" The light switch flicked on.

Eric jolted up.

"Tamara!" her mom flew through the room and seized his arm heaving him off the bed. "What the? Who the hell?" she was screaming at him. "How dare you?" She took her shoe off and started to pummel him with it.

He clearly was intoxicated because he weeble-wobbled around and fell to the floor without much force.

Tamara's mom, screaming expletives at him began to kick him again and again. "Get out! Get the hell out!" she screamed. "How dare you touch my daughter! How dare you come into my house and even think you can touch my child. I'mma kill you. Get the hell out of this house before I throw you out of the window!" she screamed loud enough that people on the other side of the planet could hear her.

As he tried to stand up she pushed him over and he fell into Tamara's desk crushing it into several pieces. "Bitch!" he bellowed. "Kill me? I'mma kill you, hoe. Don't you know about me?"

He tried to stand up again, but as he did, she kicked him in the face and then pressed her foot as hard as she could onto his shoulder and looked at him straight in his eyes. Realizing that he was nowhere inside the shell of a person at that moment she took control of him.

"No, bitch!" she stared him down. Nostrils flared and her pupils fastened on him. She gritted her teeth with all the self-control she could possibly withstand and threw her hand into the air pointing toward the door. "You clearly don't know who you messin' with." She pressed harder with her foot. If there was one thing her mom wasn't, it was a pushover. She was fierce.

She released her foot, walked calmly over to Tamara's phone on the floor, and dialed 911.

Eric didn't move from the floor. He laid there still and silent, slowly blinking his eyes in and out of consciousness.

"9-1-1, What's your emergency," the agent answered the phone.

"Yes, hi. My name is Sharon Hudgenson, I live at 9232 Sycamore Lane. I need to report a drug abuser and probation violation in my house and an assault on my daughter. I need a cruiser here immediately to pick up Eric Locke before I kill him myself," she flared her nostrils as she stared him down.

Still clearly unaware of what was going on, Eric lay on the floor of Tamara's room and stared at the ceiling.

After hanging up the phone she walked back over to her brother laying on the floor.

"I trusted you, Eric," anger welled up in her voice again. "I know you have had it rough, but I thought at least you had enough sense to not touch my children." She threw her hands into the air. "After everything that I have done for you in this life, and this is how you repay me? How dare you," tears began to surface in her eyes as she spoke. "The worst part is, I still care about you. I am so disappointed in you, Eric. You make me sick, but you need more help than I can give you," she pierced through his soul with her glare. "I will tell you this one time and one time only so you better be listening," she pointed her finger at him and tensed her whole body leaning forward in his direction. "If you ever, and I mean ever, come near my daughter again, so help me God, I will kill you. You will never so much as breathe the same air as her again. Do you understand me?" She was almost towering over him now. Before he could utter a rebuttal she followed up with, "Now get the hell out of this bedroom."

Her demonic, angry calmness sent shivers down Tamara's spine.

Slowly, he staggered to his feet, mumbling cuss words under his breath. Tamara slowly sat up on her bed, still shaking.

Her mom glanced her direction but kept her death stare fixated on him as he exited the room. He went to walk into his bedroom to get his clothes, but she followed him and interrupted. "Oh, hell no. You don't get to step foot in there. Ever."

"What? I need my clothes," he babbled.

She cocked her head and hip simultaneously, "Get out!" she screamed, and shoved him down the hallway toward the staircase.

Finally starting to realize that gravity of the situation in his inebriated state he began to weasel back, "Come on, sis, I'm sorry. I didn't mean to, I can fix this, come on. Let me fix this," he began to jabber.

"Do you see stupid written across my forehead?" as she said this she grabbed him by the top of his ear pinching and twisting with all her effort. "Get the hell out!" she roared as she began dragging him down the steps with his ear in her hand headed toward the front door.

Just then the police knocked on the door and with his ear still in her hand she opened it and gave them a look that let everyone know she was the boss.

"Ma'am," the police officer said. "Ma'am, please let go of him."

"Oh, I am happy to let go," she said as she squeezed a little harder then flicked him into the officer. "You can have him."

As her mother turned around her teenage daughter was standing like a small scared child in the living room by the staircase. "Oh, baby. Baby girl, come here." She opened her arms and Tamara fell into her. "Shhh. Shhh.. There, there baby. It's gonna be alright," she consoled the weeping child in her arms. "I am so sorry, baby."

Tamara wrapped her arms around her mother's waist and just cried. She cried like a baby. She sobbed and dripped snot all over her mother's blouse.

Her mother just let her daughter cry and consoled her with kisses on her hair line and stroked her head with her fingers.

"I'm so sorry, Mama. I hate," she choked. "I," she gasped for air. "He… hurrr...hurt Wesley," she stumbled over her words. "Mama, I," gasping again, "I'm sorry." Tamara's face and tank top were covered with her salty tears.

"Oh, baby. Is that what you were trying to tell me earlier? Are the boys okay? Is Wesley okay? Oh, Tamara, I am so, so sorry. I am so sorry." She was flooded with tears now too.

"Yeah." She took a loud breath, "Yeah, he's okay, he was really scared." Her tears grew harder, "I'm scared," she said as she buried her head into her mother's chest.

"Baby, look at me." She pulled Tamara's face away from her chest and held it in between her palms. "Baby, look at me," she repeated. "You have nothing to be scared of. I will never let anyone hurt you. I am so sorry, baby. I am so, so sorry." She pulled her daughter in for another hug. "Baby, did he," she gulped back her fear as she couldn't utter her question. "Did he… Oh, God. Has he done this before?" she stammered.

"No, Mama. No. He always says stuff but this the first time he tried."

"Oh, God. Oh, baby. I'm so sorry." She squeezed Tamara tighter than she has ever before.

Just then the officer walked into the house and Tamara's mom put her finger in the air to let him know they needed another minute before being interrupted.

"I know I've been busy working, but things are gonna change around here. Trust that. I'm gonna turn this around. I just been trying to stay busy cause I miss Daddy so much." She squeezed her daughter even more. "It's no excuse. I knew it was a risk taking Eric in, and your daddy would have never allowed it, but I felt like it was the right thing to do. I didn't think he would hurt you guys. I didn't realize how bad it was. I didn't know he was so out of control. I didn't know. I'm so sorry I let this happen to you. I am such a horrible mom. I am so sorry," she garbled through her tear soaked face. "Trust me, he will never step foot here again."

"I'm okay, Mama. I'm okay. He didn't hurt me. You're not a bad mom. I think Candice has been coming around and it's only gotten bad in the last couple of months," Tamara began to slow down her breathing, melting into her mom's embrace.

As the tears began to slow, Tamara released herself from her mother's grip and the two of them made eye contact for the first time in a long time. Neither one said a word but they smiled as they held on to one another.

CHAPTER 10
White Lights

"Mom?" Sarah shouted as she walked in the house from school. "Mom, Zoe came home with me. She's staying for dinner then we're gonna go to the game tonight." Not caring whether or not her mother heard her, the two girls set their backpacks down by the front door and went into the kitchen. "You want a juice box?"

"Sure, thanks," Zoe said as she pulled out the stool under the island and plopped down. "So, is your dad here then?" she whispered as she looked around the room.

"No, his car wasn't outside. Mom's is. I don't know where she is. I wonder where Ben is?" Sarah pulled out two juice boxes from the refrigerator and handed one of them to Zoe. She walked over to the back door and looked out to see her brother and his best friend jumping on the trampoline in the neighbor's yard. "Ben's over at Ethan's house. I don't know where my mom is. Let me run upstairs real quick. The TV remote is in the drawer of the coffee table if you want to turn on something or whatever. Can you let Emma out in the backyard for me? I'll be right back," Sarah set down her juice and raised her eyebrows as she contemplated where her mother could be.

"Mom?" she spoke quietly as she walked up the stairs toward her parent's bedroom. "Mom?" she spoke a little louder this time as she poked her head into the room.

The bed was disheveled but no sign of her mother. She made her way further into the bedroom to look in the master bathroom. "Mom?"

She heard a water noise come from the bathroom so she quietly opened the door calling for her mother once again.

Her mother was lying in the bathtub staring at the ceiling. She was surrounded by bubbles and her hair, which was normally perfectly kept, was in a messy bun on top of her head. Sarah walked over to the tub and her mother, seeming startled, jerked out of her trance.

"Sarah? When did you get home? What time is it? Are you okay?"

"Yeah, Mom, I'm fine. Are you okay?" she replied softly.

"What time is it, honey? I must have dozed off? Where is Ben? Is your father home yet?" realizing what she had just asked, a tear clouded her eye, and said, "I mean. Never mind. Sarah, honey, can you hand me that towel?"

Obediently, Sarah handed her mother the towel, unsure of what to say. She knew her mother was sad, but so was she. "Mom, Zoe's here. She's gonna stay for dinner and then we're gonna go to the game."

"That's nice, dear. Let me get dressed. I'll be down shortly," there was no joy in her mother's voice. No love or passion for life. She seemed empty.

For some reason though, Sarah couldn't be mad at her mom in this moment. It was like she was a child or something. Sarah nodded and closed the bathroom door behind her as she left.

She went back down stairs to find Zoe texting and watching cartoons. "Cartoons, Zoe? Really? How old are you?" the two girls giggled, because even though they were teenagers they both loved to watch cartoons after school.

"Hey, is your mom alright?"

Sarah had disclosed everything to Zoe and Jesse on the car ride to school this morning. She nodded at her friend and offered a half smile. The two girls sat on the sofa and watched cartoons for the next twenty minutes before anyone said another word.

Finally, lightening the mood Sarah asked, "So, what's up with you and Toby, Miss Thing? I saw the two of you at lunch eyein' each other like you were about to jump all over each other and start making out right there!"

Zoe blushed, "I know, right! I am totally into him, Sarah. He is so hot. I really think he's gonna ask me out at the game tonight. I mean, but whatever. I really would just settle for making out with him, or maybe a little more," she smiled a devilish grin.

"No way girl. You wouldn't do that with him already would you?"

"What do you mean already? We've known each other for like three years now. Besides, it's not like we'd be each other's firsts. Like you with Brody," she teased.

"Shh. Keep your voice down. I don't want my mom to hear you. Brody and I haven't done anything anyway."

"Yet!" Zoe interrupted.

"I don't know Zo. I really like him. I mean oh my goodness, he is so hot. When he hugs me, I swear I am melting. He makes me think about nothing but what it would be like. I just don't know though, girl. I want to but I really wanna save myself."

"Save yourself for what? It's better to just get it out of the way so you are more experienced. Besides, Brody really likes you. I bet he would be really gentle with you since it's your first time."

"I don't know girl. He told me he loves me."

"What? When? Why didn't you tell me?"

"It was yesterday. I was busy dealing with all the drama here, I forgot."

"Oh my God, Sarah! What did you say back?"

"I didn't really know what to say. It was the middle of the night, he probably didn't even realize he said it. Maybe I love him, but I don't know. We have only been talking for like a month and I know he makes me feel something, but is it love?"

"What isn't there to love about the guy? He is sexy, he is sweet, he adores you, and did I mention he is sexy?"

Blushing, Sarah began to smile, "You think? Well maybe I do," the two girls giggled together as Sarah began to convince herself she could truly be in love with Brody. "Okay, so maybe I do. Maybe I should tell him tonight."

"No way. Tell him tomorrow night at the party. You can totally take him up in one of the rooms and you guys can be alone and not worry about any parents walking in or anything. You don't have to have sex with him, just tell him how you feel and let your gut guide you the rest of the way."

"Okay, that's a good idea. Oh my gosh, I can't wait to see him at the game tonight."

"Sarah?" her mother interrupted as she came into the room.

Sarah's face turned bright red and her stomach did a small flip inside her. She looked at Zoe with large eyes in hopes that her mother didn't hear their conversation.

"Sarah, can you go get your brother for dinner? We are gonna have leftovers from last night again. Hi, Zoe, sorry, I didn't see you sitting there."

"Hi, Mrs. Benson," Zoe replied.

"Yeah sure, Mom. I'll be right back," Sarah gave her friend a secretive grin and danced toward the back door. Once she opened the door she shouted, "Ben! Dinner's ready, come on."

"Sarah! I asked you to go get him, not shout out the back door," her mother yelled as she slammed down the plates on the counter and stared at her daughter.

"Mom? Sorry. I didn't mean to make you mad," annoyed by her mother's attitude, Sarah rolled her eyes at her mother. "Zoe, let's go get ready, we can eat in a few." Sarah glanced at her mother who didn't seem to be paying any attention to her. She waited for Zoe to turn off the TV, then quickly marched out of the kitchen and went to her room, Zoe trailing.

"God, she is so annoying," Sarah fussed as the girls were getting ready.

"She is going through a rough patch, Sarah. Don't be so hard on her."

"I know, I'm trying not to be, but Zoe, she cheated on my dad. You know how hard it is not to hate her right now? I mean if I'm this mad, think about how mad my dad must be."

"Haven't you ever done something you regretted Sarah?"

"Whatever, Zoe. Your parents are still together, and they let you do whatever you want, so I don't think you really understand."

"Yeah, Sarah, I do. My parents let me do whatever I want because they are never around to see what I'm doing. My mom is so busy working at the office and my dad is stupid busy traveling all the time that neither one of them see each other. It wouldn't surprise me for one second if I caught my mom sleeping with some of the dudes she works with, or for that matter, I bet my dad sleeps with half of the flight attendants he totes all over the place. So trust me Sarah, I do know what it's like. The only reason my parents are still together is because they never see each other." Zoe looked away from her friend and into her reflection in the mirror. "Sarah, all I'm saying is to cut your mom some slack."

"Zo, I'm sorry. I knew I shouldn't have said that. I know you hate it that your parents are never home. I don't know. I'm just frustrated."

"I know," she said with a smile on her face turning back to Sarah, "but at least you get to kiss on your sexy boyfriend tonight."

Sarah rolled her eyes and grinned at her as they finished putting on their make-up and getting dressed.

Once they were ready Sarah and Zoe took a selfie together and posted it online saying they were headed to the game. They headed downstairs to Ben and Ethan sitting at the dining room table eating dinner.

"Where's Mom?" she looked around the room for her as she asked her little brother.

"She's laying on the couch in the family room," Ben mumbled with his mouth full of food.

Sarah glanced into the family room and saw her mom laying on her back with her arm over her forehead. Sarah rolled her eyes and went into the kitchen and fixed her and Zoe a plate of food before they headed out for the game.

"Is Jesse picking us up?" Zoe asked.

"Yeah, I just texted him. He should be here in a few minutes."

The girls ate as fast as they could and got their stuff and headed to the front door to leave.

"Sarah Nicole, can I talk to you for a moment?" her mother asked as the girls were almost out the door.

Rolling her eyes, she told Zoe to head on out and she would be right there. "Yeah sure, Mom. What's up?" she walked over to her mom laying on the couch.

"Sarah, your father and I spoke today and he is going to come and get you Sunday for the afternoon. Okay?"

"That's cool," she smiled and headed back for the door then stopped and turned back around to her mom and said, "Oh yeah. By the way, I forgot to tell you, I have a project I have to do with this girl from class, and she has to come over here tomorrow, and I have to go to her place too. I don't know where she lives but we are probably gonna take the bus to her place. I need you to take me up to school in the morning at nine, and then pick us up and bring us back here so we can finish our project."

"That's fine. I will be dropping Ben off at the field at eight, but I can come home and get you or you can just ride with us."

Sarah squinted her eyes at her mother.

"What, Sarah? Your brother still has to play soccer. I'm not going to make him miss out on that just because I," she paused. "Just let me know when you're ready to leave in the morning. What time are you going to be home tonight?"

"I don't know, whenever the game is over. We might go out for pizza or something afterwards."

"No, that's not a good idea Sarah, Just come home right after the game so you can get a good night's sleep for your project tomorrow."

"What? Mom!"

"Sarah, I'm not going to fight with you. Come home right after the game. If you need a ride, call me, but you aren't going out afterwards. I assume Jesse will bring you, correct?"

"Yes, but whatever. That's stupid," she yelled as she grabbed her purse and stomped out the door.

"Yo. What's up?" Jesse called from the driver's seat as she climbed in behind Caitlin sitting next to him.

"Hey, sorry about that. Mom is so annoying. She wanted to know what the plan was. Where's Brody? I thought we were taking him too?"

"Na, I guess he has some stuff to do, and he got his truck back. He said he'd just meet us there," Jesse responded as he looked in the rearview mirror at her, noticing how flustered she looked. "You good?" he questioned.

"Yeah," she responded, making eye contact with him. "I'm good. I just don't know how to navigate all this stuff. I just don't want to deal with her," she sighed, thankful for his listening ear.

"Just be you. You don't have to fix things with them. They are adults. They will figure it out. Just pray for them, love them, keep it moving," he softly smiled and winked at her.

"Thanks," she sighed as she stared out the window.

Thank God for Jesse in my life. He so knows how to make me feel calmer about stuff. Did he say Brody has stuff to do? How does he know? Stuff to do? What kind of stuff does he have to do? He didn't say anything to me about it. I didn't even know he got his truck back. Huh.

As they pulled into the high school parking lot Sarah's phone began to vibrate. She looked at it and a message from Brody read, "Hey, baby. I gotta take care of something, I'll see u later though."

"What do u have to do? My mom wants me to come home right after the game so I can't hang out," she texted as they got out of the car and headed towards the game entrance.

"Don't worry, baby. Ill be there b4 the games over. Ill drive u home so we can see each other 4 a min."

"Brody said he has some things to take care of. I don't know what though. But he said he'd drive me home," Sarah announced to her friends as they approached the ticket counter.

"I already said that," Jesse teased her and followed up with an elbow nudge. "If he doesn't come though, I will take you home," he said as he smiled at her.

"Thanks, Wild West Jess," she giggled back. "I kinda told Mom you would take me anyway, but for sure, if he isn't here then you can take me."

Rolling her eyes, Caitlin interrupted, "Hello?"

Both Jesse and Sarah looked innocently at her and waited for her to say what was on her mind.

Blatantly rolling her eyes again she looked at Jesse and said, "Jesse, some of my friends are going to be here from Saint Mary's. Can we go sit with them tonight instead of our usual student section?" she pouted her lips and started pulling on his arm.

He shrugged his shoulders and gave Sarah a look that she knew to be his annoyed face.

"Jealous much?" Zoe whispered to Sarah as Jesse and Caitlin walked away.

"Who me?" she turned to look at her friend.

"Uh, no. Duh! Her," she said as she rolled her eyes.

"Oh. I know, right!" Sarah dismissed the observation.

Once they got into the game they headed for their usual spot in the student section of the bleachers in front of the cheerleaders. Where you stood in the student section was a big deal as far as your social status was concerned. The closer to the field, the cooler your status, and the further up top you got, the less popular your status. Sarah and her friends were just above the most popular crew. Brody was actually one of the main guys in the front row but his absence seemed to throw everyone off.

"Hey, Sarah, where is Brody?" one of the senior girls asked as she and her friends piled into the rows below them. All their eyes turned to Sarah to see if she had an answer about his whereabouts.

"Um," nervous, because these girls never even noticed her before she started hanging out with Brody, "he said he had to take care of something, but he said he'd be here."

Satisfied with her response, the girls all smiled at her and one of them even complimented her hair.

Sarah looked at Zoe and the two of them shrugged their shoulders and smiled. It felt good to be admired by the senior girls.

The first half of the game went by rather quickly even though Brody hadn't made it yet. Toby made his way down to the group and was standing extremely close to Zoe.

At half-time everyone sat down to relax for a minute before the game started back up. Sarah noticed Toby had his hand on Zoe's thigh really high up almost completely under her skirt. Sarah elbowed Zoe and gave her a nod and a raised eyebrow toward Toby's hand and it was reciprocated with an ear to ear grin, and a sigh of happiness.

Zoe leaned in and whispered in Sarah's ear, "Oh, my God. I seriously want to jump on him right now."

"Girl, you are too much. I'm not even getting involved."

"Where is Brody?" Zoe inquired with a pouty lip.

"I don't know. He said he had to do some stuff. That's so weird. He is always here. I don't know what he had to do. You don't think I made him mad by not talking to him about my feelings today after he said that to me last night, do you?"

"Girl, no way. If anything, it only made him want you more. He said he's taking you home right?"

Sarah nodded.

"Okay then. He will be here. I'm sure he just ran out of hair product and he had to go to the nearest modeling studio to get some more," Zoe teased and winked at her friend as they both laughed because there really could have been some truth in that statement.

Just before the second half of the game started, everyone had made their way back to the bleachers when Brody came up the stairs carrying a single rose in his hand looking directly at Sarah.

She heard the senior girls around her all get quiet and swoon as he walked up the steps. He, however, didn't seem to notice them, he had his gaze zeroed in on Sarah and made his way in between everyone to get to her.

As soon as he got to her, he handed her the rose and followed it by kissing her softly and gently in front of everyone. For a moment she forgot where she was as she pressed her lips against his allowing her eyes to close and fall in love with him.

"I'm sorry I'm late, beautiful. I had to take my grandma to the doctor's office after school and then I had to go see my dad for a minute," while still holding her in his arms and looking in her eyes he continued, "God, you're beautiful. You are even more beautiful in these white lights than ever. How did I get so lucky to get you? You are definitely my girl. I'm not ever letting go of you."

Not being shaken from her gaze at him, she smiled shyly and smelled the rose then leaned up to kiss him once more.

This moment was interrupted by a huge eruption from the crowd screaming for one of the players on the football team. Sarah and Brody both unlocked their gaze and threw their hand up in the air and began screaming for the new broken record at the school.

Brandon Harris, a stud football player had just broken a school record for most tackles ever. The crowd went nuts for Brandon.

Sarah jumped up and down and cheered for him as well.

"Dude! That's my boy!" Brody shouted. "He's gonna play in the NFL one day, just wait!" he turned and gave everyone a high five and shouted again at the top of his lungs for Brandon's accomplishment.

The rest of the game went by so quickly for Sarah. She didn't want it to end when the game clock ticked down to zero. She smiled at Zoe who was on cloud nine with Toby's arms around her.

As the game ended, everyone piled their way down the bleachers toward the exit. Brody led the way for everyone in the group with his hand clasping Sarah's.

He is so amazing. I am totally in love with him. I can't believe he would kiss me like that in front of everyone. He is so amazing.

"Watch your step," Brody whispered.

She almost lost her balance because she was staring at him, admiring his manners.

Once they reached the stadium gate he shouted, "Well, I gotta go now," in a playful manner as he hoisted Sarah up and over his shoulder as if carrying a bag of grain and started slapping her butt.

Startled by this, she shrieked, rather loudly, then giggled and squirmed to be put down.

He finally set her down then placed his arm around her neck.

As they were walking Sarah noticed Tamara standing outside the locker room doors with a group of her friends. She saw two smaller children and wondered if they were Tamara's.

When she got closer to Tamara, she smiled at her. She could do nothing but smile. She was so in love with Brody and nothing was going to bring her out of the clouds. She thought she noticed Tamara smile back which gave her the feeling that tomorrow wouldn't be as bad as she was making it out to be in her head.

"Looks like your boy showed up," Jesse said quietly enough for only the two of them to hear.

"Yeah, I guess I won't need you to take me home after all. My chariot has arrived," she winked at her friend.

"You going alone with just him?" Jesse inquired.

"Yeah, Zoe told me she was going with Toby so it will just be me and Brody," Sarah smiled.

"Okay. Well, I'm happy to take you if you prefer."

"You're silly. Go be with Caitlin. Look, she is staring at us right now. She probably thinks we are about to make out. No need to make her more jealous than necessary."

"God, I know. I'm sorry. But look, Brody's staring at us too. He probably thinks the same thing."

They both giggled.

"Well I'm gonna hug you anyway. She can be jealous for a minute," she said as she wrapped her arms around him. "You guys be good and get home safe. I'll talk to you tomorrow."

"Deal," he said as he hugged her back. "You be safe too."

Sarah said her goodbyes to everyone as Caitlin announced that she and Jesse were heading home too.

Brody gave all the guys high fives and agreed to catch them all at the party tomorrow night.

When he mentioned the party, Sarah got goosebumps down her spine. *I can't believe I'm going to tell him I love him. I want to tell him right now. I want to jump on him. Maybe we can be alone tomorrow night up stairs and it can be special. Oh my God, I really think I love him.*

"You still going to the party tomorrow night right, babe?" Brody asked as he opened the door for her to climb into his truck.

"Yeah, of course," she smiled.

When he climbed into the driver side of his car he just sat there without starting it up. He sat still and quiet and looked as if he was thinking rather hard about something. Taking a deep breath he finally said, "So, now that we're alone, I want to tell you how sorry I am about yesterday."

Sarah turned to look at him. He was looking out the window but she could see how serious he was.

"I mean, I don't want to force anything on you. I really like you, and I really want your first time to be special. I shouldn't have forced you into the janitor's closet like that. I'm really sorry, Sarah," he said as he turned and looked at her, looking right through her as his blue eyes seemed to be almost filling with tears.

"Aw. Brody, it's fine. It's okay. I really like you too. I do. And it's not that I don't want to with you. I think maybe someday, but honestly, I just don't know how. I know that sounds stupid, but I don't know, it just needs to be special, and yesterday didn't seem right. I'm not mad at you though. I'm crazy about you."

"Really?" shocked by Sarah's response, Brody looked at her and wrinkled his eyebrows appearing baffled by her.

"What do you mean 'really?' Of course, why wouldn't I be?"

"I don't know, Sarah, you are just such a good girl and you come from such a good home, and me, well I don't know--" he paused and looked out the window again. "I come from a shitty home, my mom freaking hates me cause I look like my dad, who by the way is in prison for the rest of his life," he stopped and looked at Sarah's puzzled expression. "Damn, I shouldn't have told you that. I'm sorry. I don't want you to think bad of me. I just feel so comfortable with you, like I have known you my whole life, like I can tell you anything, you know?"

What? In prison? I wonder what he did. That sucks. I don't think anyone knows about that. I can't believe he's telling me this.

"Oh my God, Brody. I had no idea," she consoled him as she leaned over and hugged him.

His eyes looked wetter now.

She scooted her body over the seat and propped herself up into his lap with her legs stretched out across the interior of the front seat and wrapped her arms around his neck trying to comfort him. "Brody?" she whispered.

He didn't say anything, he just looked at her with fear that she was going to leave him. "What happened to your dad? I mean, like, what did he do?"

"You really want to know? You won't go running off on me once I tell you, will you?" he stared at her.

"No, of course not. Of course I want to know if you want to tell me about it. I would never judge you. I just didn't know that about you, so I'm curious. But you don't have to tell me if you aren't comfortable," she said.

"I don't really know the whole story. Well, I do, but it honestly just boils down to some stupid broad," he began. He paused as he stared out the window trying to decide if he wanted to confide more in her. Letting out a deep sigh he continued, "Some broad he hooked up with after he and my mom split, I was like two or something. He went a little crazy over this chick. I guess he got her pregnant and my dad was gonna propose but then they got into an argument about something and she miscarried. But, my old man thought she killed their baby just to get back at him for the argument, so he kind of went nuts on her," he examined her to see if she was ready to run yet.

Without hesitation, Sarah gently stroked her thumbs across his eyebrows to show him his words were safe with her.

"Both my parents have different versions, but my mom tells me that my dad is a serious psychopath. She says that he like stalked this chick or some crazy shit. Like he was obsessed with her and she wanted nothing to do with him.

But, whenever I ask him about it all, he always says that woman was the one that got away. He says they were in love. He tells me he and my mom got married right out of high school and they were better off friends. But when he found this other chick, he said she was the best thing that ever happened to him. He said that she ended up putting a bullet in her brain for the guilt she felt about the baby, but the law pinned it on him anyway. He always tells me that once I find the right one, I'll know it and I need to hang on for dear life and not mess things up like he did." Tears began to well up in his eyes as he stared into Sarah. "But," he swallowed and began to stammer, "Sarah, I don't want you to think bad of me because my dad's in prison," he looked at her as if he was begging for her to say something, anything just to know she wasn't going anywhere.

Filling the silence he continued, "It's just that he has been there since I was two, and once I turned ten my mom started letting me go see him once a week and he's my dad. I care about him. I just want to make him proud of me."

"Brody, I would never think bad of you because of your dad. I'm sure you are a different person than him. I'm sure your mom knows that too. I'm sure she loves you. One thing I can tell for sure is that you are the sweetest guy I have ever met and I don't think you would ever hurt a fly and I am really happy you are in my life." She kissed his forehead and the brim of his nose, over and over until she reached his lips where they kissed for a long time.

He then pulled his face away from her and held her. He held her so tightly and buried his head into her shoulder. She could feel tears soaking through her shirt.

He seemed so vulnerable to her, so real. She embraced him and comforted him, neither one speaking a word, except for an occasional sniffle from Brody.

Maybe I should tell him I love him right now. Maybe he wants to know. I think it would make him feel better. I want to tell him, but I don't want to make this about me. I would have never guessed that about his dad. I wonder if he has ever told anyone that before.

"God, Sarah, I really do love you." Brody squeezed her tightly and then grabbed her by the face with both hands to make direct eye contact. "I don't know what kind of spell you have put on me, but I am so in love with you. I have never told anyone any of this, but you are so amazing. I want to make you feel like the most important person in the world, Sarah. I am going to love you like you have never been loved before. You need to know that you are stuck with me. I'm not going to let you go. You are all mine." He pulled her face in a little closer, "I will wait as long as you want me to. You are my girl."

She leaned in just a little more and kissed him.

Sarah took a deep breath and exhaled, smiling at him she began to open her mouth to tell him that she loved him too, but right then her phone began to vibrate in her purse. She looked at her watch and saw it was five till eleven.

"Oh crap. It's probably my mom," she said as she hurriedly grabbed her phone from her purse.

"Hello?" she answered.

"I know, Mom. We're on our way. The traffic in the parking lot was crazy. I'll be home in ten minutes." She climbed off of Brody's lap as he started the car.

"I know, Mom." She buckled up her seatbelt as he pressed the gas pedal.

"Brody's bringing me home. Jesse had to leave early."

Brody put his hand on her thigh.

"No, she went with Toby," she said as she glanced over at her boyfriend who was smiling at her.

She smiled back. "I know, Mom. We're almost there. Fine. Bye." She hung up the phone and looked back at Brody who seemed to be incredibly calm.

"Everything alright, babe?"

"Yeah, Mom's just flipping out because I am alone in a car with a boy right now."

"Correction, I am a man, not a boy."

"Oh!" she laughed. "Excuse me," rolling her eyes she continued, "She's flipping out because I am alone in a car with a *man* right now."

"Well she has nothing to worry about. I'll protect you. I'm not gonna let anything happen to you. I'm gonna treat you like a queen. Your wish is my command," he rubbed her leg and smiled.

"Brody, thank you for sharing that stuff with me," she said as she watched his hair flutter in the wind.

He squeezed her hand tightly and a small, but deeply sincere smile flashed across his face.

"So, I'm gonna go to the party with Zoe tomorrow, but I will see you there. I have this stupid project all day tomorrow with this girl from my Social Studies class, but Zoe and I will be there."

"You want me to pick you up?"

"Na, I think we're gonna ride with Jesse and Caitlin. Thanks though."

"I don't have anything to worry about with you and Jesse do I?" he asked as he looked at her sideways.

"Oh my goodness. No," she laughed. "You know that Jesse and I grew up together. He is my best friend," she playfully rolled her eyes to set him at ease.

"Okay, then. But I didn't like it when he had his paws all over you at the game back there."

"Well, I promise you have nothing to worry about," she replied very matter of factly.

"I trust you," he smiled at her and brushed her cheek with the back of his fingers.

She couldn't help but smile. She was totally in love and ready to tell him.

"Thank you, Brody. You are so sweet."

He pulled into her driveway, and quickly turned off his headlights. It didn't matter though, because Sarah's mother opened the door immediately and stood in the doorway waiting for her to exit the vehicle.

"Oh my God. She is so annoying sometimes!" Sarah looked over at Brody who didn't seem to care who was watching.

"Let's give her a little show then," he smiled and leaned in to kiss her.

Backing away, Sarah settled for a peck on the cheek because she did not want to have the birds and the bees talk with her mother, especially after the recent events in the house. "Bye. I'll see you tomorrow."

She began to climb out of the car and he grabbed her by the hand as she got out. She turned toward him.

"I love you," he said as he looked her directly in her eyes.

She took a deep breath and opened her mouth, but as soon as she was about to say it her mother opened the storm door and firmly said, "Sarah Nicole."

Distracted, she looked at Brody who was eagerly anticipating her response, and she shut the car door. As she walked in front of his car he flipped the headlights on and she looked up and gave him a big smile.

"Sarah, I told you to come home straight from the game. Where have you been?"

"Mom, chill. I told you. The traffic in the parking lot at school was crazy."

The two walked into the house and as her mother shut the door she stared down Brody in his big truck in the driveway.

"Who is that boy, Sarah?"

"It's Brody," Sarah said as she began walking up the stairs.

"I don't know him. You know how I feel about you riding with people I don't know. You could have been killed, Sarah. Do you even know that boy?"

"God, Mom, yeah I do. You are being so annoying right now." Sarah got to the top of the stairs and looked down at her glaring mother. "He is really nice. He's my boyfriend. He wouldn't let anything happen to me, Mom. I promise." She gave her mom a reassuring look. "I'm going to go to bed, okay?"

"Well, we're not finished with this conversation. You can go to bed, but we are going to need to talk about me meeting him and set some boundaries about what having a boyfriend looks like, you know?"

"Okay, Mom. We can talk later. I have to get up early."

"Okay. Goodnight."

Sarah walked into her bedroom and closed the door behind her. *Oh my. Why is she so on it right now? I thought she was wallowing in her depression. She should be passed out by now. Ugh. God, he is so hot. He is so amazing. I can't believe I didn't just tell him I love him. I am totally going to tell him tomorrow.*

As she changed into her pajama shorts and tank top her phone vibrated. She looked at the incoming text message that read, "Sarah, do you love me?"

She really wanted to tell him, but for some reason, she couldn't figure out what to say back to him. *It doesn't seem like I should say it in a text. What should I say? I guess I could just text it, but I really want to tell him face to face. I just need to go to bed. I have a long day tomorrow.* She put her phone on the charger and went to the bathroom to wash her face and brush her teeth.

When she came back she looked at her phone one more time. *Oh my goodness. Three new texts? Are they all from Brody?*

She began to read the series of texts.

"Don't answer that question. I want to wait till you are ready.

I mean, ready to love me.

Okay, sorry. I can't stop thinking about you. Good night. Hope ur not mad."

Taken back by his words, she put her phone back on the charger and climbed into bed. *Zoe's right. I will just tell him tomorrow.* Seconds after she turned out the light her phone buzzed one more time.

"Sweet dreams."

CHAPTER 11
Whatever

Oh my goodness. Tamara rolled over and hit snooze for the third time. "I don't want to get up. I don't want to do this stupid project." She closed her eyes again but the dreaded sound of the alarm kept her from relaxing. Instead of opting to hear it again, she decided to turn it off and get up. As she walked out of her room, her eyes swollen from last night's crying, she opened her brother's bedroom door to make sure they were still sleeping and then poked her head in her mom's room to see if she was still sleeping.

She quietly went into the bathroom and hopped in the shower, even though the noise from the water was sure to wake up everyone.

"Tamara, honey, is that you?" her mom called from outside the bathroom door.

"Yeah, I'll be out in a minute."

"Okay, baby, I just wanted to make sure it was you. What you want for breakfast, baby girl?"

"I can't, Mama, I got to do a project with a girl from school today. We meeting up at school at nine."

"Oh, well you better move it; it's almost 8:30."

Tamara quickly finished up in the shower and got ready to go. She noticed her mother wasn't wearing her usual Saturday leggings and hoodie, but instead she had on an old pair of baggy sweat pants and a baggy t-shirt. "Mama, you alright? You look a mess."

"Oh, well I love you too, baby," she snorted back as she sat on the couch.

They smiled at each other.

"Hey, you want to talk to someone, like a therapist or something? About what happened last night?" she asked as she studied Tamara's reaction.

"No, I'm good. He just scared me. I'm good though. Nothing happened. We're gonna be alright," Tamara spoke softly, glancing at the time on her phone. "Mama, we gonna come back here and work on this project for a minute then we gotta go to her house too."

"Why you gotta go to both places? You two can just stay here. I'm not going to work today or tomorrow. I need to get Eric's things outta here and love on my babies some," she said as she sipped on a cup of coffee and smiled at Tamara.

"We have to learn about the other person's culture or life. She has to see my home and I have to see hers. She's this prissy white girl, probably dumb as a box of rocks. I'm sure she lives in a big glass house with a cute little fall wreath on the door and a yappy dog barking at people walking on the sidewalk."

"Tamara Michelle. Now, I know I taught you to be nice. You don't get to judge her like that. You ain't no better than anyone else."

Tamara rolled her eyes at her mother.

"Besides, I think it's nice your teachers are making you do this. I'll get cleaned up and clean up around here." Her mother stood up from the couch and walked over to hug her daughter. "You want me to drive you to school and bring y'all back here?

"Na, it's cool. You don't need to get the boys out of bed. Besides, I kinda like the bus sometimes. It's fun to watch all the different people come and go. I mean I have a bus card, so I might as well use it."

"Okay, suit yourself, but I'm gonna make me some fried eggs and bacon. You want me to save you a piece of bacon?"

"Sure," she smiled at her mom.

"You'd better be nice to her, you hear?" she gave her a concerned look.

"Okay, Mama. We'll be back soon." She opened the door and headed for the bus stop.

She knew her mom was right. Since Tamara could remember, even before her brothers were born, her mother was always reminding her not to judge people before you know them. She would take her and her brothers to church where they would hear it there too.

"We are all God's children," the pastor would say. "Do not judge others, or you too will be judged." He'd continue on about how if we judge people, then we are no better than them. It's our job to love others, not judge them.

Okay, so maybe Mama has a point. Sarah won't be that bad. She seems nice enough.

Tamara got on the bus and headed for school.

*   *   *

Sarah was just as resistant to getting up to her alarm. When it went off she hit snooze four times. Finally, she tossed and turned and threw a mini temper-tantrum with her arms until she realized it was useless, so she resolved to get out of bed.

Before she got dressed, she opened her blinds in her room then made her bed.

She then turned her music on and went to shower, but was immediately stopped by her little brother who just happened to be taking a bath. "Ben! What are you doing in here? I have to shower."

"Mommy said I needed a bath. She said I stink."

"No, Ben, you don't stink, you suck," Sarah shouted as she closed the door on him in the bathroom. "Mom!" Sarah exclaimed as she let herself into her parent's bedroom. "I'm showering in here since you thought it would be a great idea to put Ben in the bathtub when you know I have to get ready."

"Oh, Sarah, I completely forgot. I'm sorry."

Sarah quickly got in and out of the shower, deciding not to wash her hair since she was short on time. "We need to leave in like fifteen minutes, Mom."

"I'm waiting on you, honey," her mother calmly stated as she headed into the bathroom with Ben to get him out and dressed.

"What happened to Ben's soccer game? I thought he had to be there by eight?"

"All the games are pushed back an hour because there was a transformer down. So he needs to be there by nine. Are you ready yet?" her mother shouted from the hallway.

Sarah rolled her eyes and threw on an old pair of holey jeans and a fitted hooded sweatshirt. She put her hair in a pony-tail and put on some make up and perfume to finish up. She grabbed her phone without noticing the messages and went straight to Snapchat to update her story with a selfie and to say that she hates Social Studies and she hates projects, and most importantly, she hates getting up early on a Saturday. She knew none of her friends would be up to see it right now but it still made her feel good to see how many people reacted to her picture. Sarah threw her phone on the bed, grabbed her backpack, and went downstairs and put on her sneakers by the front door. "Mom, I'm ready."

"Okay, let's go," her mom said as she came walking down the hallway from the kitchen with Ben trailing behind them holding a pop-tart.

"Oh, wait a second. I forgot my phone!" Sarah ran upstairs to grab her phone off her bed. As she grabbed her phone she realized she hadn't checked to see if she had any new texts. Looking at it she saw she had four new messages from Brody.

"Sarah Nicole, for someone who is in a hurry, you are taking a long time. Let's go!" her mother exclaimed from the front doorway.

Before she could read the messages, she rolled her eyes accidentally putting her phone on silent as she put it in her purse.

After she climbed into the passenger seat she turned around and tore off half of Ben's pop-tart. "Thanks," she said as she stuffed it into her mouth.

"Hey. I'm telling."

"Mom's right here, dummy. You can't tell on me, she already knows."

"Sarah, don't call him dumb, and stop picking on your brother."

"Well he is a dummy. I can't help it, he's your kid."

"Sarah, I'm warning you," her mother gave her a sideways glance and tightened her lips.

"Whatever, Mom." She turned around and looked at her brother. "Sorry, Ben. I don't think you're dumb."

"We're not supposed to say that word, cause it can hurt people's feelings."

"That's right, and Sarah knows better than to say those words too, and if she says those words again, she is going to be grounded for a month."

"Okay, so anyway," trying to change the subject, "Tamara and I are going to go to her place and then come to our house. I'll call you when we get close to school."

"Where does Tammy live?"

"It's Tamara, Mom. She lives down on Sycamore Lane I think she said."

"Is she a white girl or a black girl?"

"She's black. What's that matter?"

"Well, Sycamore Lane is really nice and has beautiful houses on it. Million dollar homes some of them."

"Okay. And?" Sarah rolled her eyes as she realized her mom

was being rather judgmental and racist.

"Nothing," she started backpedaling. "I shouldn't judge a book by its cover, now should I?" she shook her head. "I would like to meet her though before you go with her."

Breathing in a deep sigh, Sarah looked out the window as they approached the school. "She's right there by the flagpole. Do you see her?"

"Yeah, I see her. What did you say her name was?"

"Tamara."

The car pulled up in front of the flagpole and Sarah opened the door to get out.

Tamara nodded and smiled at Sarah and started walking closer.

"Hi, Tamra. I'm Mrs. Benson, Sarah's mom."

"Hi. Nice to meet you. I'm Tamara."

They both gave each other a fake smile, aware of the mistake her mom just made.

"Yes, Tamara, sorry. You girls want me to drive you to your house?"

"Mom, I said no. It's fine. I'll call you when we get back here." Sarah shut the door before her mother could protest.

"You girls be careful. Sarah call me if you need anything. Nice to meet you Tameia," Mrs. Benson announced out the window as she rolled it down driving away.

"I'm so sorry about her," Sarah looked at Tamara and shook her head in embarrassment.

"Oh, it's cool. I've been called worse."

Not sure how to respond Sarah giggled uncomfortably and readjusted her backpack on her shoulders and looked around to the empty parking lot. "It's crazy how many cars this lot holds, it's so big. How many kids go to our school anyway?"

Thankful for the subject change, Tamara quickly answered, "I don't know, I think we have like 2000, or something. There's like 500 kids in each grade level."

"Really? I guess that makes sense. Whenever I get my report card it says like I'm like eight or something out of 511, I guess that doesn't mean for the whole school."

"Are you for real number eight in our class? I'm currently number two, but I think after this semester I'm going to be number one. I am taking a couple heavy weighted courses," Tamara paused and smiled.

"You are number two? Who is number one?"

"Kimmie Launder."

"Oh, I know her. She's in my English class. She is so smart."

"Well, I'm smarter," Tamara sassed back and smiled. "Seems like so many people at our school don't care about their grades."

"I know what you mean. I care, but I get so nervous anytime there is a partner or group project because I always get stuck doing all the work. And the worst part about it is that I like doing it all, because I'm a control freak and I don't want to get a bad grade," Sarah glanced at Tamara to see if she was offended.

"Girl, you ain't gotta tell me. I'm the same way."

Both girls looked away from each other and smiled at their first connection.

"I can't afford to get bad grades," Tamara continued. "I got big plans after high school. I gotta change the world." She looked out into the horizon and nodded as if she could see herself in the future. "What about you? You gonna change the world someday?"

Surprised by Tamara's interest, Sarah confessed, "A part of me wants to be a pharmacist someday, but I hate math so I think I'm considering journalism. I do want to change the world. I want to tell people's stories. I want to shed light on the world's problems and fight for justice."

"What?" Tamara sounded surprised. "A journalist? That's cool. You know, a well-told, powerful story can bring about serious change. Good for you!" Tamara nodded.

"Thanks," Sarah walked a little taller. "What about you?"

"I want to be in the medical world. I want to be a pediatrician. I love kids. I have two little brothers I would die for," she looked at Sarah and smiled. "Math isn't that hard. You have Ms. Panacinni, right?"

Sarah nodded.

"She cool. She's for real a good teacher. She said she gonna write me a recommendation letter to get into Howard."

"She's nice," Sarah agreed. "She saved my butt the other day."

Both of the girls stopped walking and looked at each other waiting. Then they both broke out in laughter.

"Yeah, she sure did," Tamara snorted and laughed as the two began walking again.

"So you have to take the bus every day?"

"Not for real. I could walk. But my mom takes me a lot. She has been working a lot lately so I've been taking it home so she doesn't have to leave work early to pick me up. Our school doesn't have yellow busses so we got me a bus card to make it easier."

"That's cool," *That must suck. I wonder what her mom does for a living.* Sarah thought to herself.

They stood there in silence both not knowing what to say to the other as they waited for the bus to arrive.

I wonder if she's ever even been on a city bus? "Have you even rode the bus anywhere?" Tamara asked.

Embarrassed, Sarah responded quietly with a quick, "No."

"For real? Oh girl, we gotta get you up to speed," Tamara teased. "There some rules to the bus system you know," she smiled at the wide-eyed white girl standing beside her.

"Yeah? Like what?" Sarah asked.

"Okay, so first, if someone looks shifty, they probably are. Don't sit in the back, and don't sit in the front. You got a bus card?"

"No. Do I need one?"

"Na, it's cool, you just gotta pay two bucks to ride without it."

"Oh, okay, I have five on me. I have my credit card too." Sarah started to pull her wallet out of her purse.

"The five works, don't get your credit card out," Tamara snorted and half smiled at Sarah. "Just follow me." Tamara moved closer to the curb as the bus pulled up. As she climbed on she swiped her bus card and Sarah handed the driver her money.

The driver looked annoyed that she had to get out change and Tamara and Sarah exchanged smiles over it.

Sarah then followed Tamara about half way down the bus to an open seat. The bus had already started moving which caused Sarah to stumble into the seat. She looked up at the driver who looked back at her and just raised her eyebrows.

"Don't pay her any attention. She just be mad cause she gotta work on a Saturday morning and she probably didn't get to go out last night," Tamara said as she shot the bus driver a look.

Sarah settled down into the same seat with Tamara waiting for the next new thing to come her way.

"So who do you live with?" Sarah asked.

"My mama and my two little brothers."

"Oh, was that who you were with last night at the game?"

"Yeah, those were my little guys," she giggled. "You know Brandon right? Brandon Harris?"

Sarah nodded.

Tamara continued, "We talkin'. I guess he's kinda my boyfriend. We going out tonight so he's something like that. Was that your boyfriend you were walking with last night after the game?" Tamara questioned.

Are we really having a boyfriend talk right now? She is really nice. Does she really care about this or is she just being nice because she has to?

"Yeah, we kinda made it official last night I guess, so yeah, he's my boyfriend. We've only been talking for like a month though."

"That's cool. I don't really know him. I guess Brandon does

though."

"That's what Brody said last night at the game when Brandon broke the record."

"Yeah, that was really awesome wasn't it? I was so proud of him. I think he's gonna play division one someday," Tamara smiled as she thought about the kiss he gave her last night along the fence when he broke the record.

Sarah noticed the smile, "Aw. That's so cute. You really like him don't you?"

"Pshh. Na. I mean. You know. He's a'ight," grinning from ear to ear Tamara couldn't hide her crush for him.

"That's so sweet. You two are really cute together."

"You think?"

"Yeah! Of course."

Looking up Tamara realized they were getting close to her stop. "We need to get off here," she said as she nudged Sarah to stand up and head toward the front of the bus.

Once the bus stopped the two girls climbed down the stairs and stood there looking at long street ahead of them lined with large Victorian homes on both sides.

"Is this where you live?" Sarah asked.

"Yep, this is my street."

The two girls began walking toward Tamara's house.

"So, we had a little incident here last night with my mom's brother, or whatever you wanna call him. It was a wreck, but my mom ended up kicking him out, so I'm just warning you now, there may or may not be a mess."

As the girls walked down the sidewalk, Sarah noticed a tall skinny white woman with bright blonde hair walking up behind them rather quickly. Sarah nudged Tamara to get her to notice too.

"Ah, dang it. Candice, what do you want?" Tamara sounded annoyed as she realized Candice had followed them from the bus stop.

"Where is Eric? Why your mama kick him out? Do you know where he gone stay now? When he comin' back?"

"Candice, I will tell you this one time, she kicked him out cause he ain't no good. Now, please get away from us, for real."

I can't believe this is happening right now. Sarah probably thinks this is truly the ghetto.

Who is this woman? I don't think Tamara likes her. I wonder if she's on drugs.

Tamara and Sarah quickly walked into the house. When they walked in it smelled like bacon.

"Baby, that you?" Tamara's mom hollered from the kitchen.

"Yeah, it's me and Sarah."

With her black leggings on and fitted hoodie, Tamara's mother came out of the kitchen. "Oh hi, honey. I'm Sharon Hudgenson, Tamara's mama. You hungry? Tamara left out of here so quickly this morning, it's no wonder she so skinny. But I saved you that bacon."

Startled by the warm welcome, Sarah took a deep breath and smiled at Tamara's mother. "Yeah, sure," she shrugged her shoulders and looked at Tamara who was smiling at her mother.

"Oh, good. I fixed up some scrambled eggs, and hash brown casserole with some bacon. You like bacon, Sarah?"

Laughing, Sarah couldn't help but enjoy Tamara's mom. "Yeah, I love bacon. You have a beautiful home, Mrs. Hudgenson."

"Oh, please, call me Sharon. Thank you. We bought this home many years ago," she said as she smiled and looked at the walls as if lost in a memory. "Wes. Dom," she hollered down the hallway into the playroom. "Tamara is home, come on and eat," she called out.

Tamara leaned over to Sarah and whispered, "I'm sorry, my mom is a little nut-so sometimes."

"Oh my gosh, I love her. I think she is so nice."

As Sarah was saying this, she was interrupted by the two boys who surrounded Tamara at the football game.

"Sissy!" Wesley jumped on his sister's back as Dom attached himself to her leg.

"Uh-oh. What do we have here?" Tamara's voice changed into a playful tone. "Mama, I seem to have this big wart growing on my back, you think you can help me get it off?"

Tamara's mom looked at Sarah and winked.

"Oh my. Let's see here. Oh yes. It is a big wart," her mother played along, while the two boys giggled. "I'm not sure how we can remove this thing. Hmm. Let me think, maybe we can tickle it off!" she shouted as she began to tickle Wesley on Tamara's back and pull him off cradling him in her arms.

Tamara was laughing and giggling with her family as Sarah watched the family love each other.

Tamara bent over and pulled Dom off her leg and pulled him up to her chest to hug him. She gave him a kiss and whispered something in his ear then set him down.

Almost immediately, he came over to Sarah and said, "Hello, Sarah. I am Dominick. Thanks for coming to our home."

Sarah laughed out loud and shook the little boy's hand. "Thank you, Dominick, I'm glad to be here." Sarah couldn't help but feel comfortable. She was smiling uncontrollably.

After Tamara's mom put the food on the table, the family sat around the table and gathered hands to pray. Dominick took Sarah's hand while Tamara's mother took the other and said a quick blessing over the meal.

"So, girls," Tamara's mother began as she dished out the eggs, "What do you have to do for this project?"

Sarah looked at Tamara who stuffed eggs into her mouth so she didn't have to respond. "Um, well I don't really know. We weren't really give too much instruction on it. I guess I have to get to know what Tamara's life is like and she has to get to know what my life is like and then we have to write about it."

"Well, I don't know if all that can be done in a day. Seems like an awful big undertaking. You two didn't know each other before this?"

"Um, I guess, not really. I mean we have seen each other, but I don't think we've ever taken the time to get to know each other before this," Sarah bashfully responded.

"Aw, that's such a shame. It's a good thing you got this project then, huh?" she smiled at Sarah, who then smiled at Tamara.

Tamara was glad her mom was home so that Sarah could see the real version of her family. Tamara was glad everything unfolded the way it did last night with Eric so that he was gone and she could finally have her mom back without him around.

They remind me so much of my family when Dad was there. We were so happy. They seem so happy together. Sarah reflected as she finished up her breakfast.

Once everyone was finished, the two girls went into Tamara's room to work on their project.

When Sarah walked into Tamara's room, the first thing she noticed was all the pink. "Wow, you like pink, huh?" Sarah teased.

"Yeah, I'm a little obsessed with it really," Tamara teased back.

"It's cool, cause my room is totally decked out in purple, so between the two of us we have all the girl power we need," Sarah giggled at her joke and then noticed the broken desk on the floor and walked closer to it. "Oh, gosh. That sucks," looking to Tamara for a response.

"Yeah, my mom's brother. He was a mess."

Sarah realized there was more to the story but she didn't push it. She walked over near Tamara's bed and read a poster on the wall that said the word "Whatever" really large across it. Inside the word there was a Bible passage that read, "*Whatever. Whatever is true, whatever is noble, whatever is right, whatever is pure, whatever is admirable, whatever is honorable…think about these things. Philippians 4:8 Remember… God is with you- whatever, whenever, wherever, forever."*

"Oh my gosh, Tamara. I have this exact same poster in my room."

"Shut up. Really?"

Surprised by this, the girls both read it to themselves.

"Yeah, my dad gave it to me when I turned thirteen. He told me since I was a teenager now I needed to keep my focus on God and not on all the bad stuff."

"Yeah, my granny gave it to me before she died about six years ago. She told me that I need to always focus on the Lord cause He is the only one who can save me from myself."

Silenced by this revelation, the two girls began to feel more comfortable with each other.

Wow, she believes in God. Maybe she isn't as promiscuous as she seems. I wonder why she's dating a guy like Brody then? She is actually normal. How weird we have the same Bible quote on our walls?

Oh my God. I can't believe she is so normal. I thought for sure she'd have like Lil' whoever posters or something on her walls. I can't believe we actually have the same Bible quote poster. That's so cool.

Tamara and Sarah both looked at each other and nodded with a smile. They were beginning an unspoken friendship, a respect for each other, one they never knew existed.

They decided to get out their notebooks to start asking each other questions.

"Okay, I'll go first," Tamara began. "Let's see," she looked at a list of conversation starter questions she had printed out at school before she left yesterday. "Okay, this is an easy one. What is something you are obsessed with?"

"Oh," Sarah smiled. "Besides my phone?" she smiled again, giggling under her breath. "Okay, for real, not a lot of people know this about me but I totally care about waste management. I mean. Let me clarify," she laughed at the absurdity of her response.

Tamara just looked at her with bewilderment.

"I mean. Okay so did you know that most of the garbage that enters the ocean is plastic? Seriously, like water bottles, yogurt cups, grocery bags, milk cartons, none of them are biodegradable. You know that I read somewhere once something like 11 million tons of floating plastic covers over five or six million square miles between California and Hawaii alone," Sarah started to get louder now, "I mean what?" she said as she threw her hands in the air. "We have got to do something about this."

With wide eyes and a slight smile Tamara just looked at her. "Oh," she finally let out, and the two of them giggled again.

"Yeah, so, I guess I'm kinda obsessed with the trash in our oceans."

"Okay then," Tamara smiled. Realizing there was a lot more to this girl than she had initially thought. She wrote down some notes as Sarah looked at the paper for question ideas to ask back to her.

"Tell me something about yourself you've never told anyone else," Sarah asked.

"Um, wow. Let's see," She stared into space for several moments contemplating her response. "So, I know this gonna sound crazy, so don't get me wrong here, but, I'm glad I'm black and I'm glad God made me the way He did, but sometimes, I get so annoyed with people judging me because I'm black. I feel like I'm always the minority. Like I gotta prove to people I'm not gonna steal their purse or act all crazy, you know?"

Sarah didn't know. She didn't know what it was like to be anything other than white. She hadn't even ever thought about it. "I mean, I guess I understand what you're saying."

Tamara went on, "I'm just saying, white people never get judged like black people do. You've probably never walked into a store and been followed around by the manager to make sure you didn't take anything. You've probably never been accused of having a baby just cause you got your little brother hanging around."

Guiltily, Sarah shook her head, knowing she made the exact judgment on Tamara last night at the football game. Feeling uncomfortable she looked at Tamara and said, "No, but white people get judged too. White people are automatically rich and live in perfect houses or listen to country music and watch NASCAR. All us white girls care about is our hair and boyfriends."

Realizing what they were both doing to each other, the room went quiet. It stayed quiet for several minutes as both of the girls began to write in their notebooks about what they were recognizing in the other.

"I killed my dad," Tamara revealed.

Sarah looked up at the girl sitting across from her on the bed.

"Two years ago, coming up in February. I was in eighth grade. I got a stupid detention for not doing my homework assignment. Which was a stupid assignment anyway. It was a word search," she rolled her eyes. "There was a lot of ice and snow that day and my mom told me since I didn't do my assignment I had to walk home after the detention. So I called my dad and begged him to come get me so I didn't freeze to death," she took a deep sigh.

Sarah scooted closer to her and leaned in to listen more intently.

"But I've never told anyone this part before," she looked at Sarah. "I told my dad that I left my winter coat at home that day, which is why he finally agreed to come and get me. But, I really had it. I was just going to stuff it into my back pack when he got there to pick me up." A tear came into her eye. "But he never showed up. He lost control on I-75 and slid over the embankment into a tree. He was killed on the spot. It was my fault. I lied to him and said I didn't have my coat. All because I didn't do that stupid assignment," she said as she shook her head to try and shake her rising emotion away. "But, ever since then, I haven't missed one assignment. Not even the stupid ones."

Sarah looked at her and gave her a soft smile. She then reached out her hand and touched Tamara on the shoulder. "In a way though, he is indirectly responsible for your education. It's like every single academic decision you make is for your dad."

Tamara wiped the tears from her eyes and smiled at Sarah. "What time is it? We probably better get to your house."

They looked at the clock which read 11:39, and agreed they needed to go.

As they were getting their bags and saying goodbye, Tamara's mother hugged Sarah tightly and thanked her for coming over. Tamara kissed both her brothers and led the way out of the house.

Once they were on the bus headed back to school, Sarah pulled her phone out of her purse to call her mom. Before she could call her mom though she realized Brody had texted her sixteen more times since this morning's texts. "Oh my God," Sarah announced.

"What?"

"Brody has literally texted me like a thousand times today."

"What? Why?"

"I don't know." Sarah quietly read the messages to herself; which the first four were about how he couldn't sleep because he was thinking about her and how he can't wait to see her. Then the next six were apologies for texting so much, which then were followed by ten more about whether or not she was mad at him because she hadn't texted back.

Realizing that her phone was on silent and taken aback by the number of messages she decided to return a text to him just to stop him from worrying any longer. "Hi. Sorry I missed your texts. My phone has been on silent. I'm w Tamara working on our project. I'll see u at the party later. Kisses;-)" She finished typing and took a deep breath. "I guess he just wanted to see how I am and tell me he's been thinking about me."

"He had to tell you that a thousand times? Girl, he want you for real. You haven't slept with him have you?"

"No, why?"

"Cause it's obvious. He obviously wants to have sex with you cause he can't stop calling you. You need to make him wait. Actually, as a matter of fact, you need to not have sex with him at all. You still a virgin?"

"Yeah."

"Don't give it up to him, girl. He too thirsty for it. You need to read your poster more," she smiled at her. "Look, I know we don't really know each other for real, but the way I see it, he is a player. He has been forever. He talks a smooth game just so he can get some and then as soon as he does he drops the girl. He's a player. At least that's his reputation anyway."

"Is it? I know. I don't know. I don't think it's all about sex with him and me though. He seems to really like me. Like, he told me he loves me. He seems to be genuine with me. I do like him a lot though. I don't know. Maybe you're right. You're probably right." This was the first time Sarah had actually considered that Brody could be playing her. "I'm not ready to have sex though. It scares me. Like, I don't want to disappoint God, you know. I don't want to do it yet."

"So don't," Tamara laughed, and Sarah smiled back.

The two girls felt a sense of closeness as if they had been friends for years, rather than just a few hours.

Sarah called her mom to come get them as they got closer to the school.

"See, the bus wasn't that bad was it?" Tamara asked as they were getting off.

"No, well other than the bus driver this morning."

"Ha. Right!"

Sarah's mom pulled into the school parking lot shortly after the girls arrived. Ben was sitting up front so Sarah and Tamara climbed into the back. Sarah could tell her mother had been crying, but decided against bringing it up just in case Tamara hadn't noticed.

"Hi, Sarah bear." Ben exclaimed, excited to see his sister.

"What's up, Turd? Ben, this is my friend, Tamara."

"Hi, Tamara. It's nice to meet you," Ben said as he turned around in his seat to take a good look at his sister's new friend.

"Hi, Ben, it's nice to meet you too. What you got there?" pointing to the toy in his hand.

"Oh. This? This is my transformer. He's cool. Look what he can do." Ben showed off his talent of morphing the car into a fighting monster.

"Wow, look at that. I bet he protects you, huh?" Tamara asked.

"Uh-huh. And he sleeps with me too. I have two more at home. I can show you them. They are cool. But they don't change into a transformer as good as this one. Sometimes they get stuck when you try to turn it into a car."

Sarah noticed her mother smiling in the rearview mirror at Tamara who seemed to be winning over Ben within the first minute of meeting him.

"So, Tamara?" Mrs. Benson questioned.

Sarah sighed a sign of relief, thankful her mom got the name right this time.

"Yes ma'am?"

"What grade are you in?"

"Oh, I'm in tenth grade."

"That's nice. Do you play any sports, like basketball or anything?"

"Mom!" Sarah interrupted.

"Na, it's cool," Tamara stopped Sarah from getting upset. "No ma'am. I'm in a math club, but I don't play any sports. I try and save that for the real athletes. I'm about as uncoordinated as they get," she smiled at the woman looking at her in the mirror.

Sarah smiled at Tamara for playing it so cool, but whispered,

"I'm so sorry."

Once they pulled into Sarah's house, everyone got out and the girls headed for the living room while her mother went directly upstairs and shut her door.

"Ben? What's wrong with Mom?" Sarah asked.

"I don't know. Coach came over to the house to see me after the game and then she got all upset about it. I don't know. They were up stairs for a long time talking."

Realizing she didn't want to hear any more of it, she told him to go play so she and Tamara could work on their project.

"Where's your dad?" Tamara asked after Ben left the room.

"It's a long story," Sarah huffed. "Do you want any juice or anything to drink?"

"Well lucky for you I got nothing but time," Tamara pushed. "And sure, I'll take a glass of water."

"I don't know," Sarah sighed. "I just found out that my mom is having an affair with my brother's soccer coach," Sarah began to tell the story trying to avoid making eye contact with the wide-eyed Tamara across from her. "Well, I told my dad and now he's not here, and they're probably getting a divorce. Mom is acting so distraught over the whole thing but she is the one who was literally cheating on my dad. And apparently, the coach is moving in." Sarah handed Tamara a glass of water.

"What makes you think he's moving in?"

"Ben just said he was here."

"That don't mean he's moving in, Sarah," she paused and looked out the back door. "You gotta give it to God and let him control it. It's not yours to control. You just gotta hope your mom and dad figure it out."

Sarah smiled at her.

"You have a nice place, girl. I mean you don't have no NASCAR posters or nothing, but I guess it will do," she smiled at Sarah who couldn't help but giggle.

"Whatever, right?" Sarah looked at Tamara to see if she picked up on the shared understanding of the word from their posters.

"Whatever!" Tamara nodded in agreement to show she understood exactly what Sarah was saying.

"So, I say we should just go start typing our project out and put it together into a scrapbook style. We can take some pics with our phones and just print them out."

"Okay."

The girls went up to Sarah's room and laughed when it was indeed as purple as Sarah had described. Sarah sat next to Tamara on her bed and they took some silly pictures of each other and began printing them out. They even exchanged phone numbers and sent some pictures to each other's phones.

After they had the pictures placed into the scrapbook they sat together and typed out a reflection to their day.

They decided the key ingredient was the word WE. They weren't going to say I and me in the reflection, but only say we, because as Sarah put it, "WE discovered how similar WE really are," she smiled as she put the final sentence down.

"Girl, you probably going to that party tonight, right?" Tamara asked.

"Yeah, I am."

"Look. You cool. I like you. So I'm gonna tell you this on the real. Don't be stupid. Don't do anything you don't want to do. Okay?"

Sarah took a deep breath and looked at her new friend. "Okay, deal."

The girls got up and hugged each other, thankful for the new friendship they had found. They decided to make their friendship official so they Snapped a selfie together and added #NewBesties to the image and put it on their Instagram and Snapchat stories.

Sarah's mom agreed to take Tamara home and Sarah rode along to make sure her mom didn't say anything stupid again.

"Alright, girl. Catch you Monday. Be good. It was nice to meet you, Mrs. Benson," Tamara spoke as she got out of the car.

"You too, Tamara."

"Whatever, Tamara," Sarah smiled. "You be good too. See you Monday."

The two girls smiled at one another through the window and waved.

CHAPTER 12
First Date

"Tamara, hurry up. Brandon's been out here waiting for almost five minutes!" Tamara's mom smiled at the young man quietly waiting in the doorway.

"Oh, Ms. Hudgenson, it's cool, for real. I'm in no hurry. My daddy always said you should never rush a woman," Brandon smiled and adjusted the collar of his button up shirt, seeming slightly nervous.

"Sorry." Tamara came bouncing down the staircase in her red high heels and short black dress. "I'm so sorry. I couldn't find my mascara. Somehow it ended up in the toy box in someone's room," she glanced at her brothers sitting on the couch staring at her in wonder.

Noticing the glance toward her brothers Brandon jumped to their defense, "Well, when I was little I used to always take my mom's makeup and use it as grenades for my G.I. Joe men to blow up."

"It must be a guy thing, Tamara," her mom teased as they all stood awkwardly in the living room looking at each other. "Well, baby, you look stunning. There is no sense in you wasting your good looks around here. Take this handsome man outta here before he changes his mind."

They all smiled, then the pair headed toward his car. Brandon opened Tamara's car door for her and she noticed him smiling as he walked around the front of the car to get into the driver's seat.

"So," he began once he got into the car, "I have reservations for us at The Sector. Do you like that place?"

"I never been," she smiled at him.

"What? It's so good. It's a steakhouse but taken to a whole new level. The steaks just melt in your mouth. You like steak?"

"Yeah, steak is good," she giggled.

There was a long silence as they drove down the road, both obviously nervous. "You look amazing tonight," he finally broke the ice.

"Aw, thank you. You lookin' good too."

"Na, I mean for real. When I saw you walk down the staircase, I was like oh dang, keep it together, B.," he laughed.

"Whatever. You're a fool," she blushed as she looked at him.

He smiled at her and put his hand on her knee over her hand.

She felt his palm sweating and thought it was cute how nervous he was, because she was just as nervous.

Instead of having the valet take the car, he parked it around the back of the building, and again, opened the door for Tamara. He held his arm out for her to clasp as they walked into the restaurant.

"Good evening," the hostess greeted.

"Hello," Brandon nodded at her and responded in a deeper voice than his usual.

"Do you have a reservation this evening?" she continued with a smile.

"Yes, under Harris. Brandon Harris," he cleared his throat.

"Ah. I have it right here. For two?"

"Yes, ma'am," he reciprocated the smile.

"Welcome. We have your table waiting for you. Please, follow me." She headed toward the inner part of the dining room. Brandon motioned for Tamara to go ahead of him and he followed.

"Here you are. Will this table suit you this evening?"

"It's perfect," he smiled.

The hostess pulled the chair out for Tamara to sit, but Brandon rushed over behind her and said, "Please, allow me," motioning for Tamara to take a seat so he could push it in for her.

"Thank you," Tamara exhaled, feeling overwhelmed by his charm and chivalry.

He smiled at her, went to the other side of the table, and sat down. Once he was seated the hostess handed both of them their menus and took the cloth napkin out of the wine glass on the table and laid it across each one's lap.

"So fancy," Tamara whispered.

Brandon smiled and nodded his head in agreement.

"Please," the hostess began, "take a moment to look over the menu. If you have any questions don't hesitate to ask. Your waiter's name is Eugene. He will be with you momentarily."

"Thank you."

"Enjoy your time with us," she clasped her hands and walked back toward the front of the restaurant.

"Oh my goodness," Tamara said, as her eyes gleamed.

"I know right?" Brandon smiled back. "This place is amazing. I couldn't imagine bringing such an amazing girl like you to any place other than this place for our first date."

Aw. What a gem. I don't think he could get much sweeter. She exhaled slowly and allowed herself the opportunity to just take it all in.

"Hello," a waiter approached their table smiling. "My name is Eugene. How are you this evening?"

"Good evening," Brandon returned the smile. "We are doing well. Thank you."

"Excellent. Welcome to The Sector. We have an outstanding menu this evening. Would you mind if I went over it with you?"

"Sure," they agreed.

"Excellent. You will find our hors d'oeuvres located near the top of the front page," he continued.

Tamara was completely zoned into Brandon. She didn't hear a

word the waiter said because she was so caught up on watching him being so dashing. *This man. Oh my. He actually really cares about whatever Eugene is saying. Look at those dimples. I am melting. His jaw line. Stop. Can he really be this handsome? He has got me. I am hooked. Why are they both staring at me?*

"Tamara?" Brandon questioned. "Are you alright?"

"Oh my goodness," she blushed. "Yes. What was the question?"

"What may I start you with to drink this evening, ma'am?" Eugene knowingly smiled.

"Oh, I'll just take a Sprite."

"Excellent choice," he smiled at the two of them and walked away.

"You good?" Brandon gave her a sideways glance.

"I am more than good. I'm great. I guess I just zoned out," embarrassed to admit she was admiring him and got lost in her thoughts.

"Excellent," he mimicked the waiter and smiled.

She blushed and smiled back.

Throughout dinner, Tamara was amazed by Brandon's manners and his knowledge of etiquette. For the first time in her life she felt like a grown up. They laughed and teased each other. They quietly made inappropriate jokes about some of the people around them, but mostly they enjoyed each other.

"So, how'd the project go today with that girl?" Brandon asked.

"Oh, I can't believe you remembered. It went well. Turns out she is really smart and super cool, for real. We got just about everything done and we prolly gonna end up with an A. But, would you expect anything less, honestly?" She posed as if she was on the cover of magazine and smiled at him.

"Well, I don't know the girl, but if she anywhere near as smart as you, you'll prolly get a double A++."

"Oh my goodness," Tamara groaned a little later as she rubbed her stomach. "I don't think I can eat another bite."

"What?" Brandon quipped. "Well, if you ain't gonna eat it then lemme have it. This stuff is so good. How can you be full, they barely put any food on your plate," he reached for her plate and slid the rest of her steak and mashed potatoes onto his and began shoveling it into his mouth.

She laughed at his silliness, "You're a mess," she teased.

"Hey, I'm a growing boy," he argued as he hovered over his plate of food with his knife in one hand and his fork in the other. "I gotta get my protein in so I can get big for the NFL one day."

"Oh, is that it?"

"Yeah!" he smiled as he put a scoop of potatoes in his mouth. "What? You think I'm fat or something?" As he smiled, a piece of potato fell onto his chin from his mouth.

The two of them broke into laughter, causing the people at the tables around them to look over in annoyance, which sent them into an even bigger fit of laughter. They tried to conceal their giggles by taking a drink of their soda.

Tamara was trying not to be so loud, but the harder she tried it seemed the harder it was to stop laughing. She even snorted a little as she took a drink, which caused her to choke on her soda, and laugh even harder.

In the midst of their laughter, the manager came over and asked if they needed anything. The two tried to gain composure and politely Brandon apologized and told him they were fine.

"Very well then," the manager said as he signaled to their server. "I'll have your waiter bring the dessert menu over so you may see if there is anything you would like to try."

"Oh, na, man. For real, we're full," Brandon hesitated, "I mean, would you like anything for dessert, my lady?" he smiled at Tamara across the table from him.

"You must be crazy if you think I can eat anymore. I'm straight. Thank you though."

He looked up at the manager and the waiter now standing over them. "We will just take the check when you get a moment. Thank you, gentlemen," he said as he immediately turned his gaze back to Tamara and took a drink.

He is so amazing. I can't believe how wonderful he is. I'm in heaven. Tamara took a drink as well and looked at the tables around her. "I wonder what everyone here does for a living?"

"I don't know, but I can tell you one thing, they better work some place that pays a lot if they like eating out like this, cause this place ain't cheap," he looked at the bill. "You bring your apron? Looks like we gotta do some dishes," he winked at her as he pulled his wallet out of his back pocket.

Tamara's eyes opened wide, not realizing he was only kidding.

"Relax," he laughed. "I'm just playin'. I got it. I got this. You know, you hang with me long enough, you'll realize just how much of a queen you really are," he grinned at her as he handed the check presenter back to the waiter. "Keep the change, man."

"Yes, sir. Thank you very much, sir. You two have a wonderful evening," the waiter smiled at both of them and took the remaining dishes into the kitchen.

Tamara smiled at his coolness, "Thank you for dinner."

"You are very welcome. It was my pleasure."

He stood up and Tamara followed suit. Brandon took Tamara by the hand and led her to the door of the restaurant, past the valet crew to the car. "Brrr," he shivered when he got into the car. "It's getting cold out for real. This is when you know it's football season," he smiled and rubbed his hands together quickly and blew warm air into them as he waited for the car to warm up.

"They are predicting it being a real snowy winter," Tamara said as she shivered alongside him.

"That's awesome. We can go skiing. You ever been skiing?"

"What? Skiing? No, I ain't never been no skiing," she laughed. "I thought only white people skied?"

"I must be white then, cause this little black boy loves to ski. It's awesome. You'd love it. I'll take you on our first snow day."

"Snow days! I love snow days!" she smiled. "There is nothing better than waking up, looking outside, seeing all the snow, and turning on the news to wait for your school's name to show up at the bottom of the screen."

"What? You wait for it on the news? I just stay sleepin' an wait for a text alert," he laughed.

"Oh, yeah, I get those too," she contended. "But I can never go back to sleep, so I love to get up and just go out into the living room and watch it on the news," she shrugged her shoulders. "Guess I'm old school like that."

"But you know since we live in the city the bus routes never stop running. So we don't never get called off for real. If the busses can drive, we can ride."

"Ugh," she agreed.

"So, you for real about that NFL thing?" Tamara questioned as they started getting closer to her house.

"Well, I'm for real about the college thing. I got a lot of scouts lookin' at me right now. You know how many high school players actually make it to the collegiate level? And then, how many of those players actually make it to the NFL? It ain't a lot. Not saying I don't want to, but I gotta keep my options open, and my mind in check. I can't allow myself to get caught up in a dream and not keep my focus on what my circumstances are right in front of me. I definitely wanna play at a division one college, but I also think it'd be real cool to be a teacher or something like that one day, you know?"

"I don't know about no teacher, but I hear ya. I couldn't be a teacher if it was the best paying job on the planet. I know what kind of attitude my friends give the teachers at our school. I am sure I would get stuck with a bunch of kids just like them," she huffed. "No, not me, I wanna be a doctor."

"A doctor?" he looked over at her and smiled.

"That's awesome. I can't even say the names of the medicines I get prescribed when I'm sick, so I know I sure wouldn't make it as no doctor," he smiled again at her. "But that's cool, Tamara. I think that's real cool you wanna be a doctor. I hope you do. As a matter of fact, I'm gonna see to it that you do. Ain't no excuse from here on out with me. You want it, you gotta go for it," he encouraged as his car approached her driveway.

"Okay then, well if you want the NFL, then no excuses for you either. If you want it, you gotta go for it," she grinned at him as she reached for the car door handle.

"A'ight," they both nodded in agreement to the challenge.

She glanced at the clock and realized her mom would probably be asleep in bed by now. "You wanna come in and watch a movie or something?" she quietly asked. *Please say yes. Please say yes. Please say yes.*

"Okay, sounds good to me, but wait before you get out," he grabbed her hand before she could open the car door. "Let me come around and open it for you."

Before she could utter a response, he was already out of his door approaching hers to open it.

"Thank you, Brandon," she blushed at his kindness.

As soon as they got inside Tamara immediately took off her heels. "You want something to drink?"

"Ah, na, I'm cool. Is your mom here?"

"Yeah, but she's in bed. Ain't nothing waking her up now."

"Cool. You mind if I use your bathroom right quick?"

"Na, you cool. It's on the other side of the living room down the hall on your right."

Oh my God. He is so amazing. I need to text Porsha. She took her phone out of her purse and noticed she had a missed call from Sarah. *Hm. I wonder what she wanted? When'd she call? 10:17. Huh. Hope she good. She'll call back if she needs something.*

Tamara scrolled down to Porsha's name in her phone and sent her a text to tell her how awesome Brandon was.

Brandon came quietly back and startled her as she walked out of the kitchen into the living room, holding a glass of water for him. "Oh, I'm sorry," he gently put his arm around her neck.

Mmmm. He smells so nice. "You almost got water all over you," she teased.

He put his hands on the back of her head and pulled her lips into his. He held onto her head and neck as they kissed and her body fell into his chest as she relished his embrace.

"Thank you for going out with me tonight," he looked her directly in her eyes as he pulled his lips away but still kept her body pulled in closely.

She closed her eyes and kissed him again. "I had such an amazing time," she whispered as she gazed back at him.

"I think I am going to leave. As much as I would love to stay here with you and your beautiful self, I know I should prolly be a gentleman and leave you alone," he reasoned with himself, more so than with Tamara.

"You don't have to leave," she contended.

"I like you. I don't want to do anything stupid and ruin anything."

Tamara knew he was trying to be a gentleman so she didn't pressure him to stay any longer. "You are so sweet. Thank you for everything, Brandon."

"No, thank you. You are so beautiful." He hugged her and kissed her once more. "I'll text you in a few."

"Cool." She shut the door behind him.

As soon as he walked out, there was a quiet tap on the door. She opened the door and he poked his head back in and kissed her one last time before he left.

"You a mess," she teased as she kissed him back.

"A'ight. Bye."

"Bye."

Aw. I am totally head over heels crazy about that guy! She locked the door and grabbed her high heels from the floor to carry them up to her room. On her way to her room she got her cell phone from the kitchen and turned out the lights.

She took off her dress and got into her shorts and tank top and crawled into bed. Once she was in bed she looked at her phone.

Porsha had returned her text, "U got it bad."

Tamara laughed, *if you only knew how bad.* She thought to herself. *Mmm. What a gentleman. He was so respectful. I can't believe they make men like that. I definitely do got it bad. I wonder what's up with Sarah? I should text her. She's probably at that party. I hope she didn't do anything she didn't wanna do.*

"Hey girl! It's Tamara. Missed your call. Sorry. Hope ur cool. Remember do what's good 4 u, don't worry bout no one else. Call me back if u need me."

Just as she hit send she got a message from Brandon.

"Hey boo. U amaze me. Sweet dreams."

Aw. He is adorable.

"G'nite;-)" she texted him back. As she reached for her light switch, she smiled from ear to ear playing the night over in her head. She fell asleep dreaming about his kisses.

CHAPTER 13
Party of the Year

"Thanks so much for picking us up," Zoe said as she and Sarah got into Jesse's car.

Sarah got into the front seat since it was empty and Zoe sat behind Sarah.

"You know I'd take you anywhere," he smiled and winked at Sarah.

Sarah smiled back at him. "Where's Caitlin?"

"Oh. She's gonna get off work around six so she said she would meet us there," he sounded nonchalant about it.

"Hey, you good?" Sarah asked, noticing his lack of zest.

"Oh, yeah. I'm good. We're good. She just is sometimes a little crazy, you know? Of course you do, you're a girl. All you girls are crazy," he laughed.

"You need me to put her in her place. I mean I am practically your sister," Sarah teased.

"Ha," he rolled his eyes. "Yeah, that wouldn't go over too well, I don't think," he snorted.

"Oh my God. Please don't tell me she is jealous of Sarah?" Zoe chimed in from the back seat. "I mean you two are best friends. You have known each other forever. She is dumb," she declared. "I mean, don't get me wrong, people ask me all the time if you two ever dated, but once I tell them you guys are like brother and sister they drop it."

Sarah and Jesse smiled and looked at each other.

"Is that it?" Sarah questioned. "Is she worried about our friendship?"

"I guess," he shrugged his shoulders. "She says that I do anything you ask me to do and I would drop everything to come to you, but I'd do the same for her so I don't know why she gets in her own head all the time about it."

"Jesse, I can stop calling you for rides and stuff and leave you guys alone for a little while so she doesn't have any issues?"

"Heck no," he jerked his head and looked at her. "No, no. I ain't getting rid of you for her. She can get over the fact that you are in my life. You were in my life before her and you and I are friends. She will get over it. It's good. You aren't going anywhere," he made eye contact with her as he said this and nodded his head.

Sarah smiled and allowed their eyes to stay connected for longer than usual.

"Okay, well you guys are weird," Zoe interrupted. "If you don't want her to think something, definitely don't look at each other like that in front of anyone ever again."

"Ha," Jesse said as they both blushed and awkwardly averted their eyes.

"So can we talk about me now?" Zoe begged from the back seat.

Sarah rolled her eyes, "Of course, Princess Zoe."

"So. Jesse, you probably already know this, but Sarah doesn't."

"Oh, what? That you hooked up with Toby last night?" Jesse teased her.

"Oh my God. He told you?" her face turned bright red. "I didn't think he would actually tell you!"

"What?" Sarah shrieked from the front seat.

"Yeah, so, uh," Zoe made eye contact with Sarah.

"Spill!" Sarah demanded the details.

"Okay, so Jesse, I don't know what he told you," she paused, waiting on a response from him.

"He didn't go into the details," Jesse assured her. "He just said he stayed the night at your place cause your parents weren't home."

"Okay, so he didn't say anything bad?" Zoe pushed.

"What? No. I think he is into you. I mean I wouldn't start planning your wedding or anything because I highly doubt that dude will ever get married. But he likes you. He isn't going to just sleep with you and be done."

"Okay, good," Zoe sighed.

"But, he also isn't one to keep his mouth shut. Don't count on it being a secret for too long," Jesse warned.

"Okay. So, what? You and Toby hooked up last night or he just stayed the night?" Sarah was still trying to dig for the details.

Zoe smiled, "Yeah, so after the game," she said as she flipped her hair. "He drove me home and he was touching my thigh like all night."

"Yeah, I remember he was all over your thigh at the game."

"I know, right?" she laughed.

"But on the way home, he, uh, you know? Went a little further," She shrugged her shoulders.

Sarah's face still showed her complete shock and confusion.

"What? Why are you looking at me like that?"

"I'm just surprised is all. I mean I know you joked about it, but I didn't think you were serious," Sarah said as she stared at her friend.

"Well, nothing major happened in the car. It wasn't like we had sex in his car."

"Oh, but letting him touch you in the car is okay?"

"What is wrong with you, Sarah? You aren't my mom. Why are you being so judgy?"

"I'm not. I'm just surprised is all," Sarah tried to fix the look on her face.

"So when we got to my house he walked me in because it was dark. There was a note on the counter from my mom that said she would be back Sunday, she had to go out of town and that Dad was on international flights for the weekend. So, I asked him if he wanted to watch a movie," she looked at Sarah still staring at her with her big eyes fixated on the punch line.

"And?" Sarah pressed.

"And, we were making out and one thing led to the other. That's it. That's all."

"That's it? That's all?" Sarah snuffed. "Well, did you guys use protection?"

"Yeah, so, um. That's kind of the problem," Zoe put her hand on her forehead.

"What?" Sarah's jaw hit the floor.

"Well, it just happened. It was all so fast and I was so distracted by it all that I forgot until it was over."

"Oh my God, Zoe," Sarah remarked. She turned to look directly at her friend in the back seat.

"Yeah," Zoe shrugged her shoulders.

Jesse gave a sideways glance to Sarah as he stayed silent in the driver's seat.

Sarah rolled her eyes as if she just turned into Zoe's mother. "Zoe! What if you get pregnant? What if you get an STD? That is so, so reckless."

"Oh my goodness, Sarah. Stop it. I'm not pregnant and I don't have any STD's. Settle down."

"Zoe?" Sarah calmed her voice down. "Zoe, I hope you're right. I hope nothing happened like that, but you are gambling with your life when you take big risks like that," Sarah shook her head.

"Okay, whatever, Sarah," Zoe snipped. "Just wait until you are alone with Brody. You will finally understand exactly what I mean by you just get caught up in the moment."

"Okay," Sarah huffed back and turned around in her seat to look out the front window.

"So what's the deal with this party anyway?" Sarah changed the subject, still annoyed though.

Jesse, seeming grateful for the subject change said, "So, Dylan and Connor's parents go out of town every year for the Notre Dame homecoming game. And since they are like stupid rich, the brothers always throw a huge bash."

"They're seniors right?" Sarah asked, her tone sounding a little less angry.

"Connor is, but Dylan is a junior," Zoe mumbled from the back seat.

"I thought they were twins?"

"They are, but Dylan got held back in like fourth grade because he got in trouble for blowing up a cat," Zoe snorted.

"Shut up!"

"Nope," Zoe lightened up slightly. "I remember it. We were all in like second grade, but you would have thought the world came to an end that day."

"What?" Sarah gasped. "So if he's like a bad kid, why do their parents trust them to go out of town each year?"

"They don't know about the parties," Zoe continued. "I don't know how they haven't found out, but according to Dylan, they have no idea."

"That's crazy. So how do they get all the kegs and alcohol?"

"Their dad works for some major beer brewing company, he's like really high up in management there, so they have endless beer. But I think their older cousin always hooks them up with the liquor."

"Yeah," Jesse interjected again. "Dex, he's like a cop or something, but he's cool. He always hooks them up with it, and he makes sure he is the one patrolling the area the nights of the parties so whenever there is a call, he's the one that responds."

"Wow," Sarah remarked. "It sounds like they got it all planned out."

"Yeah, it's crazy, but wait 'til you see their house. It's freakin' huge. It seriously has like a thousand bedrooms."

"But don't you worry guys," Jesse said as he looked at Sarah, "I'm not drinking."

Jesse's older brother died in a car accident when Jesse was nine. His brother was sixteen. He wasn't the one driving. His friend who was driving started messing with the radio and lost control of the wheel and both boys died at the scene. Even though the accident didn't involve any alcohol, Jesse didn't want to take any chances on getting into an accident so he was determined not to drink if he was the one driving.

There was an awkward silence in the car as Sarah and Zoe looked over at Jesse. He felt their stares, smiled at them, and quickly changed the subject, "So are you two good?"

Sarah looked back at Zoe who was half smiling at her.

"Yeah, we're good," she tilted her head. "I just worry too much I guess."

"I'm thankful I have a friend like you who is willing to worry about me," Zoe smiled back at her.

Feeling the tension leave the car, everyone smiled as they pulled into the neighborhood.

"Oh my God. Look at all these cars," Sarah commented.

They pulled onto the street of the party, which was lined on both sides with cars of kids from school.

Sarah nodded at the truck parked near the house. *He's here. I can't wait to see him. I've like actually missed him today. I just want to be real with him. I just want to be honest. I'm not ready to have sex but I am so ready to love him. I hope he is serious about not wanting to pressure me. I definitely don't want to end up in Zoe's shoes and not know how I got there.*

"Sarah, there's Brody's truck," Zoe pointed out. "You ready to tell him you love him yet?" she pressured as the three looked for a parking spot.

Jesse raised his eyebrows and Sarah avoided eye contact with him and smiled back at Zoe. He pulled into the closest spot he could find which was still almost a block away.

"Text him and let him know you're here," Zoe nudged Sarah. "Ask him if he's with Toby."

Sarah pulled out her phone sent him a message, "We just got here. I think I saw ur truck. R u and Toby here?"

Almost immediately he texted her back. "Hey beautiful. Ive been waitn all nite 4 u. We r out back by fire. I got a beer 4u.;)"

"They're out back by the fire pit," Sarah announced to the group as they walked down the sidewalk toward the music. She looked at the time on her phone and noticed it was just past seven.

"Toby too?" Zoe whispered.

"I think so. He said we. I asked if he was with him."

The two girls smiled at each other.

As they approached the party, the music grew even louder. When they walked into the house, they were immediately greeted by Connor Patterson.

"Yo! Wasssssup!" he wiggled his way around to them. "Grab a beer yo! We got a fire goin' out back, got some pizza in the kitchen. Help yoself," he winked at Sarah as he finished his greeting and made his way over to another group of people coming in the door.

The three of them made their way through the crowds of their classmates toward the kitchen. Jesse grabbed four cups and handed one to each of the girls. He pumped the keg a few times and one by one filled up each cup and then his own.

"I thought you said you weren't drinkin'?" Sarah questioned as they began walking toward the back screen door.

"Oh, well, it's all for looks," he smiled. "If I have a full beer in both of my hands, then no one will try to get me a beer or top me off. I'm set. What, you my mother now?" he leaned into her and smiled.

"There you are," Brody came dashing up to them with a beer in each hand. "You already got a beer?" Noticing the beer in Sarah's hand.

"Hi! Yeah, Jesse just got me one." She put her arm around his waist to hug him.

His shoulders slumped a little, "Oh. Okay, well I had one for you, but I guess I'll just drink it." He lifted his beer up and gulped it down quickly, then slid his empty cup under the beer he had waiting for her. "What's up dude?" Brody said as he and Jesse bumped fists.

"Dude, a lot of people here," Jesse shouted above the noise.

Sarah noticed Zoe standing close to Toby next to the fire pit in what seemed to be an extremely funny conversation based on the way she was giggling.

Everyone was having fun with each other. The night was turning out to be awesome. Sarah noticed how cool Brody was being with everyone around the fire, reinforcing her adoration.

Brody went inside to grab another beer, leaving Sarah and Jesse by the fire.

"Caitlin just texted me," Jesse leaned in to alert Sarah.

"Yeah? She coming or not?"

"Yeah. She said she's almost here," he smiled. "I'm sorry about her."

"Oh my goodness, Jesse, don't be," she put her hand on his arm. "You're right, we are best friends, no one can come in between that," she smiled as he leaned his shoulder into hers and smiled back.

"Hey, am I interrupting something here," Brody came up behind them.

"Dude, na. You good. I was just telling Sarah that Caitlin is about here. I'mma go out front to catch up with her. I'll see you all in a bit," Jesse said as he smiled at the two of them and walked away.

"You two sometimes seem awful close. Are you sure you never dated him?" Brody interrogated.

"Brody, don't be ridiculous. Jesse and I are friends. That's all. He is like my brother," she looked up at him and smiled. "You have nothing to worry about, I promise," she leaned up and kissed him on the edge of his mouth.

Sarah could smell liquor and beer on his breath but he didn't seem to be drunk so she didn't pay much attention to it.

He kissed her back and hugged her. "Good. I'm telling you, I ain't letting you go for no one. Even if he did want you, he can't have you," Brody squeezed her tightly around her waist, leaned down, and kissed her very passionately.

Okay, then. He is definitely enjoying his alcohol. At least he is having fun. Sarah thought to herself as he released her and winked at her.

He looked up and saw a group of his senior friends over near the back fence. "Hey, I'll be right back, you good?" he kissed her and walked over hooting to his friends in a playful way.

"Op. Okay. Yep, I'm good," she stated to herself as she looked around to see who else she could talk to. She found herself floating around the back yard talking to random friends and faces, but she also noticed Brody talking to one of the senior girls a few times.

What is he saying to her? She thought about their conversation after the game last night. The senior girl he was talking to was giggling the same way Zoe was giggling with Toby. *Is she flirting with him? Is he flirting with her? Maybe Tamara was right. Maybe he has us all wrapped around his finger.*

Sarah felt her cheeks redden as she watched the girl flip her hair behind her ears and smile at Brody, who had momentarily forgotten that Sarah even existed. Annoyed by this, Sarah chugged her beer and went inside to the kitchen to refill her cup.

"Yo! Wasssup girl," Connor Patterson approached out of nowhere and took Sarah's cup from her hand and began filling it up.

"Hey, Connor. This party is awesome," she shouted above the

music and conversations in the kitchen.

"Yeah, that's cause you're here," he smiled at her. "Where's Brody?" he asked as he looked around the kitchen to see if he could see him.

"Oh, he's out back talking to Rachel Worthington by the fire."

"Ha. What?" Connor handed her cup back to her. "What, are you jealous? We can make him jealous back if you want," he put his arm around her neck.

"Yo! Connor!" Brody's voice came shouting from outside the screen door.

"See, I knew that wouldn't take long," he whispered to Sarah as he smiled up at Brody. "Yo, my man! How you gonna leave a beautiful lady all alone like this? And Rachel? Dude, com'on."

Brody walked up to the two of them and they slid hands together and grinned.

"And, I mean dude, look at this girl here, so fine. In my house. You better watch your goods," Connor winked at Sarah and playfully smiled at Brody.

Sarah couldn't tell if Brody was being seriously protective, or if he was just being playful with Connor, but still she couldn't help but feel better about him being away from Rachel. Though she didn't want to admit to being jealous, she did feel somewhat uneasy about it.

"Hi," she smiled at Brody and looked up into his eyes to see if she could tell what he was thinking.

"Hey, baby. Why'd you run off like that? I turned around and you were gone."

"Oh, sorry. I didn't wanna interrupt, you know."

"Girl, you are never an interruption," he said as he lightly kissed her on her forehead. "So how was your day? I feel like I haven't talked to you in forever."

"I know. I've been busy with that project all day."

"Oh yeah, that's right. With that black girl from school right? I saw your Snap."

"Yeah. It was awesome. She was actually really cool. I like her a lot. Maybe we can go out with her and her boyfriend sometime, like a double date."

"That means I would have to share you and I don't wanna share you with nobody." He put his arms around her waist and swayed her to the bump of the music.

Aw. That's so sweet. Maybe he really is all about me. Would it be weird if I just blurted out I love you? "You're so wonderful," she leaned into his swaying body and kissed him. She felt his hands tighten around her waist and tug her closer to his body.

He continued to kiss her and wrap his arms around her body leaning his lips into her ear. "I love you, Sarah Benson," he whispered into her ear then followed it with light kisses on her neck.

Here it is. Here is my chance. I love you too. "You want another beer?" *What? Sarah? Tell him.*

He leaned back from her and looked her in her eyes. "You wanna go someplace quiet for a minute?"

"Okay."

He smiled at her response and looked deep into her eyes again, then took her by the hand and led her through the party. Every few feet or so they were stopped by this person or that, some of the guys giving him a fist bump and then checking Sarah out to make sure she was sexy enough for a guy like Brody. It was obvious everyone agreed with his choice, because they all nodded and smiled at her as she followed him around the corner.

"Oh, sorry," jolted by laughter the two of them were bumped into by Rachel, the girl Brody was outside talking to earlier.

Brody let go of Sarah's hand and shoved his hair back out of his face.

"Oh. It's cool. You good, babe?" he asked.

"Yeah," both Sarah and Rachel responded simultaneously and

looked at each other in confusion.

What? Did he just call her babe or me? Did she hear him right? What is going on here?

"Oh, my bad, I am so clumsy. I so didn't mean to bump into you guys. I was just," Rachel took a drink of her solo cup filled with beer, "I was just seeing what was going on over there and oopsy."

"It's good," Sarah remarked, noticing the beer on her own shirt. "Oh, man," she said as she tried to wipe it off. "Dang it. This is new. I need to go wipe it off, Brody," she looked at Brody who seemed to be approaching drunk. "Brody, I'll be right back."

She scurried away leaving Brody and Rachel there to sort out whatever just happened. As she approached the bathroom, she saw Toby and Zoe standing near it.

"Toby," she ran up to him.

"Hey. What's up? Where's Brody?"

"He's back there. He's with Rachel Worthington," Sarah sighed. "Toby, is there something up between them? Is there something I need to know? I don't want to get played."

"What?" he snorted at her. "Sarah, you females are something else. You always try to find a way to make us guys look like jerks, and you just can't accept it when you actually get someone who is head over heels for you. Sarah, no. Nothing is going on between them. That was almost three years ago. They have been over forever. She flirts with everyone and he broke up with her and she never got over it. And, she is probably drunk. Besides, he is crazy about you. He texted me like three times today to see if I had talked to Zoe to see if she had talked to you cause he hadn't heard from you," he tried to reassure her.

Somewhat calmed by this she took a deep breath and exhaled, "Okay. Thanks, Toby." Instead of heading to the bathroom, she walked back toward Brody and Rachel who were still standing there talking. She watched from afar for a moment. Brody kept looking around the room. He would smile at people as they walked by, and as Rachel talked to him, he participated in the conversation but it was clear from afar that he wasn't into her like he was Sarah.

Assured by this, Sarah approached the two of them. Immediately, he greeted her with a kiss right in front of Rachel, then grabbed Sarah's hand, and pulled her away before Rachel could get another word in edgewise.

He led her into the back part of the house where there were only a few people standing around talking, but mostly couples making out. She thought they were just going to stop there but he kept walking and pulling her hand along.

At the end of the back room there was a door which Brody opened, revealing an entire other part of the house. This part was apparently off limits to the party guests but Brody winked at Sarah as he shut the door behind them indicating it was okay since he had VIP status.

"Wow. I didn't even realize this part of the house existed."

"Yeah. This is their parent's private wing. No one's allowed back here, but Connor told me if I needed to get away for a few I could come over here."

Oh my gosh. This house is crazy. I can't believe it's this big. They must be loaded. Why are we still walking? We're all alone now. Where is he taking me? Brody kept Sarah's hand locked in his as he continued to walk toward the staircase on the other side of the room.

"Let me show you this place. It's amazing." Slowly, and gently he led her up the stairs toward a dimly lit master suite. "This is their parent's room."

"Oh my God," Sarah gasped. "This is insane. It is gorgeous."

"Right!" he looked at Sarah as she admired her surroundings, then he looked at himself in the vanity mirror. "Check out the bathtub. It has a Jacuzzi in it."

"Shut up, are you serious?" She went into the bathroom that was three times the size of the one she and Ben shared at home.

When she came out of the bathroom, Brody was sitting on the edge of the bed staring at her.

"Come here," he plopped his hand on the edge of the bed next to him.

She set her drink down on the dresser and walked over to him and sat down.

"Brody, what's up with you and Rachel?" looking for one last bit of reassurance.

"Oh. Man. Well, nothing. You know she and I dated a few years ago, right?" he asked.

"Yeah."

"Well, she is one of the only other people that know about my dad being locked up. I don't tell people about him. But, nothing's up with us now. She's actually kinda crazy if you ask me. She's always texting me or sending me snaps. She couldn't accept that we were over when it ended."

"Why did it end?" Sarah pushed.

"Well, we were sophomores. It wasn't a forever thing. We were just hanging out. She fell in love, I didn't."

"Oh," Sarah waited for him to continue hoping for more information.

"What?" he asked defensively. "It just wasn't right. She wasn't you. You are my forever girl, she wasn't. I know I have the reputation of being a player, but I'm not. I'm just not going to waste my time on a girl that doesn't make me feel alive; like the way you make me feel. You make me feel like I could stand on top of the world. You make a darkness inside of me a little brighter. Why waste my time with anyone else when I found you, my forever girl?" he stared deep into her eyes.

This is it. This is right. I can do this. He is so sweet. He is perfect. I do love him.

"I love you," she blurted out without hesitation.

He didn't return the words but put his hand on the back of her neck and lightly began kissing her lips.

She was so overcome with the realization that she just told him she loved him, that she fell into the moment and allowed her body to fall into his hand, on down to the bed, as she kissed him with her eyes closed.

At first, his other hand caressed her cheek and hair while they lay side by side kissing. Slowly, his hand fell to her collarbone. There he lightly swept his fingers over her shoulder as he continued to wrap his lips around hers.

Feeling her body relax, his hands began to explore. He kept kissing her and moved his hand up under her shirt, barely brushing her bra.

Her body tightened but he kept kissing her more seductively.

Okay. This is okay. I am fine. He is being sweet. He's not doing anything bad. This is okay. He is such an amazing kisser. This is totally PG.

Slowly his hand went to her stomach just under her belly button. Every couple of seconds his finger would brush across the zipper of her jeans, which caused her body to raise slightly off the bed. *My heart is beating so fast. I can't let this go too far. Oh my God.*

He climbed on top of her and started grinding his hips over hers. He felt her body getting warmer so he leaned onto his elbow and began unbuttoning her jeans.

Just then, her shoes slid off her feet thudding to the floor.

He chuckled as he heard her shoes hit the floor. He stood up off the bed in front of her and took off his shirt, then pulled her jeans off of her, then her shirt, leaving her in nothing except her underwear and bra. He then leaned down and grabbed hold of her by the waist.

"What are you doing?" she whispered.

"I just wanna show you how much I love you. I wanna make

you feel so good," he closed his eyes and continued to kiss her. *Oh my God. This is happening. I can't believe this is happening. Is this really happening? This can't happen. Oh my God. What is he doing?*

As he kissed her, his hands kept exploring further and further down until he began playing with the top elastic on her underwear.

Oh... so many things going on. Oh my God. God. God... Oh my God. I can't do this. This isn't right. This isn't right. I can't do this yet. Oh God. Oh my God, Sarah, what are you doing? You can't do this. This isn't right.

"Brody?" she leaned onto her elbows and looked at him. "We can't do this. I'm not ready for this."

Without missing a beat, he looked up at her with his piercing blue eyes and swept his hair out of his face, "Relax, baby girl. This is love. I'm so hopelessly in love with you," he said as he went back to caressing and kissing her.

Is it? Am I supposed to have sex just because I said I love you? I don't want to get pregnant. I'm not ready. I want to do the right thing. The WHATEVER.

"Brody," she tightened her body. "I can't do this, Brody. I am just not ready," she said, feeling ashamed.

"What? Sarah?" His shoulders slumped down and his hands fell into his lap. "Sarah, you just told me how good it felt."

I did? "Yeah, but I can't Brody. I am so sorry. Brody, I'm scared. I'm not ready. I do love you but I'm not ready for this."

"That's such bullshit, Sarah."

"What?" shocked by his response, she sat straight up on the bed. "Brody? Are you mad at me?" her heart raced.

"You just told me you loved me. Why wouldn't you want to be with me? Like I'm some sort of monster or something."

"No, Brody," she put her shirt back on.

"Whatever, Sarah. This is what people who are in love do. They give each other themselves. They make love. This is love, Sarah.

How can you say you love me if you don't? It's such bullshit."

"What?" realizing how angry he was getting she reached for her jeans beside him on the floor.

"You're such a tease. You know how much I want you right now?" his voice was louder now. "You just told me you loved me. What? Now you don't? Am I not good enough for you, Sarah? What the fuck?"

"Brody stop it. Why are you acting like this? What's wrong with you? You said you would wait as long as I needed to?"

"What's wrong with me?" he yelled as he stood up.

Sarah stood up, pulled her jeans over her hips and buttoned them.

"How about, um let's see. I tell you how much I freaking love you. I practically pour my entire heart and soul out to you last night, for what? For what!" he yelled. His face was bright red.

"Okay, I don't know what's gotten into you, but I'm leaving." She began to step around him when he stepped in her way.

"You're not leaving," his voice wasn't as loud this time, but still stern.

"Oh really? Watch me," she said then pushed his shoulder out of her way and placed her feet into her shoes.

"So that's it, huh?" he said as he forcefully grabbed her by the arm. "You really don't love me do you? You're just gonna lead me on, and for once I think that I've actually found my one true love, and most importantly someone who I can trust, and then bam, just up and leave."

Sarah looked at him and for a second started to feel bad. "No, that's not it, Brody."

He squeezed her arm tighter. "Bullshit!" he bellowed again. "You are mine."

She tried to pull her arm away, but his grip was too tight around her wrist.

"You aren't leaving! You don't walk out on me. This isn't over until I say it's over!" His eyes pierced through her.

"Ouch, Brody, that hurts!" She whipped her arm out of his grip and hurried over to the door, "I meant what I said, I do love you, but you obviously don't love me like you say you do because if you did you wouldn't be giving me this guilt trip right now." She opened the door, "Maybe I was all wrong about you. Maybe you are just like they say." She slammed the door behind her and hustled down the stairs before he could catch her.

By the time she got to the door leading out to the party she heard him open the door.

"Sarah! Wait. Sarah!" he shouted from the top of the steps as he began running down them.

She didn't turn around. She walked quicker than ever through the party and out back to where Jesse was standing. He could see there was something obviously wrong with her so immediately he stopped his conversation with his friends and looked at her. "Sarah? What's up? What's wrong with you? You okay?"

"Jesse," she whispered. "I need you to take me home," she glanced into the house and saw Brody looking around for her. "Never mind. I'm gonna walk. Just act like you never saw me. Okay?"

"Sarah, what's the matter with you?"

"Never mind, just forget you saw me. I'll text you when I get home."

He noticed Sarah look at Brody in the house who seemed to be looking for someone. "No, Sarah," Jesse grabbed her hand pulling her closer to him. "I'll cover for you. Go to my house not yours. I'll meet you there after I stall him."

Before Brody could spot her she vanished. There was a gate at the back of the yard she slipped out of without being seen by anyone. She looked back through the cracks in the privacy fence and saw Brody walking up to Jesse. She saw Jesse shrug his shoulders and hand Brody a beer to keep him around for a few minutes while Sarah had time to get away.

The Patterson's house was only about ten minutes away from their neighborhood, but it seemed to take her much longer to walk. She didn't want to stay on the main roads but her heels kept getting stuck in the mud and the sod, so she took them off and jumped over a fence and walked the path between everyone's back yards.

Oh my God. Sarah, what is wrong with you? I can't believe he acted like that! I can't believe you almost had sex with him. I can't believe he was such a jerk. I need to call someone. I can't call Zoe, he's probably right next to her waiting on me to call her. Who can I call? I'll call Tamara.

She dialed Tamara's number but it just rang and rang. Finally, it went to her voicemail. She hung up.

She's probably still on her date. She was right. I can't believe how right she was. I can't believe he was such an asshole.

Sarah climbed a few more fences and cut through a few more backyards. By the time she was almost to Jesse's her phone started ringing. It was Brody. She hit the ignore button. As soon as she ignored the call, it rang again. She hit ignore again.

It rang a third time but this time it was Jesse.

"Hey?"

"Sarah, where are you?" Jesse sounded frightened.

"I'm about a minute from your house. Are you coming?" her heart raced.

"Sarah, he's on a warpath right now. I just left. I'm on my way. When I left he was dropping the F bomb left and right and throwing logs and beer and cups into the fire like a wild man," Jesse paused. "Are you okay? Did he hurt you?"

"I'm fine. Is anyone at your house? Can I just use your garage code to get in? I really don't want to see your mom right now. She will totally call mine and I have zero interest in dealing with her."

"Yeah, Mom is there, but she's in bed. Just use the back sliding door. It's usually unlocked. Go downstairs to my room. I'll be there in like two minutes."

"What about Caitlin? Is she with you?"

"No, I left her there. What do you mean? She has her own car. I'll text her after I get to you."

"Okay, I'm here. The back door is unlocked. I'm going in."

"Cool. Sarah, don't answer your phone if he calls you."

"Okay. See you in a minute." She hung up the phone and saw a text from Brody.

"Where r u? I can't find u. Don't leave me here. I'm by the fire. Please come talk to me."

She went downstairs into the basement where Jesse's bedroom was. She laid on his bed and pulled the comforter up over her head. *Oh my goodness. I am such an idiot. IDIOT. I can't believe I fell for him. How could I be so dumb?*

She started to cry. *How could he be so mean to me? I thought he loved me. He told me it was okay to wait. Oh my God.*

Just then the door to Jesse's bedroom flew open, "Sarah? Are you in here?" Jesse sounded out of breath.

"Here," she announced from under the covers.

He walked over to his bed and sat beside her.

She flopped the covers down to reveal her tear stained face.

"Hey. What happened?"

"Nothing. Everything," she rolled her eyes while Jesse sat motionless waiting for her to open up. "I told him I loved him."

Jesse gave her a confused look. "So why are you freaking out then? Seems like you should be happy," he nudged her.

"Well, apparently in Brody's mind, love means we have to make love. And since I didn't want to do that, he got all angry and said I didn't actually love him," she pouted her lips and began to tear up again. "But it wasn't okay. Like he went crazy on me. He like started cussing at me out and he grabbed my arm really hard and he really scared me."

Jesse's fist clenched. "I'm going to kill him, Sarah. Like legit. I'm going to kill him."

"No you aren't, Jesse. Don't be ridiculous," she snorted. "Thank you for letting me come over here."

Her phone began to vibrate again. It was Brody. She hit the ignore button. It rang again. Him again. She hit the ignore button again and looked up at Jesse staring at her with his nostrils flaring.

"Come here," he pulled her up into a hug. "You are safe here with me." He held her for a long time while she soaked his shirt with her tears.

"Sorry," she looked at the mascara mess forming all over the front of it.

He laughed, "It's all good," he said as he climbed into the bed and the both of them laid there under the covers. Jesse just held his arm around her while she lay next to him, thinking about all that had happened.

"Did you let Caitlin know you left the party yet?" Sarah looked up at him.

"Kinda. She texted me when I pulled in. I told her I had to take care of something and I'd catch up with her tomorrow. I'm sure she will probably break up with me when she finds out I came running to you, but oh well, I guess she is right. I'd move mountains for you," he said as he looked down at her and gazed into her eyes.

As their eyes met, so did their lips. Gently, as if neither one had kissed anyone before, they felt the electricity of their friendship zap to life. Shock waves radiated through them as they lingered on each other's lips, tasting the breath of each other, merging all of their friendship and love with a passion that overcame them both. As they kissed, he shifted his body so that he was facing her and holding her. Neither one wanted to stop kissing the other. They both melted into the warmth of their embrace.

Her phone rang again, sucking the air out of the room. They locked eyes and realized how truly essential the other one was. Jesse took Sarah's phone from her hands and hit ignore, then he turned her phone on silent.

As they laid on the same pillow together staring into each other's eyes, they didn't say a word. They didn't need to. They knew. This was exactly what was meant to be. She didn't have to have sex with him. She had loved Jesse her entire life. She didn't need to prove it by hooking up. She could be herself and he was completely okay with all of her. He felt the same for her. There was nothing to prove.

As they gazed at each other they started to smile.

"What is this?" she laughed and rolled her eyes and looked at him.

"This is perfect," he said as he kissed her again allowing their friendship to be a thing of the past.

Sarah sighed and allowed herself to be kissed by her best friend. In this moment she realized she had substantial feelings for Jesse welling up inside of her.

Sarah finally looked at the clock and realized it was ten after twelve. "Jesse, I think I need to get home. Will you walk me?"

He kissed her one last time on the lips and then on the forehead. "Of course. You want to borrow a sweatshirt?"

"Thank you," she smiled at him. *This is so okay. I have been way too lost in being something I'm not. Everything I have ever wanted in a guy was right here in front of me the entire time. This. Yes. This is very much okay.*

"I'm so not ready to deal with all of this," Sarah looked at Jesse and slumped her shoulders.

"Deal with what?" he asked as he gestured for her to go first up the basement stairs.

"All of it, you know? Brody. My mom and dad. You and Caitlin. I really felt something for him, you know. But, I am just sick over how he behaved tonight. And this." she looked at him as they walked out the back door. "Jesse, what is this?" she asked again.

"He shrugged his shoulders and pulled her in for a hug. "It's right. I think this has always been the right answer. Sarah, I've been crazy about you since Bible Camp back in third grade. You remember when you made me that friendship bracelet there? I still have it. You have been my person since then. Well, really since we were in diapers, but for real, that was when I knew you were going to be in my life forever."

She nodded in agreement and hugged him around his waist. They continued cutting through a few more yards until they got close to hers. She noticed the lights were all still on in her house when they approached it from the back. She didn't want to seem weird for walking in the back door so Jesse walked her around to the front porch. Her mom didn't have the front porch light on so it appeared drastically darker than the back of the house.

"Hey," he looked at her and smiled, "It's gonna be all good. Besides the fact that I might kill Brody myself, but for real, you did the right thing. I'm so thankful he didn't hurt you. I'm proud of you for standing up for yourself." He nudged her on the shoulder.

"Thanks, Jess. I'm good. As long as I can avoid interrogations from everyone and avoid him, it will all be fine. I'll text you tomorrow sometime," she gave him a half smile.

"Don't hesitate to text me if you need something tonight. He was acting crazy and I don't want him to do anything stupid."

"Thank you. I will for sure. I don't think he would be stupid enough to keep bothering me tonight. He will probably just go hook up with Rachel," she snorted then kissed him on the cheek before entering the front door.

She heard her mom in the living room laughing at the TV, but she must not have heard her come in, so she shut the door behind her and took her muddy heels upstairs to her room and changed into her sweatpants but left Jesse's sweat shirt on.

After she changed, she went back downstairs to her mom. "Sarah, I didn't hear you come in." She sat in the recliner across from her. "How was your party, honey?"

"It was fine." She turned her phone off of silent and saw she had four new text messages.

Zoe had texted her and said, "Girl where ru? Brody's looking everywhere for you. He's kinda going crazy. I'm having so much fun with Toby."

Brody also texted her. "Sarah. Where r u? Im lookn everywhere."

Tamara also responded reminding her not to do anything she didn't want to do.

She is so sweet.

Another text from Brody saying, "Sarah, don't be stupid. I kno ur still here. Come back over to me & we can talk about this."

Shortly after sitting down in the living room her phone buzzed. It was Brody. "Im sorry I said those things."

Yeah, I'm sure you're sorry. Sorry you didn't get laid. She rolled her eyes and looked over at her mom laughing on the couch at the movie.

Just then Jesse texted her. "Hey. I know you and I have a lot to talk about, but I want you to know that this friendship and you mean the world to me. You mean more to me than anyone ever has. I am here for you. I think tonight was supposed to happen. Everything about kissing you feels like the right thing. Good night, Sarah."

Another text message, this time from Brody, "Sarah. I am so sorry. I've had too much to drink. I over reacted. Did you go home? Let me come over."

Another text from Brody, "I'm coming over. Meet me outside in 5 minutes. We can talk."

Brody texted her again, "I love you. I don't want to hurt you."

She looked at her phone and realized that if she didn't respond to him he was going to show up and she was going to have to explain things to her mom.

"Brody. Please don't text me again tonight. I can't talk to you right now. I am so angry with you. Do not come over to my house. I will not answer the door. You and I are over. I will not be disrespected like that. Please leave me alone."

She decided to text Jesse back too, "XOXO." After hitting send, she turned her phone back to silent and began staring at the TV, but not really watching it.

I'm such an idiot. I can't believe I fell for a guy like him. I really thought he was great. I can't believe I'm such an idiot. What the heck just happened with me and Jesse? Did that really happen? Did I just dream it?

She pinched her arm to see if she was truly in real life and not a dream. *He's always been like a brother to me, I didn't even know I had feelings for him. When he kissed me it was magical. What? Jesse and I kissed. Oh my goodness. Caitlin is going to kill me. Brody is going to kill him. Oh my goodness. I need to go to bed.*

CHAPTER 14
Sunshiny Sunday

"Morning, baby," Tamara's mom smiled at her as she came out from her bedroom.

"Morning," she smiled in return as she wiped her eyes and stretched to the ceiling.

"Baby, you don't look ready for church? Just cause you had a date last night don't mean you get to skip out on church today!" She tied Dom's shoes as she looked up at her daughter.

"What time does it start?"

"10:00. Same time every week," she giggled.

"Yeah, Tamara," Dominick interjected his playful opinion into the conversation.

"Oh, okay, smart aleck," she smiled at her brother and looked at the clock. "It's 9:15, what time we leaving?"

"As soon's you're ready," she said as she looked back at Dominick as he got off the couch, "Wesley, come here so Mama can tie your shoes, baby."

"Okay, lemme get ready," she turned around, went back up to her room and picked out her clothes.

On their way to church the sun came peeking out from behind the clouds. "Looks like it's gonna be a sunny day," she looked at her children and smiled. "So Tamara, how was your date last night? That Brandon sure did have some manners. You didn't scare him off now did you?" she glanced at her daughter then looked back at the road.

Squinting her eyes at her mom she replied, "No, it was awesome. He was so cool. We had a great time. And no, I didn't scare him off, thank you very much. In fact, he told me he can't wait to see me again, so what?"

"Aw, I'm happy for you, sweetie," she smiled. "Didn't you say he was pretty good at football?"

"Yeah, he is for real. He probably gonna get a full ride or something into a division one school."

"That's great. Where does he wanna go?"

"I'm not sure, his dad went to Ohio State, but he' told me he'd rather go to Notre Dame or something like that, but he wouldn't mind going to one of the West Coast schools like USC or something."

"West Coast, huh?" her mom's tone implied more than what was really being asked.

"I know, Howard is in Washington DC, but you the one who told me not to worry about guys and I have the rest of my life to deal with their nonsense so I best get my education before I worry about that."

"That's right! I did!" smiling proudly. "But you think it might affect you wantin' to go to Howard?"

"Na. Not at all, Mama. That's been our dream forever."

"Alright. Just makin' sure. But don't push him away just cause you might not wanna go to the same college. You got two more years of high school before you have to worry about that, so just have fun."

"Whoa," Tamara laughed at her mom. "You musta really liked him, cause normally you tell me to get my head outta the clouds and to keep my focus on my homework."

"Yeah, baby, but you know I want you to be happy too. And Brandon seemed like a good guy so I just like to see my baby girl happy, that's all."

"Thanks, Mama."

"Speakin' of Howard, I been meaning to talk to you about that."

"Yeah?"

"Yeah, so I just want to make sure you know I am in total support of you going."

"I know that."

"Wait a second, I'm not finished," she put her finger up to stop Tamara from saying anything else. "Now, I know you're trying to keep your grades up and we talked before and I said you need to get a full ride just like your father did."

"Yeah?" Tamara raised one of her eyebrows and looked at her mom.

"Well, I didn't want to tell you this, but you know how your daddy and I put away a college fund for all you kids? Well, I decided to put his life insurance money into it as well. There was enough of it that it allowed for me put plenty in each of your accounts so that the three of you can go to any school you'd like," she said as she put her finger back in the air so Tamara couldn't interrupt her. "And, I know we have been pushing you to go to Howard, but I want you to know that you can go anywhere you want. You gotta live your dreams baby, not ours."

Tamara was silent as tears made their way up to the brim of her eyes.

Her mom looked at her and grabbed her daughter's hand. "Your happiness and success is our dream, and we are gonna make it happen."

Tamara squeezed her mother's hand and wiped the tears from her cheek, "Mama, I don't know what to say."

"Well you can start by saying you will go ahead and take those College Credit Plus classes your Math teacher keeps pushing you to take," she said as she cocked her head toward her daughter in the passenger seat. "Now just remember," her voice got stern again, "this doesn't mean you get to slack off for the rest of high school and not do your work. You still gonna bust your butt getting them grades and tryin' for those scholarships, but I'm just sayin' you're going to college and you're going to change the world, but it's gonna be on your terms, not mine."

"Yes ma'am," she said wiping another tear from her cheek. "I will, I promise. I will take the math courses too. I will be good. But Mama, I want to go to Howard. I want to follow in daddy's footsteps. So it is our dream."

By the time they arrived at church the sun had completely come out and all but a few clouds disappeared. *What a beautiful day. I'm going to Howard. Ah! I'm so excited. What a great day. I can't wait to tell Brandon.*

"Life is going to happen," the pastor began his sermon.

Tamara loved this particular pastor. He made church not so boring. He had jokes, and he was like a real human.

"Life is going to give you lemons," he continued. "Life has a way of sneaking up on you and beating you up and then kicking you while you are down," he studied the congregation. "But one thing I know. One thing I know for sure is Romans 8:28. 'And we know that in all things God works for the good of those who love Him, who have been called according to His purpose.'"

"Amen!" several people exclaimed.

After church ended the four of them went to lunch at the diner around the corner. This was one of Wes and Dom's favorite places to go because the manager always let them get free milkshakes.

Tamara loved going there too for the same reason.

"Say thank you, boys," she smiled.

"We already did, Mama," Dominick argued.

Which was returned with a quick look from their mom.

"Thank you," they all said in unison.

As they were leaving the diner they waved to a few people who had also come over after church.

"Well guys, what you wanna do on this beautiful sunshiny day?"

"Moon!" Wesley was infatuated with anything that had to do with outer space.

"No, that's silly. We can't go to the moon, Wesley," Dom interrupted his little brother. "We can go to the park and you guys can push us on the swings."

"What if I wanna get pushed?" Tamara teased her little brother as she bent over and scooped him up to tickle him.

He giggled and snorted at the attack.

"Does that sound good to you? The park?" her mother asked.

"Fine by me. We never go to the park together anymore, well since Eric's been around so it sounds great to me."

Her mother smiled at her and touched her shoulder in an apologetic manner. "The park it is. We'll make these boys push us on the swings," she smiled at her daughter and the four of them headed to play.

"Mama, so let me tell you 'bout this steak we ate last night."

"Where'd ya'll go?"

"The Sector."

"Oh, I don't even wanna hear it. Makes my mouth water just thinkin' about it."

Tamara pushed Dom as her mom pushed Wes. "It was so good. I'm for real gonna have to go back."

"He buy?"

"Yeah. Was I supposed to?"

"Oh, no. You're a princess, you can let him wine you and dine you, there isn't any need for you to be given him no money."

The two looked at each other and laughed.

"Higher!" Dom exclaimed.

"Higher!" Wesley followed in suit.

They pushed the boys so high that their rear-ends bounced in the seat on the way down. They giggled uncontrollably and kept shouting to be pushed higher.

Tamara and her mother enjoyed the time together and adhered to their requests, pushing them even higher.

"Okay, boys. Your mama is tired now. I'mma need to sit down," she halfway teased as sat down on the swing next to them.

"Yeah, me too," Tamara agreed.

"No," Dom whined.

"Well, come sit on my lap and I'll swing with you," she offered her son.

"Okay." He put his feet down and skid them across the mulch to slow down his swing. Once he was off, he stopped Wesley's swing and helped him down. They jumped onto Tamara and her mom's lap and they began to race to see who could swing higher. The boys were overcome with delight, as was Tamara.

She noticed all the smiles coming from her family and she couldn't help but smile herself. It was the first time in a very long time she had seen a genuine smile on her mother's face. She wanted this moment to last forever.

CHAPTER 15
Wave A Magic Wand

Sarah woke up earlier than usual for a Sunday. Her mind was all over the place and sleep wasn't happening for her. She looked at the clock and it said 6:32. She hesitated to look at her phone because she knew without a doubt there would be a message from Brody. But, she was still so baffled by the whole scene that she decided to turn it off silent and look at her messages. Twelve new messages from Brody alone.

Message One 12:45am: "Sarah, I'm not playing. I can't do this. I'm so sorry. Please talk to me, babe."

Message Two 12:54am: "I love you. I didn't mean to be so mean. I'm drunk. I'm sorry. I'll never drink again. Please call me."

Message Three 1:26am: "Sarah, I'm outside your house. Your light is off. I need to see you. Please come to your window."

Message Four 1:30am: "I'm not leaving until I see you."

Message Five 1:42am: "Did you call the cops on me? They just drove by. How could you do that? I'm not going to hurt you. I just want to see you. I love you."

Message Six 2:21am: "I NEED TO SEE YOU. I AM SORRY."

Message Seven 3:11am: "I'm going to go home. Or drive off a cliff. I'm sorry. I guess you hate me. I can't believe you don't love me. I should have never let myself fall for you. You are so perfect and I am so not. I can't believe I could mess this up so badly. Damn it. Bye."

Message Eight 4:01am: "DAMN IT!!! I'm leaving for real this time. I'm getting you back. You can't get rid of me that easily. This isn't over. You are mine. You belong to me. If you actually love me, which I think you do, then you won't give up that easy either."

Message Nine 4:22am: "Just got home. In case you wanted to know, I am safe. I love you baby. Sweet dreams, good night."

Message Ten 5:01am: "I'm sorry baby. I will tell you forever. I will make this up to you. I'm sorry."

Message Eleven 5:02am: "I love you. I love you. I love you. I love you. I love you. I can't wait to hold you again. I love you."

Message Twelve: 6:27am: "I can't sleep. You awake yet?"

Oh my God. What in the world? He is losing his mind. I feel so bad for him. But, what? Is he actually this crazy? This can't be him. I think I need to throw up.

She got out of her bed, went to the bathroom, and walked over to her window. She didn't open the blinds but peeked through them to make sure he wasn't anywhere to be seen. It looked as though the street was empty except for her elderly neighbor walking outside to collect the newspaper. She let out a sigh of relief.

Should I tell someone about this? No. They would think I'm making it up. They would tell me that I asked for this by dating an older boy. They would tell me it's my fault for going into a room alone with him in the first place. I can't tell anyone. I don't hate him. I don't want him to get in trouble. I just don't want to be with him. No, I can't tell anyone. He will be fine once he gets some sleep. I should just message him later after he has had some sleep. No. I'll just see him at school tomorrow. He and I should end this face to face. Maybe I did lead him on. I need to make sure he knows I'm not getting back together with him.

She rummaged through her closet looking for some comfy clothes since she was just hanging out with her dad today.

Once she was ready she went downstairs and ate a bowl of cereal and turned the TV on but started scrolling through her social media feeds instead of watching it.

Jesse had recently posted a meme of a person laying in their bed awake and angry with the caption, "When you want to go back to sleep to finish the storyline of your dream but can't." Under his post he wrote the words Banana Pancakes.

When Sarah read this, she knew in an instant it was for her. Their secret code their entire friendship had always been Banana Pancakes. They only used it with each other and no one knew what it meant, except the two of them. It had been several years though since either of them had said it.

When they were in sixth grade they made a pact that if their parents ever forced them to move out of the house when they got old that they would get a house together and fill it up with banana pancakes and eat them for every meal of the day. Silly really. But it was so funny to them at the time that it just stuck.

I wonder if he was dreaming about us? Where did that come from? How have we missed this for so long? How have I missed it? I'm so thankful for him. What an amazing friend.

She texted him, "Banana Pancakes though?"

"Ha. Just wanted the world to know I was dreaming about something great."

"Yeah? What?"

"Eating banana pancakes, duh!" he messaged back with a winking emoji.

She smiled and set her phone down.

Her phone buzzed again, "Did everything end up okay last night? Nothing crazy after I walked you home right?"

Should I tell him about how crazy Brody was? I can't. No, I can't. He will tell me to call the cops or something. It's not that big of a deal.
"Yeah. Everything was good. Just went to bed."

"Sarah?" he pushed, knowing that she was leaving something out.

"How do you know me so well? Okay. So, apparently Brody was outside my house for most of the night, but my phone was on silent so I had no idea. He texted me like a million times and I think he is losing his mind, but he probably just needs to sleep for a little while. But, everything is fine. It's fine. I promise."

"SMH. Are you for real? Is he still there?"

"No. I didn't see him. He hasn't texted in a while. He probably went home and passed out."

"Okay, well, I'm here if you need me. Don't hesitate to call me. Okay?" Jesse insisted.

"Okay. Dad is coming over to get me in a little while. Have a good day," Sarah responded back and smiled at how easy it seemed with Jesse.

"Sarah bear?" Sarah's dad hollered from the front entryway at their house.

"Dad?" she yelled as she rushed to the edge of the stairs. "Daddy!" She ran down the stairs and wrapped her arms around his neck. "I've missed you so much, Dad." She hung onto his neck as he hugged her back.

"Aw, hey, princess. I've missed you too. Where's my little man?" he asked as she let go of his neck.

"Oh, I think he's in his room. You want me to go get him?"

"No, I'll just go up and surprise him. I'll be right back down. Get your jacket and tell your mom bye," he smiled at his daughter.

"Okay," she smiled back and grabbed her jean jacket out of the closet. "Mom?" she yelled into the kitchen as she watched her dad go into her little brother's room. "Hey, Mom. Dad is here. He went upstairs to see Ben real quick then we're leaving."

"Your dad's here?"

"Yeah that's what I just said."

"Oh, well I want to at least see him before you leave."

"Mom, he's in a good mood, maybe you should just let it be for a little while, you know?"

Her mom noticed her maturity was starting to come through

because she smiled at her and nodded her head.

"Okay. Maybe you're right," she agreed. Just tell him I will have dinner ready around 5:30 if he'd like to join."

She smiled at her mom as she heard her dad's footsteps coming down the stairs. "Okay, Mom. See you later. Love you."

"Love you too."

Sarah climbed into the passenger seat of her dad's convertible BMW. "What do you think you're doin'?" her dad asked her as he held the keys at his forehead jingling them in a taunting manner.

"Are you serious? I can drive?" she exclaimed as she jumped out of the passenger seat and ran behind the car to the driver's side. "Ah! This is so awesome."

He smiled at his daughter as he walked around the front of the car and got into the passenger seat. "Buckle up," he sounded a bit nervous as he put his seat belt on.

"I'm a good driver, Daddy," she retorted, sensing his nerves.

"Well you have to be, I taught you everything you know," he winked as she put the car into drive. "It's just that this is my baby, Crystal." He petted the dashboard of his car.

"You're so stupid," she laughed and pulled out onto the road.

"You can put the top down if you want."

"Na, I don't wanna mess up my hair," she giggled. "So, where are we headed?"

"Well, I figure you have the homecoming dance coming up and I could take you to get a dress if you want?" he smiled again. "Your mom told me you have a new boyfriend who drives, so I am assuming he's taking you to the dance?"

She slouched in the seat.

Yeah, DID have a boyfriend, until I realized what a psychotic jerk he is.

"Yeah, I don't think I'm gonna go," her voice gave away a hint of awkwardness.

"Really? I thought the homecoming dance was one of the

biggest dances of the year. Well, at least that's what you said last year when you needed a dress for it." He put his hand on the back of her head. "Everything alright with you, Sarah?"

She was silent then took a deep breath. "Yeah," she exhaled. "It's just that there was this party last night and Brody wasn't the guy I thought he was, so we're not really together anymore."

"Oh, I see," he sighed. "Well, it sounds like you made the right choice then, honey," he paused. "You know, relationships aren't easy. If you want it to work out, you gotta work for it, that's the bottom line. But, if you don't want to, then you won't. It comes down to what you really want. Do you like the guy?"

"I did."

"But you don't anymore?"

"No, it's not that, it's just that," she didn't know how to say it without getting anyone in trouble.

"What happened at the party?"

Sarah couldn't concentrate on driving anymore so she pulled the car over into a gas station parking lot, and put the car in park. She looked over at her dad and a tear began to roll down her cheek. "I'm sorry, Daddy." She broke out into tears, and put her hands over her face.

"Honey, what's the matter?"

She continued to cry into her hands, so he unbuckled his seatbelt and put his arm around her leaning her into his shoulder.

"Shh," he tried to comfort her.

After a few minutes, her sobbing began to lighten and she wiped her face on his shirt. Laughing, yet still crying, she apologized as she realized she got makeup on his shirt.

"Oh, I'm not worried about that, what's going on? What happened last night sweetie? You know even though I'm not staying with you guys right now doesn't mean I'm not here for you. Is everything okay?"

"Yeah," she choked in the air as she looked at her dad. "It's just that Brody," she was scared to tell her dad about it, but she knew he would be the one to give her the best advice. She had always been able to talk to him about her boy problems because he seemed to understand them better than her mom did, perhaps because he was once a guy their age too.

"Did he hurt you, Sarah?"

"No," she paused and looked out the window. "No, it's just that he tried, or maybe I let him," her tears began to come back. "I don't know, but when I realized what we were about to do I stopped it," she started sucking in the air harder again. "And then he got pissed, and he was really rude." She put her hands in her face again.

"Oh, honey," he pulled her in again. "I am so sorry," he stroked the back of her hair to try and calm her down. "People can be so awful sometimes, honey. But believe me, you did the right thing. If he can't respect you, he doesn't deserve you."

She coughed into his shirt.

"If I could wave a magic wand for you, honey and make everything alright, I would. I am so sorry you have to go through this," he consoled.

"I know. It's just that he's a senior, and all the kids at school are having sex, and I don't want to, but now, I look like the idiot and I'm sure he's gonna spread rumors about me and I'm gonna look like a slut," she said as she wiped her face again.

"A slut?" he questioned. "Trust me, you are far from that. Has he tried to contact you?"

"Yeah, like a hundred times. He's been blowing up my phone."

Should I tell Dad that he was practically stalking me last night by sleeping outside our house? No. Dad would lose his mind. I can't. I don't want to freak him out anymore.

"You want me to take care of him? I'll show him not to mess with my little girl."

Sarah laughed, thinking of the similar threat Jesse had made,

"No. I just really liked him and I feel like an idiot because I thought he really cared about me, you know?"

"Oh, trust me, I know," he looked out the window.

"Oh, I didn't mean it like that, Daddy, I'm sorry," realizing she had forgotten about the fight he and her mom just had.

"You know, Sarah, I may not be the best husband around but I love your mom. And I don't know what's gonna happen with your mom and me but that doesn't matter right now, Sarah. What matters is this boy tried to take advantage of you and you deserve better than that," he furrowed his eyebrows and looked at her. "I don't want you to see this boy again, Sarah."

"Dad, I know."

"I know how these young men are and he sounds like trouble. How well do you know him?"

"I thought I knew him really well, but I guess I don't. I don't know."

"He'd better leave you alone. Maybe I ought to talk to his parents. He wouldn't try to hurt you or anything would he?"

"Oh, no. He's not like that at all, Dad. He really is cool. He said he loves me so I know he wouldn't ever intentionally hurt me. "

"No, he tried to take advantage of you, so he's not really as cool as you think, Sarah."

"But."

"No buts, Sarah. I mean it," he interrupted. "I am not going to let my daughter be taken advantage of. I think I need to talk this over with your mother, but we should probably meet with your principal at school this week and make sure this boy gets in trouble. I am not okay with it. What's his last name? You said Brody?"

"Dad, no. Lemme handle it. Don't do that. I would be so embarrassed," her eyes were huge as she pleaded. "Seriously, Dad, I know what he did was wrong. And I know I can't see him again, but it happened at a party. He can't get in trouble because it was off school property. I didn't tell you so you could get him in trouble, Daddy. I told you cause I didn't want to tell Mom. I didn't want to tell anybody. I'm so embarrassed and I feel so stupid," she put her face in her hands again and began to sob.

"I'm sorry, honey," her dad consoled. "I know it hurts," he pulled her to his shoulder again and let her cry it out.

"I'm sorry," she choked as she wiped her eyes and sniffed in the mucus dripping from her nose.

"Don't apologize, Sarah. You have nothing to be sorry for. This Brody guy does."

"Yeah. I know," she sighed. "It's just that I wanna do what's right, but now it seems like it woulda been a lot easier to just give in than deal with all this. Ya know?" She looked at her dad.

"No, kiddo. It wouldn't have been. Cause had you let it get further, today you would just be another number to him. Today you wouldn't matter. And that would hurt worse than this, I can promise you that."

"I just don't get it, Dad. I don't understand why guys can be such jerks. I mean do they teach you this in school at some point? How to be a jerk?"

"Aw, baby. Not all guys are jerks. You will find the right one someday."

She looked up at him and smiled, "That's another part of the problem, Dad."

"Huh?" he looked baffled.

"So, Jesse kissed me last night after all this happened," she looked at her father to see if he approved.

"Wild West Jesse?" her dad perked up.

Wild West Jesse was a nickname Sarah's dad had given him when they were in fifth grade because Jesse had decided to do a book report on Jesse James the American Outlaw. For a month after, he only introduced himself as Jesse James to people, which Sarah's dad found endearing, and decided it would be his nickname for the rest of his life.

"Yeah, Dad," she rolled her eyes annoyed by his constant need to refer to Jesse as Wild West.

"Okay! Now I really have to worry," her dad gave her a stern look.

"What do you mean?"

"Your mother and I knew it would only be a matter of time before the two of you realized how great you would be together. You guys have been inseparable since you were little, so it only makes sense that he would kiss you," he looked at his daughter seeing all the self-inflicted torture of not knowing what to do on her face. "Are you glad he kissed you?"

"Dad!" she nervously giggled.

He smiled at her.

"I mean, yeah. I think so. But I'm kinda in the middle of this thing with Brody that I have to figure out how to get out of, and Jesse has a girlfriend too."

He put his hand on the back of her head. "What can I do for you, my dear? How can I bring you a little bit of comfort today?"

She wiped her tears again. "Maybe we can just go get some ice cream and then go to that little boutique around the corner. I've been wanting a new scarf, and I think they have it, and I think ice cream is good when you are going through a break up, so we could both use a little ice cream in our lives," she looked at her dad and shrugged her shoulders.

He smiled, "Well I can certainly spring for some ice cream and a scarf." He pulled a tissue out of his jacket pocket and handed it to her. "But honestly, Sarah, what did you say Brody's last name was?"

"It's Paulson. Brody Paulson."

"Paulson?" He put his hand on his chin and looked out the windshield. "That name sounds familiar to me. Hmm. Paulson," his voice began to fade as he pondered. Snapping back to reality he looked at his heartbroken daughter, "You want me to drive?"

"What?" her playful voice came back a little. "If anyone knows where the best ice cream in town is, it's me, so I will drive us there."

"Oh, yeah?" he laughed. "Okay, then. Let's see you in action." He buckled up again as she began to pull out of the gas station.

She drove him to the ice cream shop and then to the boutique. All the while, she enjoyed the simplicity of the day with her dad. For the first time, she felt like a true adult. She had the keys to prove it too. When it was time to head back home though, she let her dad drive so she could look at the three new scarves and fashion jewelry he had purchased for her in place of a homecoming dress.

"Well, kiddo. Thanks for hanging with your old man today."

"No, thank you for taking me today."

"If you don't mind, I'm gonna come in and talk to your mom before I hit the road. I'd like to see Ben again too."

"That's fine. We are having dinner at 5:30 and she said you can stay for dinner if you'd like."

"Oh, yeah? Well, we will have to see about that," he partly grinned as he got out of the car.

As the two headed toward her front door, she glanced down the road and saw a truck idling at the stop sign.

Why is that truck just sitting there? Is that Brody's truck? She felt her phone vibrating in her pocket and she knew that it was indeed him. She hit the ignore button but tried not to make it obvious to him or her dad.

Her heart started beating faster. *Should I tell Dad? No way. He will go out there right now and kill him.*

They walked into the house.

"Honey, is that you?" her mom called from the kitchen.

"Well, I don't know about honey, but I'm here," her dad hollered back and smiled at Sarah.

"Daddy!" Ben came racing out from the kitchen to greet him and be swept up for a big hug.

"You guys have fun today?" her mom questioned.

"Yeah, look what Dad bought me." Sarah pulled out her scarves and jewelry from the bag to show them off to her mother.

"Oh, that's nice, dear. But I thought that maybe you were going to go do a little bigger shopping today?" she questioned as she looked confusedly at her husband. "I don't know, like say for a dress?"

"Oh. Well, Dad wanted to take me, but I don't need a dress."

"You don't? The dance is coming up, sweetie, and Brody came over here today to meet me and make sure it was okay that he took you to the dance with him. He seems like a super sweet kid. We should have him over for dinner this week."

"He came over today?"

"Yeah, he left probably about an hour ago. He stayed around and hung out with Ben for a little while. He said he had to put something in your room, but yeah, he was here."

"Sandy," Sarah's father interrupted.

Sarah looked up at her dad in disbelief.

"Sarah, why don't you take your things upstairs. I will talk to your mom real quick."

Sarah, not knowing whether to be surprised, mad, upset, or angry, grabbed her bag and left the kitchen for the stairs.

"What was that about?" Sarah heard her mother question as she walked up the stairs.

Oh my God. He is going to tell her and she is going to freak out. I can't believe he was here. Who does he think he is? Sarah got to her bedroom and found a single rose on her bed with a note.

Sarah,

I know you still love me. Please don't ignore me. We will fix this and be together again soon. Nothing can keep us apart. This isn't over. You belong to me. I can't live without you. I love you.
With love,
Brody

Are you kidding me? Sarah thought to herself. *He seriously thinks that we are going to fix this? What a jerk. I can't believe he was here in my room. What was he thinking?*

Sarah's phone began to vibrate.

She had a message from him that read, "Did I see a smile when you read my note? I'm glad you like it."

Sarah looked up and realized her blinds and curtains to her window were wide open. She walked over to them but didn't see anything or anyone outside, nonetheless, she shut the blinds and pulled the curtains closed.

She started to get a nervous feeling in her stomach, like something bad was going to happen. Then her phone vibrated again.

This time the message said, "Don't shut me out."

Sarah dropped her phone. "Dad!" She raced out of her room and into the kitchen. "Dad, I think Brody is outside," her voice was trembling

"What? Why?" He looked back at his wife who seemed to be wrestling with whether or not she wanted to be mad or sad. He walked to the front door and stepped outside.

Both Sarah and her mother stayed quiet in the kitchen and waited for his return or for any out of the ordinary noise, neither of them breathing.

Her dad came back in a few moments later. "I don't see anyone. Why do you think he's here?"

"When we got home, I thought I saw his truck down the road. He left a note on my bed, and then he texted me and said he is glad I got his note. Then, I shut my blinds and he texted me again and said not to shut him out," she was breathing heavily.

Her mother covered her mouth with her hands trying not to gasp.

"Well, I didn't see anyone out there. But I will stay here tonight if that's okay with you?" he nodded at his wife across the counter top.

"Yeah, of course. I'll make the couch up for you, or you can sleep up stairs or whatever," she took a deep breath in. "Oh, Sarah. I am so sorry this boy has done this to you. Are you okay, honey?"

Taking a deep breath, "Yeah. I'm fine. It's whatever. Are you sure you didn't see him outside, Dad?"

"I'm sure, sweetie. I will take a walk around the house in a little bit as well. Your mom and I have plenty to talk about so I am sure it will be good for us to stay up and chat for a while," as he said this a realization came over him. "Paulson?" he looked at Sarah.

"Yeah, Brody Paulson. Why?"

"Daggone it!" he shook his head in nervousness looking at his wife.

"What is it, Dad?"

"If it's the same Paulson I know, he is probably the son of a man we put in jail several years ago, back when I worked for the District Attorney. The guy's name was David Paulson."

Sarah's face froze. "Yeah, he said his dad was in prison."

Her dad nodded his head. "Sarah, you are absolutely, under no circumstances allowed to see this boy again, do you hear me?" his voice was loud and stern now.

"Dad, yeah, but why? What are you referring to?"

"I won't get into all the graphic details but his dad is in prison for murdering the woman he was engaged to, a clear cut case of a psychopath."

"Okay, Dad. I hear you, but honestly, I think you are overreacting. It's fine. He might be a little crazy, and honestly, I'm not interested in him being my boyfriend anyway, but he won't hurt me. He isn't his father. Don't you think you are being way to judgmental? I mean, you are the one who told me not to judge a book by its cover, and to give people a chance."

"I don't care what I said, you are my daughter, and it is my job to protect you. Even if I am being unfair in my judgements, I'd rather be safe than sorry!"

Putting on a strong face so her mom would stop looking at her with panic, she tried to change the subject. "Mom, is dinner ready yet?"

"Oh. Dinner. Yeah. I almost forgot." She rustled around and began taking plates out of the cabinet. "Ben, you wanna help your sister set the table?" she hollered toward the living room.

Sarah grabbed the plates and set the table while Ben followed her with silverware.

"Daddy's staying for dinner, Sarah bear," Ben excitedly exclaimed as he entered the room, breaking the tension.

"I know. Isn't that cool?" she tried to stay focused on her little brother, but couldn't help but think that Brody might be outside somewhere looking in on them.

"Yeah. It's super cool. I can't wait."

They both giggled.

After they finished dinner, the four of them sat around the table and laughed at each other. For the first time in the last twenty-four hours, Sarah was able to think about something other than Brody.

Ben talked about his soccer game and how cool it was that he got to have oranges after each game.

Dad talked about how his boss was throwing a company picnic at an indoor go-karting facility.

Mom talked about her aerobics class and how it is someone's

birthday tomorrow so she is baking cookies. Everyone at the table found it to be humorous that she is baking cookies for an exercise class.

Sarah talked about the project that she and Tamara did yesterday and how they will most definitely get an A, and most definitely be the best one in the class.

Sarah noticed her mom and dad glance at each other and smile. She saw the two of them enjoying the life they had built together. The only thing Sarah didn't think about for once was Brody. She allowed herself to take in the joy of her family and forget all about the recent drama that had filled her life. This break in her day from all the emotions, nerves, and worries left her feeling ready and confident for whatever the world had to offer her tomorrow.

CHAPTER 16
Broken

What the hell did I just do? I gotta get to her. How could I have reacted like that? What was I thinking? She hates me.

Brody paced around the fire pit. Several people had started to head home but there were still plenty of people at the party which left his truck blocked from getting out. He decided to text Sarah. "Sarah, I'm not playing. I can't do this. I'm so sorry. Please talk to me, babe."

"Brody?" Rachel walked over to him.

"Hey," he slumped as he tossed his beer cup into the fire.

"You okay?" she asked.

He took a deep breath and then exhaled, "No!" he shouted. "I need a damn beer!" he clenched his fists.

"Hey, hey, hey." Rachel put her hand on his shoulder. "Brody, it's me. Rachel. You are spinning out of control right now, babe."

He gave her a death stare. "I'm not your babe anymore, Rachel. I'm with Sarah. Sarah is my girl. I'm in love with Sarah. Not you. Leave me the hell alone," his voice raised to almost a shout.

Feeling the sting of rejection, Rachel rolled her eyes at him. "Yeah, well? Where is she, Brody? I don't see her anywhere? How's it feel to not be loved by someone you love so much? Serves you right! I hope she breaks you into a million pieces." She flipped her hair as she marched away.

She does love me. Sarah does love me. The hell with Rachel. She doesn't know what she is talking about. The hell with her. Sarah loves me. I know it. I just scared her. I just messed up. I had too much to drink. She said to stop and I didn't. Damn it. I can't believe I was so awful to her. I can't let her get away. She is mine. I will text her again.

"I love you. I didn't mean to be so mean. I'm drunk. I'm sorry. I'll never drink again. Please call me."

Okay. I took ownership. I remember they told my dad that once. He had to take ownership for his behaviors. I was drunk. I admit it. I was wrong. I admit it. I am sorry. She will forgive me. She has to.

"Dude!" Connor came up to Brody and put his arm around him. "Some party, man," he wobbled as he looked at all the people still having fun. "Hey! Where'd that hotty sophomore of yours go? You better go find her before I do!" Connor laughed in jest.

"Shut the hell up, man," Brody stared him down.

Connor's face twisted into confusion as he realized Brody wasn't in the playful mindset he had been in earlier.

"You know what, man?" Brody continued, "I gotta get out of here. You have any pills or anything, I think I just need to sleep it off."

"Ah, now we're talking!" Connor nodded his head as he reengaged into the conversation.

"I don't know what these things are that my boy gave me. I don't think they will help you sleep, they may make you wanna party, but maybe take a few of them and you'll be so high you'll just pass out anywhere!" he said as he pulled some tablets out of his pocket and handed Brody five of them. As he handed them to him he also gave him the full drink in his hands. "Take two for now. Wash it down with this whiskey. You won't be feeling a thing."

Without hesitation, Brody put two tablets in his mouth and the rest in his pocket. He took the full cup of whiskey and poured it down his throat. "Thanks, bro. I gotta get out of here. I'll catch you later."

"Later, gator!" Connor laughed as he wobbled away and Brody headed for his truck.

I gotta see her. I gotta get to her house.

"Sarah, I'm outside your house. Your light is off. I need to see you. Please come to your window."

Argh! I gotta see her. Why isn't she responding? Where the hell is she? Is she here? Maybe she stayed the night at Zoe's? No. I just saw Zoe at the party. Come to think of it, I didn't see Jesse at the party, but I did see Caitlin. Na. I'm just messing with my own head. She wouldn't cheat on me with him. She'd be crazy. Where the hell is she? I'm not leaving until I see her face. I don't need to talk to her. I just need to see her. I just need to know that she is in there.

He texted her again. "I'm not leaving until I see you."

After a minute passed with no response from her, Brody decided he needed to take a walk around her house.

He got out of his car and walked up to the front door. He tried the handle.

Locked.

He checked each of the front windows.

Locked.

He walked around the side of the house and into the back yard. He walked up to the sliding glass door on the back of the house.

Locked.

He tried the kitchen window.

Locked.

Every window around the entire perimeter of the house was locked.

As he rounded the other side of the house he saw a police cruiser driving past. He ducked behind her front bush to conceal himself. The cruiser stopped outside of Sarah's house and shined a light all over the house from the car. After about a minute the cruiser drove off.

What the hell? Were they looking for me? How the hell did they know I was here? Did Sarah call the cops? Hell no. No, she didn't. Why the hell would she do that? What kind of monster does she think I am?

He pulled out his phone and texted her again. "Did you call the cops on me? They just drove by. How could you do that? I'm not going to hurt you. I just want to see you. I love you."

Angry about the cops showing up, Brody ran over to his car and got in. He turned his stereo up and clenched his fingers around the steering wheel. The songs were full of angry, heavy-rage. Brody held onto the steering wheel for several minutes.

Staring out the window. Looking for the cops. Watching Sarah's bedroom window for even a hint of movement or light.

Where the hell is she? WHAT THE HELL? WHY THE HELL WON'T SHE RESPOND? WHY DOESN'T SHE CARE? DOESN'T SHE KNOW I'M HERE? DOESN'T SHE KNOW I AM SORRY? DOESN'T SHE KNOW I NEED TO SEE HER? DOESN'T SHE KNOW!

"AHHHHHHHHHHHH," Brody roared and bellowed in his truck. Angry at the world. Angry at himself. Angry at Sarah for not seeing him. He messaged her again, "I NEED TO SEE YOU. I AM SORRY." Several minutes continued to pass by and still no response. No movement. Nothing. Brody decided to take a short walk to try and clear his mind. As he began walking down the sidewalk he started to realize how creepy he was actually being so he walked to the end of the street and back to his truck.

Once he got back to his truck he decided it was time to go home. He texted her again, "I'm going to go home. Or drive off a cliff. I'm sorry. I guess you hate me. I can't believe you don't love me. I should have never let myself fall for you. You are so perfect and I am so not. I can't believe I could mess this up so badly. Damn it. Bye." He started his car up and pulled away. The entire time keeping an eye on her window.

Wait. He slammed on his brakes just past her house.

He put his truck in reverse and stopped directly in front of her house. *Did I just see her blinds move?* He stared at her room. *I know I saw it move. I know she is in there. I know I saw it. No. What the hell am*

I doing? I need to get home.

He drove down the road some more, stopping at the intersection. Instead of turning out of the neighborhood towards his house he drove around the corner to Jesse's house. *I swear to God, if I see her there, I will kill her. I will kill him.*

He parked down the road from Jesse's house and got out of the truck. He walked up to the house and started peeking through the windows.

When he got around the side he saw a TV light coming from one of the basement windows. He walked over to it, laid on the ground, and peered into the window.

Jesse was sound asleep in his bed with the TV on. No one else was in his bed with him.

Damn it. What has gotten into me? What am I thinking? She wouldn't be here. She wouldn't cheat on me. She wouldn't confide in him about me. She's in her bed. She loves me. I know she does. She clearly doesn't want anyone else. She needs me. I need her. I need to remind her that she loves me. I need to get out of here.

Brody walked back to his truck and got in. He drove around the block one final time and looked back up at Sarah's room and texted her once more, "DAMN IT!!! I'm leaving for real this time. I'm getting you back. You can't get rid of me that easily. This isn't over. You are mine. You belong to me. If you actually love me, which I think you do, then you won't give up that easy either."

This time, he pulled away. He wasn't sleepy but he knew he had to get home to try and sleep off his frustration.

Once he got home he texted her again, "Just got home. In case you wanted to know, I am safe. I love you baby. Sweet dreams, good night."

He went into his house and raided the cupboards for whatever food he could find. When he didn't find any food he wanted, he decided to hop in the shower.

After the shower he tried to talk himself into being calm. He knew he had to wait until the morning to talk to her. She couldn't ignore him forever. But, he could tell her how sorry he was.

Finally, he texted her again, "I'm sorry baby. I will tell you forever. I will make this up to you. I'm sorry."

Damn it. I forgot to tell her I love her. I love her. I love her. I love her.

"I love you. I love you. I love you. I love you. I love you. I can't wait to hold you again. I love you," he hit send.

As he laid there staring at the ceiling he decided he knew what he had to do. *I'm going to go see her tomorrow. I am going to just show up. I am going to meet her parents. I'm going to convince them to fall in love with me. I'm not letting her go. She is going to see that I am the only one she needs. I am going to ask her parents if I can take her to the homecoming dance. She will think it's cute. She'll think of it almost like I am asking for her hand in marriage and she will realize that I love her that much.* His mind couldn't shut off.

With the break of light coming into the sky he still couldn't sleep. He couldn't get her off of his mind. He couldn't stop playing the party over and over in his head. He couldn't stop thinking that he was going to get her back even if it cost him everything. He sent her a message, "I can't sleep. You awake yet?"

After several hours passed and no response from Sarah and no chance of falling asleep, Brody decided he needed to go see his dad today. Visiting hours started at nine so he got dressed and headed to the prison.

"David Paulson! You have a visitor," the guard at the prison stated as he escorted Brody's father to the visitor's room.

"Brody, my boy!" he waved to him through the glass window pane.

"Hey, Dad," Brody slumped into his chair.

"Son, what's the matter? You don't look so hot."

"Dad, I need some advice. I don't know what to do?"

"Well, I ain't got nothing but time, so let me have it. I can't promise I have any great advice and not any that would be worth your while but I do have time to listen," his dad chuckled and leaned back in his chair crossing his arms.

"There's this girl."

"The one you were telling me about the other day?"

"Yeah! That one. Sarah," Brody confirmed. "So I really screwed up, Pops!"

His dad began to look skeptical through the glass at him. "Go on, I'm listening."

"Look. I was drunk. It's no excuse, but I was. She told me she loved me and then all of a sudden she stopped messing around with me right before we were about to hook up. But she told me she loved me, so it didn't make sense to me why she wouldn't want to hook up. So I accused her of not really being in love with me and she stormed out on me. She won't call me back now. Girls are so crazy, Dad. One minute they like you, the next minute they don't. They say yes, then they say no. So how am I supposed to know?" Brody huffed as he rattled off his mind.

"What's there to know, boy?" his dad raised an eyebrow and looked confused.

"What do you mean, Pops?"

"Son, she clearly likes you. Don't you know that when girls say no, they really just want to make sure they feel heard, but they really mean yes. You just have to let her know you hear her. She will come around. Sounds like she loves you. She probably stormed out on you because you got mad. She thinks you didn't hear her, but once she knows that you are a good listener, she will be right back in your arms."

Brody smiled, "Yeah? How am I supposed to get her to see that I hear her?

"Be there. Go see her. Don't let her get away. If you really like her, don't let her slip through your fingers. Women like love letters. Hand written ones. Not that silly text message stuff you kids do nowadays. Write her a love note."

"Alright. I can do that."

"Good. But remember, if you don't get her back, someone else is going to come in and swoop her up, so you better let her know she belongs to you so no one else can have her," his father smiled at the advice he was offering.

As their conversation came to a close Brody felt assured that he knew what he needed to do.

*   *   *

Monday Morning:

I can't stand it. Brody thought to himself after not hearing back from her at all for the entire rest of the day. *I don't understand why she wouldn't text me back. I can't believe she won't answer my calls. I know she got them. I watched her. I left her my note. Why didn't she call me back? It wasn't that bad. This isn't the end of the world. Why is she being so damn crazy? I made a mess of this. I don't know what to do. How the hell did I let this girl get to me? She gets me. She'd be crazy not to want me. Who does she think she is? She can't end this with me. We aren't over. She is mine. What's her problem? How do I make her love me?*

Brody paced around his bedroom listening to his rock music as he got ready for school. He stopped and stood in front of the mirror on his closet door and looked at his bare chest.

"I can't stand it," he roared at his reflection. He then stared himself down in the mirror. "Alright, Brody!" he looked directly at himself in the mirror. "You can do this shit, bra. You got this. You gotta put an end to this. This has gone on long enough."

Like Dad said, she is mine. I can't let anyone else have her. She is mine. Mine. Mine. Mine. She is all mine. He threw on a t-shirt and put his baseball hat on backward, grabbed his backpack and headed out to his truck. *No backing down now. You got this. Stay calm.*

CHAPTER 17
Best Partners in the Class

"Are you sure you don't want me to walk you in, honey?" Sarah's dad yelled toward her as she got out of his car.

"No. I'm good, Dad, I promise. I'll be fine," she smiled back at him. "I love you."

"Okay. Love you too. Call me after school. Wild West Jesse will bring you home, right?"

"Yeah. See ya," she said as she waved at her dad and turned to walk up the sidewalk into the school.

As he drove off, something felt different in the air for Sarah. She felt new and fresh. She felt ready for her day. "Tamara?" she shouted out to the crowd of girls ahead of her.

"Hey, Sarah. How are you?" Tamara smiled when she saw her.

All of her friends stopped and stared at the two of them as if they had seen a ghost.

"What's up, girl? I'm good. How was your date?" she smiled and looked over Tamara's shoulder and noticed Brandon standing there.

Tamara smiled at her, "It was amazing. He is so sweet. Hey, so how was your party?"

"Oh my gosh, I don't even wanna talk about it. Brutal."

Tamara's face frowned as Sarah said this.

"Let's just say you were right about Brody."

"Oh no, Sarah. Are you okay?"

"Yeah, I'll be fine. But he's still an asshole. Look, here's our project. You can turn it in if you want. I really don't feel like talking much in class today. Trying to keep a low profile."

"I hear ya, girl. Cool. Well, I'm here if you need anything. Besides, we don't need to say much about our project. We got the best one in the class since we the best partners."

"Thanks," Sarah smiled at her as she walked into the building.

"Tamara, since when you friends with that white girl?" Chance asked her as she came back toward the group.

"Since none of your business, that's when," she shot him a sarcastic look, smacked him on the back of his head, and went on about her conversation with Porsha.

As Tamara headed into the school building she noticed Brody walking up from the school parking lot. *Ugh. I don't like him.* She thought to herself. *I don't like the look on his face.*

"Tamara?" Brandon noticed her looking across the parking lot toward Brody. "You good?"

"Oh, yeah. I'm good," her gaze fixated on Brody.

Brandon smiled at her and glanced at Brody who was completely unaware of the stare down he was getting from Tamara.

After Brody walked past them into the building Brandon and Tamara headed in as well to go to first bell.

"Okay, beautiful. I will see you at lunch." Brandon put his arms around Tamara's neck. "I got a big chemistry exam second bell. I gotta go see coach to see if he can help me a bit."

"Oh my," she smiled. "You studied all day yesterday. You'll be fine."

"Well, you know. You never can be too prepared," he kissed her on her cheek. "I'll find you at lunch."

"Okay. I might try and sit with Sarah because she seems upset, but you could sit with us."

"Cool."

*　　*　　*

"Sarah. What in the world happened to you the other night? I mean, we were all at the party having fun and then the next thing

203

I know, you are nowhere to be found. Where did you go? Brody was looking everywhere for you. He texted me like a hundred times asking me if you were mad at him," Zoe confronted Sarah as soon as she walked into class.

"Oh. Sorry. My mom needed me to come home. Sorry," she avoided making eye contact with her so instead, she looked at the teacher who was sharpening her pencil.

"Well," Zoe persisted.

"Well what?" Sarah snapped back.

"Whoa. What's wrong with you? No wonder Brody thinks you're mad at him. Chill out, girl," Zoe leaned away from Sarah in an awkward motion.

"Look," Sarah exclaimed at her friend, who truly had no idea what had happened. "I don't want to talk about it. I am sure everyone will find out soon enough. I'm not mad at you. I promise. I'm sorry I just yelled."

"It's okay, girl. Remember, I'm here for you. I don't know what happened, but I'm totally on your side. You're my best friend."

"Thanks, Zoe," Sarah responded but then averted her eyes. Luckily, she didn't get called on to answer anything during her morning classes because all she could think about was avoiding eye contact with everyone and especially avoiding any contact with Brody.

*　　*　　*

"Hey, Sarah, wait up," a voice called as they switched into third bell.

Sarah glanced back and realized it was Jesse, so she stopped, not noticing Brody standing at the end of the hallway watching them from afar.

"Hey, Jesse," she bashfully smiled thinking back to their last face-to-face interaction.

"Hey. How are you?" He gave her a hug and smiled as he noticed her wearing the cross necklace he had given her for Christmas back when they were in seventh grade.

I knew it. I knew he had a thing for her. Brody's body grew tense as he watched Sarah and Jesse hugging in the hallway. He was close enough to see every move they made, but not close enough to hear anything they were saying.

Not wanting to let go, she allowed herself to be embraced by him for several long seconds. "I'm okay. I just can't wait to get this day over with. I need to end things officially with Brody, but I just don't know how. I haven't seen him at all today or heard from him, so I don't know if he is even here, but if he is, I will probably just do it at lunch."

"Yeah, so I need to break up with Caitlin too," he said as he chuckled and softy smiled at her.

"Is she here today?"

"Yeah, but she has a chemistry test. So I was going to wait at least until after that class," he shrugged his shoulders.

"Well, I think that's a good idea. I also think you and I should just keep this thing of ours between us for a little while. I don't want people getting the wrong idea," she gave him a half smile.

What the hell? What is he saying to my girl? Brody stared the two of them down with daggers in his eyes.

He leaned in and whispered in her ear, "You have been in my life forever. You will be in my life forever. I'm not going anywhere. We don't have to rush into being public about anything. You're still my best friend and that's never going to change. But, now that I finally have a green light I might sneak in a few kisses here and there," he winked and slid in a little peck on her cheek as he said this.

Are you serious? I'm going to kill her. She is for real letting this little boy kiss her? She is mine, damn it! Mine. Mine. Mine. Mine. Brody's body started to shake and tremble. *This is a game changer. That's it.*

No going back. Get ready asshole. Shit's about to get real. A tornado was waging war inside of him.

She blushed and tilted her head on her shoulder and smiled at him, "Thanks, Wild West Jess," she laughed. "Okay, I gotta get to class. Good luck today with Caitlin. Text me and let me know how it goes. If you see me talking to Brody at lunch it might be best to just stay far away," she exclaimed as her eyes widened in the anticipation of his explosion.

Brody watched them walk their separate ways. He pulled the three leftover pills Connor had given him at the party from his pocket and dropped them into his mouth and swallowed them. He then disappeared into the stairwell to await lunch.

*   *   *

"Sarah?" Mrs. Panacinni, her fourth bell teacher called after her when the bell rang to dismiss for lunch.

"Yeah?" Sarah glanced into the hallway to make sure she didn't see anyone.

"I just wanted to make sure you're okay. You seem a little distracted today. Is everything alright?" Mrs. Panacinni questioned.

"Oh, yeah. I'm fine Ms. P. I've just had a crazy weekend. My parents are crazy. You know."

"Oh, okay. Well, I'm here if you need anything."

"Okay, thanks," Sarah didn't even make eye contact as she thanked her and scooted out the door.

The hallways were almost empty but thankfully, there was no sign of Brody. *Maybe he didn't come to school today. I haven't heard him in the halls. Normally he's mister obnoxious.* Sarah looked at her phone to see if she had any messages from him. *Wow. Nothing. Maybe he finally got the hint that I'm not talking to him.*

Knowing that she couldn't avoid him forever, she decided to

text him to get this inevitable conversation over with.

"Hey, Brody. Are you at school today? I thought maybe we could meet up at lunch and talk for a minute."

She headed upstairs to the cafeteria. When she got in there she spotted Jesse and Caitlin at a table along the back wall near the window overlooking the football field.

Her phone buzzed in her hand. A message from Brody said, "Yes. I am here. We can talk. Be there soon."

She started looking for Zoe when Tamara stopped her, "Hey, girl," Tamara tugged at Sarah's arm.

"Oh, Tamara. Hey," Sarah was feeling uncomfortable from Brody's cold text.

"So, you seemed a little upset this morning. You wanna talk?"

"Oh. Well," she responded but then noticed that Caitlin wasn't sitting with Jesse anymore but her books were still there.

 He gave her a confused look and shrugged his shoulders.

"Actually, yeah. Lemme go check on something with Jesse real quick. But I'll be right back." She set her books down at the table Tamara was sitting at and headed over toward Jesse.

Tamara saw Brody walk into the cafeteria. *Oh God. I hope he doesn't try and talk to her.* Tamara glared at him as he fiddled with the bill of his hat and put one hand into his pocket while the other one adjusted the backpack over his shoulder.

Sarah had her back toward him, but it was clear to Tamara that he had spotted her talking to Jesse. She noticed him stop in his tracks. *What's he doing?* Tamara thought to herself. *I don't like this.*

*   *   *

She just texted me to talk, and now she is talking to him? Brody's body temperature raised in anger as he saw her with him. *How could she do this to me? She is mine. Mine. Mine. Who the hell does he think he is? I thought maybe she wanted to work this out. Damn it. Damn it. Brody!*

Pull it together. Jesse can't have her. If you can't have her, no one can. That's it. Go time.

*   *   *

Brandon had just walked out of the lunch line when he noticed Tamara staring down Brody. Not sure what to do, he started to walk toward her.

Then he noticed Brody stop and take off his backpack to get something out of it.

Brody reached into his backpack and slowly pulled out a nine millimeter handgun.

"Oh, hell no," Brandon's heart stopped as he watched his girlfriend stand up and run toward Sarah.

"Sarah!" Tamara shouted.

"Tamara!" Brandon shouted.

Brody looked at the two people running toward Sarah and his face grew angry. "No!" he screamed at the top of his lungs.

Panic filled the room. All eyes fell onto Brody standing there pointing his gun in Sarah and Jesse's direction, now only twenty feet from her. The stunned silence turned to screams of students.

Brandon rerouted toward Brody's direction as the pandemonium unfolded.

Unaware of everything going on until this moment, Sarah turned around to see Tamara running toward her as Brody was holding a gun toward her and Jesse.

Brody fired.

Tamara tackled Sarah as the bullet sounded across the room.

Sarah screamed as the bullet from his gun exploded.

Sarah's scream was silenced.

He fired again.

Tamara shrieked.

Jesse screamed.

Students screeched, yelled, shouted, and cried in panic for their lives and ran chaotically out of the cafeteria.

Brandon ran toward Brody from the side and threw his body toward him to stop him from firing.

It was too late. He fired once more. This time, the bullet aimed for Brandon.

As Brandon fell to the floor, Brody was seized from behind by the school's security officer. He slammed Brody's body to a table. "Drop the gun," he shouted.

Brody dropped the gun and fell limp against the coldness of the table he was pinned against and stared at Jesse holding Sarah's bleeding, unmoving body.

Wails filled the air. Within minutes, sirens surrounded the building.

Police officers and medics rushed in and quickly moved to the injured students and security officer.

Brody was escorted by three officers to another area.

The moment of chaos quickly spread to devastation as the students cried over the chain of events.

Jesse held onto his seemingly lifeless best friend.

Tamara held the side of her stomach as she bled over the two of them crying in disbelief.

Jesse became hysterical as he tried to figure out what was happening.

Paramedics quickly rushed in and everything became a blur to Jesse. He watched as the medics hovered over Tamara's body, Sarah's body, and Brandon's body. He didn't know if anyone was dead, but he knew in this moment, his life had changed forever.

"Son? Son?" a police officer touched Jesse's shoulder. "Are you injured, son?"

Shakily, Jesse shook his head and put his face in his hands and began to sob uncontrollably, falling onto the floor.

"Alright, son. We're gonna need to clear the area here. Let me take you out of here."

Jesse looked up at the officer and slowly came up on his feet. He allowed the officer to escort him out of the cafeteria. But as he was leaving he noticed the paramedics placing the heart paddles on Sarah's chest.

"Clear."

CHAPTER 18
Mourning

"Three students at Vector High School were shot by a gunman today. The gunman has been named as eighteen-year-old Brody Paulson. Two of the victims have died and one currently remains in critical condition. None of the victims' names have been released at this time but as we know more, we will come to you with live updates. Now, we will take you live outside the school with our own Adam Mandrel. Adam."

"Thank you, Joanne. I am here outside of Vector High School where behind me many students have begun to gather as they await the status of the third victim. We do not have much yet on the story but in the midst of this tragedy, we may have some heroes. I'm standing here with the principal of the building, Hank Whitley. Mr. Whitley, first of all, I am terribly sorry for this tragic event. Can you try to explain to the viewers what has happened here today?"

"Without knowing the details, I am sorry but there really isn't much I can tell you. It saddens me on all accounts to lose the life of a child. Today we lost two. Our hearts and prayers are with the families of these students, as well as the one who is fighting for her life at Memorial Hospital. We are a close community and we will be strong for each other. We are a community of dedicated and loving people. Together we will pick up the pieces of our lives and stand together as we overcome this unfortunate incident. All I ask is that the media please try and keep their distance, as we don't want to make a spectacle out of this terrible, terrible tragedy."

"Mr. Whitley, is there anything you can tell us about the moment this happened and how it occurred?"

Like I said, I am not at liberty to speak freely, however, it seems that two of our students tried to stop the gunman from shooting one of the victims. One of whom has lost his life today. I'm sorry. I can't. No more questions."

"Well, thank you again, Mr. Whitley for taking the time to speak with us. Joanne, that's all we have for now. Back to you in the newsroom."

"Thank you, Adam. What an emotional day for those students. We will have more as it comes."

Channel 6 News at 11

"After a school shooting today we have learned the names of the victims and those involved. Seventeen-year-old Brandon Harris has died and sixteen-year-old Sarah Benson has also died. Sixteen-year-old Tamara Hudgenson is under care at Memorial Hospital with a gunshot wound to her ribs and abdomen. Senior, Brody Paulson, has allegedly been named as the gunman. He is in police custody at this time. Eighteen-year-old Paulson is the son of convict, David Paulson, who is currently serving life in prison for murder, menacing, and violent stalking. Ironically, one of the victims' father assisted in prosecuting David Paulson sixteen years ago. The school district superintendent has cancelled classes for the high school students at Vector High for the rest of the week, including the major talent show scheduled to happen this coming Friday and Saturday, so students can grieve and piece together the loss of their friends and loved ones. Obviously, this is still very new information, so as we get more, we will be sure to pass it along to our viewers. For now, our hearts go out to those students involved and all the families whose lives have been turned upside down from this tragedy."

CHAPTER 19
Sentiments

Dear Sarah,

I should not have talked you into going to that party. I should have watched out for you better. I'm sorry. I miss you! I love you! I don't know how I am going to get through my life without you. I hate myself right now for not realizing what happened between you and Brody. I should have been a better friend. I will forever be sorry. I love you so much. I can't believe you are gone. I know you will look down on me from heaven and keep the sun shining. You will always be like a sister to me. I love you.

Zoe

Dear Brandon,

Bra, I can't believe you're gone. GOD. How is this fair? I swear to God, B, I'm gonna live my life tryin to be as brave as you. I miss you, my man. I'll look out for Tamara for ya.

Chance

Brandon,

Oh my goodness, bra! I can't believe you gone. I think you are so brave. It's no wonder Tamara was so crazy over you. I am so sorry you died. You were gonna be a super star. I promise Brandon, I'mma take good care of Tamara. She's my best friend.
 Love you,

Porsha

Sarah,

I don't know why, but I feel real salty you and B gone. You musta been cool for Tamara to try an save you like that. I'm sorry you gone. Brandon was the real deal too. He gonna be missed for real.

Kenna

Dear Brandon,

The college scouts have all sent their condolences. I'm so sorry for you kid. I know without a shadow of a doubt that you would have gone on to play division 1 football. Notre Dame and Ohio State's head coaches even called me personally yesterday to offer their condolences. I want to tell you that it has been an honor coaching you over the past few years. I have never had an athlete who worked as hard, and played with as much passion and heart, on the field and off the field. Your work ethic and love for this team was contagious. We are going to retire your number here at school. We are going to play every game in your honor. We are going to make it to the state championships. We are going all the way Brandon, and you will lead the brigade. I want you to know that you will never be forgotten here at Vector High School. You are the glue that held this team together. Thank you for all you did for this team. You are very much loved.

  With Respect,

  Coach Daniels

Sarah bear,

We love you, Sarah. We miss you so much. No one will ever know the pain of losing a child. I can't tell you how much it hurts. I feel like a part of me died with you, Sarah. Your father and I are keeping each other strong, trying. He is blaming himself for not going into school with you that day. I won't lie, I feel like we both should have gone in with you. I love you so much. You are my baby girl. We are going to go see Tamara at the hospital tomorrow. We buried you today. Oh my God, Sarah. I can't believe you have left us. I promise you, baby, I will keep this family strong and honor you forever. We will make sure justice is served. The ache I feel is unsurpassable. I am empty without you. You are my first born, and one of my greatest loves. I will never stop loving you. It isn't fair. It isn't fair that you don't get to go to prom, and go to college, and get married, and have babies. I can't believe you will never get to do those things. Oh my God. I am so lost without you. I feel so dead. I will always miss you. I will always love you.

  Love you,

  Mommy

Sarah,

You are my best friend. I love you so much. I am so sorry I didn't see him coming. I can't believe this happened. I'm so sorry I didn't pull you behind me. I'm so sorry I didn't stop him. I'm so sorry I didn't know how to react.

I am so sorry that you are gone. I am so sorry that I didn't tell you sooner how I felt. I am so sorry that we won't get to grow old and buy a house and fill it with banana pancakes. I'm so so sorry. I love you. I remember losing my brother and being real sad, but I have never experienced a sadness this deep.

I ache all over. My heart physically hurts. I am so sorry, Sarah. I am so sorry I will never get to see you again. I love you so much. I am so sorry I couldn't save you. I am so sorry. I love you.

Forever Sorry,

Jesse

Brandon,

I am so sorry my decision caused you to die. I didn't know you were there. People keep telling me I am a hero, but I don't feel like one. I didn't do anything. I am the reason you died. I am the reason you got shot. I don't know how I can live with that. I didn't even save Sarah. I messed it all up. I am so sorry. I can't even begin to express how much it hurts to know you are gone. To know I caused you to die. I wish I had died with you. I wish people would stop calling me a hero. I hate that this happened. I hate Brody. I hate that I can't get out of this hospital bed to come to your funeral. I hate that I didn't get to kiss you once more. I hate this. I hate this. I hate this. I hate this. I am so sorry. I am sorry that I caused this pain to your family. I wish I could change it. I wish I could have saved Sarah too. Oh my God, everything is such a mess. I wish I had you here to sort it out with me. I hate that you're not. I don't know how I will make it through. I know we weren't together long, but I want you to know that I love you. Ugghh! That truly hurts my heart to say because I never told you. I love you Brandon, and you will always be my first love. I will never let my promise to you die. I will follow our dreams and rise to the challenge.

Love forever and always,

Tamara

CHAPTER 20
Hospital Visit

"Hi," Mrs. Benson stood in the hospital room doorway peering at Tamara.

"Oh. Mrs. Benson. Hi," Tamara responded weakly. "Come in. My mom just went down to the coffee shop."

"Hi, Tamara." Tears began to well in Mrs. Benson's eyes. She slowly walked into the room, which was covered with flowers, cards, and balloons. "Wow. People are really supportive, huh?" she said as she approached Tamara's bed.

Tamara could see the tears forming in her eyes and she too had to start fighting back the wave of emotion that was taking over. She opened her mouth to start to say something but Mrs. Benson grabbed her hand and sat down beside her. The tears began flowing from both of them.

Tamara choked on her sobs. "I'm so sorry. I'm so sorry," she coughed and choked in between words.

"Oh, Tamara," Mrs. Benson placed her other hand on Tamara's shoulder. "You have nothing to be sorry for," she said as she wiped her own tears from her cheeks. "You hear me?" She swallowed her breath. "What you did for my baby was noble."

More tears began to fall.

Tamara sucked in the tears that were forming around her quivering mouth.

"You were more of a friend to my daughter than most," she said as she squeezed Tamara's hand harder. "You did something for her that only a truly wonderful person can do." She wiped her tears away from her cheeks again. "Do you know what you did, Tamara?"

Tamara rolled her head toward Mrs. Benson as she continued to sob. "No," she uttered. "I didn't do anything. It's my fault she died. It's my fault they died."

"No, Tamara. Don't you say that. You listen to me," Mrs. Benson exclaimed as she Tamara directly into her eyes. "This was in no way your fault. This was the outcome of a very sick young man who didn't know how to love. But, Tamara, you listen to me. You are not to blame. You did everything right," she paused for a moment and looked at the machines hooked up to Tamara. "You loved," she squeezed her hand again and slightly lifted it in rhythm to her words and repeated, "You loved."

Tamara looked at the woman sitting beside her. The woman who only a few days ago had forgotten her name. The woman who had lost a child to a terrible act of violence at school. The woman who had uncomfortably welcomed her into her home. The woman whose daughter was so much like Tamara; beautiful, smart, kind, brave, courageous, and most importantly, loving.

Tamara took her hands and wiped her face and looked at the aching mother. "Thank you," she whispered as she blinked the remaining tears from her eye lashes.

"Thank you," Mrs. Benson whispered back.

The two of them sat there for a long time just looking at each other; both deciding that love has no color, no barriers, no conditional factors.

Both of them, in that moment, realized that pain is pain, no matter who you are. The problem with pain is that it takes a long time to heal. They both stared at each other knowing that even though they were very different on the outside, the pain and love they shared would be the tie that bonded them together. Neither one would ever let Sarah's memory die.

Sarah would live on forever giving them strength and guidance to put their broken pieces back together and do great things despite the difficult circumstances life offered.

CHAPTER 21
The Problem of Pain

Six Years Later…

"In closing today, my fellow Howard University Graduates, I want to leave you with a poem I wrote my sophomore year in high school. A poem that I have kept with me, and I hope you will all keep with you when you feel the pain of life getting too hard. We each are given special people who come and go out of our lives and they each impact us in their own ways. The friends we have today are not the same friends we will have thirty years down the road, and for many of us, we may remember your face, but your name will be forgotten. I want to challenge each and every one of you today not to forget those people who will come and go out of your lives. As we each grow into the Doctors and Researchers we want to be, do not forget where you came from. Do not forget why you are here in the first place. And that is because someone once told you that you could do it."

I Will

Written by
Tamara Hudgenson
Howard University Graduate

Pain is extraordinary
Longsuffering endures forever.
Small moments in the day bring your face back to my heart.
The problem with pain is it lacks compassion.
Undoubtedly though pain would not be pain
without love.
One cannot love without feeling pain.
One cannot have pain without love.
Do I then retreat from love to avoid pain?
I cannot crumble.
I choose love.
I will stand for you.
I will wage this war.
I will carry on.
Carry on a promise.
Hold on to your dream
My dream
Our dream.
The stars won't determine destiny.
I will.
I will.
I will.
I will shine for you.

"Once again, congratulations on your hard work and much deserved degree. Good luck to all of you in your future careers. Thank you."